Praise for **TERMIN**

"Author Kate McGuinness does a terrific job highlighting the challenges that are all too familiar to women in the working world, especially in big law. An intriguing portrayal of discrimination and harassment, *Terminal Ambition* is a must read."

Susan Estrich
Fox News Commentator
Robert Kingsley Professor of Law and Political Science
University of Southern California School of Law
Author: *Sex and Power*

"The issues addressed in McGuinness' intriguing first novel *Terminal Ambition* - from acquaintance rape to sexual harassment - are ones that will be all too familiar to her readers. Heroine Maggie Mahoney's courage in challenging the status quo will inspire young women to speak up and take action in their own lives."

Abigail Collazo
Editor Fem2pt0

"Every working woman should read this book! Author Kate McGuinness both entertains and educates, inspires and motivates women and men who work with them to claim the rights that are theirs by law and more. Brilliant, passionate, *Terminal Ambition* could revolutionize how you think about going to work and what you can do there."

Kathleen Barry, Professor Emerita
Pennsylvania State University
Author: *Female Sexual Slavery;*
Unmaking War, Remaking Men

"A gritty legal thriller, set in the everyday life of high-priced lawyers and their wealthy corporate clients, that pivots on the theme of sexual harassment. This page-turner book not only illuminates one of the most persistent and important gender-justice problems of the day—a problem that continues to burden the lives of professional women decades after the Anita Hill/Clarence Thomas incident—but it also raises thorny moral questions that challenge every woman or man who seeks success in the top professions of our society. A must read for lawyers and nonlawyers alike."

Roy L. Brooks
Warren Distinguished Professor of Law
University of San Diego School of Law

"In this engaging thriller, **Terminal Ambition** tackles the culture of sexual harassment and discrimination in a big law firm. From its dramatic opening on a mountaintop to intriguing scenes inside the walls of a powerful firm, this page-turner offers readers a wild ride they won't soon forget."

Steven J. Harper
Author: *The Partnership, Crossing Hoffa*
Retired partner, Kirkland & Ellis

"A terrific, smart, honest book. Kate McGuinness knows the inside scoop on life at a big law firm. She also knows how to write a suspenseful page-turner—one that doesn't shy away from presenting the ugly reality of workplace sexual harassment and discrimination. As important as it is long overdue."

Will Meyerhofer, JD MSW
Author: *Way Worse Than Being a Dentist*

"In Maggie Mahoney, McGuinness has created a vivid and engaging protagonist, who possesses grit, integrity and a burning desire for justice. Surely admirable qualities for a lawyer—but they may yet bring about her destruction."

Claire McNab
Past President Sisters in Crime
Author: *Lethal Care*

TERMINAL AMBITION

KATE MCGUINNESS

Marianne and Eric,
Best wishes!
Kate Mc Guinness

© 2012 by Kate McGuinness.(om
Two XX Press
PO Box 169
Fairfield, Iowa 52556
www.womensrightswriter.com
www.twoxxpress.com

ISBN: 978-0-9849901-7-7
Library of Congress Control Number: 2012935074

Editor: Melanie Rigney
Cover and Interior Design: Lewis Agrell
Cover copy: Kathryn Agrell

First Printing: 2012
Printed in the United States of America

TerminalAmbition.com

ACKNOWLEDGEMENTS

I could not have written this novel without the efforts of the women who went before me in the struggle for equality. Unfortunately, the names and roles of many of them have been forgotten. However, I acknowledge a debt to Catharine Sedgwick for her advocacy for female education and Arabella Mansfield as the first women admitted to the bar in the United States.

I am grateful to those who helped shape *Terminal Ambition* and hone my writing skills: Melanie Rigney, Claire McNab (aka Claire Carmichael), Lisa Cron, Daniel Jaffe, Robert McKee, Gina Barkhordar Nahai and Bill Thompson.

Terminal Ambition would not have been published without the guidance of my dear friend and mentor Sandy Nathan, a talented author. Others provided encouragement when my spirits flagged: Frank Carpenter, C. David Anderson, Valerie Coachman Moore and Virginia Linden.

My thanks also to those who provided technical assistance including Kathy Grow for her meticulous proof reading, Don Herion for the design of my website and my son A J McGuinness Anderson for his patient help in guiding me through numerous computer and internet questions.

Best guide to get it published

For my son

Alexander James McGuinness Anderson

Barn's burnt down —

now

I can see the moon.

— Masahide

CHAPTER 1

August 16, Saturday
Maggie Mahoney

Maggie Mahoney bit back a smile at her client's frustration. She'd watched Wade Johnson coolly negotiate deals worth billions of dollars, but he had just been shut down by their helicopter pilot, a grizzled Vietnam vet called Stoney. Shaking his gray ponytail, Stoney gave the same response to each of Wade's offers: "Not worth it."

Maggie pushed the microphone button on her headset. "You might as well promise him the moon, Wade. He won't take your offer because he doesn't think he'll live to collect it."

Wade's goal of a longer run down Valle Nevado could be satisfied only if Stoney landed above the chopper's maximum ceiling. Their planned sixty-five-hundred-foot run somehow wasn't enough for Wade. Of course, what Wade really wanted was to prove he was Wondrous Wade, King of the Street and master of all he surveyed.

Stoney wasn't with the program. As he put it, the helicopter "didn't have the guts to grab onto air that thin." He could land the sucker. The challenge would be lifting off again after Wade and party departed.

Indifferent to the prospect of Stoney's death, Wade continued to up the ante. The pilot rebuffed all offers until he heard something that overrode his instinct for self-preservation: "$100,000."

"Deal. Cash to me or my old lady."

The men shook hands, and Wade flashed a triumphant thumbs-up to the other passengers. Maggie knew she should look enthusiastic, but the best she could manage was a half smile. The prospect of Stoney risking his life to feed Wade's ego turned her stomach. But she told herself a man with forty years experience flying helicopters surely knew their limits.

The helicopter put down near the top of the twelve-thousand-foot peak and offloaded passengers and gear. The rest of the party busied themselves with final preparations for the run, but Maggie hung back to silently cheer Stoney on. She covered her ears to muffle the low thrum of the helicopter's rotor and the high-pitched shriek of its turbine engine. Swirling gusts of snow stung her face. The chopper rose, bobbed on the icy froth from the rotor's churn, then pitched forward.

When it finally leveled off, Maggie turned to share her relief but the others were focused on sorting equipment. Her husband, Bryce Chandler, worked with Wade to lay out skis and poles. The men's gear was easily distinguished: Wade was the shortest member of their foursome and Bryce the tallest.

In his matching parka and pants, Wade resembled a mustard fire hydrant as he spread his arms wide. "Just look at this! It's a day to die for. Great weather with two feet of fresh powder." To his left, the peak towered over steep, nearly vertical slopes; a vast bowl opened on the right. Brilliant sunshine lit the cloudless blue sky and warmed the air to twenty degrees.

"So, ladies, what's it going to be?" Wade asked. "Are you ready for the ride of a lifetime or do you want to dillydally down the mountainside?"

The run would be gnarly. The men fancied themselves downhill racers and would ski close to the fall line. Maggie didn't share their delusion, but she never backed away from a challenge. She lifted a shoulder in a deliberately casual shrug. "Sure. I'm up for it."

"That's my girl." Bryce winked, and a grin warmed his patrician features.

Maggie turned to Savannah Johnson. "How about you?"

"Not me." Tall and catwalk thin, she tightened her collagen-plumped lips. "I'll take my time and track back and forth."

"Let's go, guys." Maggie charged down the face in a linked series of shallow turns. She quickly established a rhythm and let it seduce her down the steep slope. Bryce and Wade followed to her left, each carving his own gently arched track.

Maggie paused on a relatively flat shoulder. As Bryce and Wade stopped beside her, she checked Savannah's progress. The other woman was proceeding cautiously, her silver parka and ski pants almost invisible against the winter panorama.

Suddenly, Maggie heard a boom that sounded like thunder. Except thunder didn't make sense on a winter day. Squinting, she scanned the mountainside for the source of the noise. The deep, muffled thunk had come from a fracture in the snow two hundred feet behind Savannah. A massive white slab was charging downhill straight at them. It picked up speed, swallowing the other woman.

Fear flooded through Maggie. "Avalanche!"

The men looked up. "Holy shit!"

Maggie pointed her ski pole at a cluster of evergreens sheltered by a rocky ledge. "Head for the trees." She rocketed away, taking a forty-five-degree line over the slope.

Bryce yelled, "Maggie, straight downhill! We'll outrun it." The men launched themselves onto the mountainside.

"You can't!"

But they passed her, their bodies tucked. She was committed to reaching the ledge. If she didn't, she'd be hit by a white freight train. The slab of snow had shattered into blocks as long as boxcars.

The short downhill run had given her speed. More speed than she had expected. She was almost past the trees. She had to turn now. Right now. Shit! The angle was very tight. She couldn't fall. If she did, she'd never get up in time. She'd be tumbled down the mountain in a giant snow-filled washing machine. And die.

Panic tightened her chest. She fought to hold her focus, telling herself to think about what she wanted to happen. *Visualize a perfectly executed turn.* As she moved her elbows forward, she set the edges on her skis. The strength of her knees and thighs held the chattering skis in the turn. Her upper body followed. She'd made it!

But she wasn't safe yet.

Her eyes flickered from the shadows of the forest to the violent white sea bearing down on her. Furiously poling and skating, she aimed for the cluster of pines sheltered by the rocks. The trees closest to her were relatively short and thin. If they broke off, they'd pin her under them—or to them.

On the far side of the grove, the pines nestled behind the ledge. She had to get there before the snow slammed into her.

She traveled across the level shoulder of the mountain almost as quickly as she had blasted downhill. Starved for oxygen, her lungs burned. She pressed on, safety only twenty feet away. Her legs quivered. Under her breath, she chanted, "Pole kick." Fifteen feet. "Pole kick." Ten feet. "Pole—"

A violent blast of wind pushed past her, shoving her into a large pine. Terror gushed from her pores. She hugged the tree fiercely as ice crystals speared her neck like a hail of needles. Beneath her, the ground shook as if jolted by an earthquake. The movement of soft, delicate snowflakes became a roar, punctuated by the snap of splintering trees.

She gulped in air and turned. With numb fascination, she watched blocks of snow hurtle by within feet of her refuge.

It seemed as if the entire mountainside had collapsed. She tried to estimate how fast it was traveling, but she had no point of reference. All she could see was a turbulent jumble of snow studded with rocks and tree trunks.

Eventually, the torrent slowed and then stopped. Everything went quiet.

She relaxed her death grip on the pine and collapsed at its base. Her pulse pounded as she took short, shallow breaths. She could still hear the rumble of churning snow as it swept down the mountainside below.

It could have overtaken the men, burying them under tons of snow. Buried Bryce. Killed Bryce. *No, that couldn't be. No, no, no.* He would survive. Wade might die, Savannah might die, but not Bryce.

Last week, when Stoney had handed out their avalanche beacons, he'd hammered on the importance of rapid rescue. Survival dropped from something like 90 percent at fifteen minutes to 20 percent in fifty minutes. Nobody made it after two hours.

Bryce needed her help, but Maggie wasn't sure if she could even stand up. She was shivering; her skin was cold and clammy. She felt dizzy, her mind fuzzy, as if she might pass out. Grabbing a handful of snow, she rubbed it roughly around her

face and the back of her neck. Her skin burned, but she felt
alert again.

Bryce was *dying*! No, she wouldn't let her mind go there. His
predicament was a problem to be addressed rationally, methodi-
cally. Step by step. Just like the thousands of legal problems she'd
solved.

For now, the only thing she had strength to do was switch her
beacon to receive, and listen. Nothing. How far could the signal
travel? She tried to remember what Stoney had said. Not very far.
Something like two hundred feet? She had to get a move on. If
she didn't, Bryce could die. She couldn't lose him now, just when
things were turning around.

Maggie rose and shuffled toward the open slope, passing
through the remnants of the smaller pines, now a handful of shattered trunks oozing sap. The air was saturated with their scent.
When she reached the open slope, she gazed uphill. The remaining snowpack looked as if a drunken plowman had groomed it.
As tons of snow had rammed boulders and tree trunks downward,
the debris carved long gouges and deep holes. Clods of earth,
rocks, and broken branches were scattered on the slope like shells
on the sand.

She'd have to walk.

Clicking off her skis, she jammed them into a snowbank,
started to do the same with her poles, then changed her mind.
They might help in clambering over the rubble and, worst case,
she could use them to poke through the snow for the others. Her
heart clenched. *Sweet Jesus, don't let that be necessary.*

Studying her watch, Maggie counted backward. It was 9:50
now; the avalanche had started no later than 9:45. Probably earlier. The quickest way to find the men would be to follow the
centerline to the end of the runoff. But she could miss a signal if
the sending units weren't strong enough.

She scanned for evidence of the skiers. Maybe she'd spot a glove, goggles, or a hat. There was nothing. She looked back at her skis and guessed she'd used five minutes to cover four hundred feet.

Whomp! She jumped. This time she knew what the sound meant. Pivoting, she spotted the rolling snow six hundred yards or so to her left. The new avalanche wouldn't get her, but it meant conditions were still unstable.

She could see in the distance a level area piled high with snow and rubble. It could be the end of the avalanche runoff.

Hobbling down the incline, she saw something red and yellow below her, about sixty feet to her left, near a jumble of broken trees. The tip of Wade's ski!

"Yes." The word sizzled under her breath.

Bryce couldn't be far away. She checked her watch—10:15. The avalanche had started about thirty minutes ago. Chances were good she'd made it in time to save him. After he was safe, she'd help Wade.

As she charged forward, the receiver beeped faintly. She stopped. Maybe it was Bryce. The display showed a figure downhill to her right, estimated distance one hundred seventy-five feet. It had to be Bryce. Squinting, she studied the area and thought she saw something tan, but couldn't be sure.

She stumped to her right, dodging the obstacles as quickly as she could. As she got closer, she realized she was looking at a hand, Bryce's left hand with his platinum wedding band glinting in the sun. Her eyes filled with tears. She staggered toward him as quickly as she could in the stiff boots.

"Bryce, Bryce. It's me—Maggie. I'm here." Ripping off her glove, she grabbed his fingers. "Can you hear me?" She squeezed his hand. "Can you feel me?"

His fingers wiggled. He was alive! She felt as if she could float.

"I'm going to get you out of there. Just hang on a little bit longer."

She kissed his hand. He was alive. Everything would be okay now.

Frantically, she pawed at the snow. Her fingers didn't even break the surface. She might as well have been trying to dig through plaster. She scratched the snow on the other side of his hand. Cement. She scraped the surface all around his hand. Cement. *Cement.* *CEMENT.* How had soft, fluffy snowflakes turned into concrete? Stoney had said something about this, about carrying collapsible shovels, but only Savannah had. The men had scoffed at the possibility, and Maggie had refused to appear fearful when they weren't.

Her husband was dying eighteen inches below her and she couldn't get to him. Eighteen goddamn inches. Angry and frustrated, she hollered, "Help! Somebody help!" The slope ended at the top of a lift; maybe they'd heard the avalanche and sent a rescue party.

No one answered.

Suddenly, she was aware of a squeaky, grinding noise. It was her molars. Christ! It she didn't find a way to get Bryce out soon, she'd explode.

And he'd die.

Then she saw the answer. The ice tip on her ski poles. It should blast through the snow. With all her remaining strength, she plunged a pole into the surface. It bowed. *Shit.* Grabbing the other pole, she positioned her hands lower on the shaft, knelt on the surface, and jabbed at the crust again. Glassy chips of snow flew out, but the pole held firm.

She chiseled the snow away bit by bit. And she kept talking to him. She told him about her escape from the avalanche, the shattered trees, the debris, the beacon—everything she could think of. Except Wade.

Her goggles steamed. Jerking them off, she tossed them aside. When Maggie turned back to her digging, she saw drops of blood.

They were coming from her face as shards of hardened snow hit her cheek. *Irrelevant.* She kept spearing the surface. All that mattered was getting Bryce out. It had taken ten minutes, but she'd reached his elbow. Forty-five minutes overall.

"Hey, here's some good news. I've gotten down to your elbow. Won't be long now." *Please, God, don't let it be much farther.*

The muscles in her arms and shoulders were burning. Her hands were sore. Her shins were freezing. After a few more minutes of chopping, her hands cramped. Sitting back on her heels, she caught her breath and shook them out. She checked her watch. Forty-eight minutes overall. Before she picked up the pole again, she squeezed his fingers. No response.

"Bryce, can you move your fingers?" No response.

Her heart skittered.

"Can you hear me?" No response.

She whacked at the snow. The ice tip bored through another inch of snow. But it had taken her three minutes. Fifty-one minutes overall. Why hadn't she reached him yet?

She chopped at the snow again. Another inch. Another three minutes. Fifty-four minutes overall. *No!* It was taking too long. He couldn't be that far down. She wiped her runny nose on her sleeve.

"Bryce, can you hear me?" Maybe he'd regained consciousness. No response. "Bryce!"

She whacked at the snow again and again. The tip broke into an opening. He had made a pocket in front of his face! It would take a long time to get him out, but now he could get air. "Bryce! Only a little while now."

No response.

Carefully, she chipped away the ice at the edge of the hole to enlarge it. She ripped off her glove and slid her hand in. The first thing she touched was the bridge of his nose. Slipping her fingers lower, she reached his nostrils. She waited to feel warm air as he exhaled. Nothing. She reached a little farther so the tips of her fingers were in front of his mouth. Nothing.

But that didn't prove a thing. After all, hypothermia lowered the respiration rate. She waited a few more seconds. Nothing. Not a single whisper of air.

She jerked her hand out. Her stomach clenched. Rolling to her side, she threw up.

Jumping up, she hacked ferociously to widen the hole. When it was big enough, she'd poke her head in there and do mouth-to-mouth. She attacked the snow again and again and again.

Once more she drew the pole back, but it stopped. She yanked, but it wouldn't budge.

"*Señora, por favor. Dejanos hacerlo nosotros.*"

She turned and looked into the face of a young man holding the end of her pole.

"Let go! I have to get him out."

"We do that. Please, to get out. You need doctor." Keeping his grip on the pole, he offered his other hand to her.

"You don't understand. It's my husband. He's the one who needs a doctor."

Strong arms lifted her up. Someone wrapped a blanket around her and walked her away.

CHAPTER 2

August 25, Monday
Maggie

Maggie stared at the motes of dust suspended in the late afternoon light. Passing by the broad window, a waiter scattered the specks. He was serving guests who'd attended Bryce's memorial service. The hum of their voices floated to the penthouse's carved plaster ceilings. The visitors drifted from the library to the sitting room to Bryce's gallery of abstract art.

She gazed at the guests in wonder. She'd never anticipated entertaining her husband's mourners. Of course, she'd never anticipated his death either. Even though he was more than twenty years older than she, Maggie had always thought of his death as a vague, distant event. Something peaceful and antiseptic in a hospital, not the booming cascade that had hurtled over him.

The memory seized her. She squeezed her eyelids as if they could obliterate the images that flickered through her mind.

"Sweetie, are you all right?"

Maggie didn't need to pretend with Ginger Marshall. They'd been friends since they'd started together at Sweeny, Owens & Boyle sixteen years earlier. The nation's best law firm. That's what they'd told themselves until Ginger was passed over for partner while Maggie made the cut.

Maggie sighed. "All right? Sure. I'm alive."

"Bryce and Wade are dead because they refused to listen to you. Typical goddamn men. If they had, they'd still be alive." A scowl tightened Ginger's long, angular face. Her blotchy freckles and red curls usually gave her a manic look, but today a mask of makeup covered her rawboned features. Her corkscrew tendrils had been tortured into waves.

"I don't know. I guess. But—" Maggie scrubbed her face with her palms. "I keep thinking there must have been *something* I could have done."

"Nope. Not your fault. You have to let it go."

But nothing could keep her from believing some magic would unwind the events. Bryce would be alive. She missed him so. And how could that be? She'd been considering divorce before he died, but now she missed him.

She'd become lonely in her marriage. In the beginning, she'd been unable to believe the great Bryce Chandler had wanted her. But, after he had acquired "the best of all his possessions," he'd grown complacent or bored or . . . She wasn't sure exactly what had happened, but he'd become aloof, almost detached, even physically remote, as if she were an artwork best appreciated from a distance.

So why did she long for him? Maybe it wasn't the man as much as something his presence added to her life. Bryce had provided an education, not just in the law but also in—she struggled for the right words—gracious living.

She had metabolized his style, and it was reflected in the reception. Bryce would have approved of the uniformed servers offering small sandwiches, scones, and miniature pastries along with tea, port, and sherry. Hard liquor only on request. A subdued contrast to the raucous send-off her father had arranged for her mother. But he'd been entitled to celebrate the departure of the crazy drunk who'd brought them so much shame.

It didn't matter anymore. Both her parents were dead now; she had no siblings. Sweeny, Owens & Boyle had become her family. With her professional achievements and social register wedding, she had erased her background.

Her marriage had been the fulcrum of her personal and professional worlds. Bryce's college roommate, Wade, had become her primary client, the keystone of her book of business when the partnership considered her admission. She'd been afraid she'd lose her relationship with Wade if she divorced Bryce.

Well, she didn't need to worry about Wade's business now. She'd worked with Kent Quigley, his partner in JJQ, before. Together, she and Kent would continue to buy and sell major corporations. She had managed to lose her husband without losing the business. Lucky her.

But, without Bryce and his relationship with Wade, she'd have the chance to prove to Sweeny Owens she could succeed on her own. Even though no one had ever said it to her face, she knew some suspected she wouldn't have made it without him.

Now she'd show them. Maggie sat straighter, her body tense with determination.

Ginger said, "What is it?"

"Nothing. Just thinking about the firm. The jerks who think I only made partner because of Bryce. They refuse to see what a terrific lawyer I am. This gives me a chance to show them what I can do on my own."

"True." Ginger elongated the word. "But don't hold your breath waiting for them to pat you on the head. If I had, I'd be long dead by now." She laughed, a short dry burst of air. "Keep being a terrific lawyer because you love what you do—not to get a gold star."

"Yeah, you're right." Maggie managed a small smile. "I *do* love it."

"All right! Good to hear some enthusiasm." Ginger wrapped her arm around Maggie's shoulder, delivered a quick squeeze, then shifted her weight on the bare wooden sofa. "Christ. Modern may have been Bryce's passion, but it's not comfortable. Or attractive. That thing looks like a plastic bucket on skis." She pointed to a molded fiberglass chair on rockers.

"I'll have you know, that chair was one of Bryce's prized possessions. An original Charles and Ray Eames."

"And what about those hideous black things Len and his wife are sitting in? Judging from the look on Len's face, they can't be particularly comfortable."

"I'd guess it's more Wendy than the chair that's bothering him."

"Problems?" Ginger asked.

"Bet on it. Her ego requires constant stroking and she's wildly jealous of any woman not in AARP."

"Then she can't be happy with that sweet young thing leaning over Len. She's absolutely stunning. Is she with the firm?"

"Yeah. Rosalinda Morales. I hired her out of UCLA a couple of years ago. She's doing very well. Great analytical skills; good writer, too."

Maggie took pride in Rosalinda's success. Of course, the girl's looks had helped. When she walked through the door to get an assignment, the first thing most men noticed was her figure. When she returned to ask for clarification, the guys were usually drawn to her large dark eyes and full lush lips. Few men felt inconvenienced when she needed additional guidance on a project.

Ginger said, "Well, she'll be out on her ass if Len's wife has anything to say. Wendy's sure giving her the evil eye."

CHAPTER 3

August 25, Monday
Rosalinda Morales

"So sad for Maggie," Rosalinda murmured.

Wendy Wang said, "Yes, but she's a survivor. Len told me she had a wretched childhood and she skated away from that quite nicely. She may be hurting now, but she'll be back on her feet in no time." The woman hoisted her glass of scotch in a mock salute.

Rosalinda fought the impulse to defend Maggie. This bitch obviously had it in for her. But it wasn't prudent to get in a pissing contest with a partner's wife. Wendy was one of the legions of people a baby associate had to make nice with.

"Wendy, please." Len Wang winced, his expression tightening his chubby cheeks and drawing twin lines between his brown eyes. "Besides, now that Bryce is gone, Maggie's not the only one who's hurting."

"What do you mean?" Rosalinda asked.

"Andy. He counted on Bryce to keep the firm ticking while he was playing politico. Without him, Andy's screwed. He wanted to devote 110 percent of his attention to Senator O'Toole's presidential campaign. Really get in tight."

"That's too bad. At his age, it's his last chance for a cabinet position—assuming O'Toole wins," Rosalinda said.

"*And* assuming Andy doesn't get derailed." Wendy lifted an eyebrow, giving her thin face and sharp features a sinister appearance.

Rosalinda asked, "Derailed? What could do that?"

"Honey, I don't think . . . ," Len began. "You don't know for certain."

"What's going on?"

"I'm a lawyer at the Equal Employment Opportunity Commission. The New York district office is investigating claims of sexual harassment at a 'major international law firm.'" Wendy pumped her manicured fingertips to create invisible quotation marks.

"Okay," Len said. "So *some* law firm is being investigated. Doesn't mean it's Sweeny Owens."

"Oh, now, Len, you shouldn't be so quick to dismiss the possibility."

Rosalinda leaned forward, propping her elbows on her knees. "So you're saying the EEOC plans to sue Sweeny Owens, alleging female employees have been sexually harassed? Is that it?"

She didn't want to sound too pleased, but an EEOC investigation might be exactly what she needed to chill Travis Benally, a senior associate she had looked to for advice. At first it had been nice to have a big brother, but now Travis wouldn't leave her alone.

"No." Len's voice was adamant.

"Not quite." Wendy said.

"Don't listen to her. All speculation. Rumor—"

"Not necessarily," Wendy said. "But people keep asking me what's typical in a big firm. If it was a big firm *other than* Sweeny Owens, I'd be working on it because I know about big firm culture. But I'm not."

"You're not working on it because your calendar is too full," Len said. "Last month you complained to your boss about it. Nothing else is going on."

"You can say that, but I think the director excluded me from the case because I'm married to a partner of the target of the investigation."

Len waved his plump hand at her. "You're a conspiracy nut. Don't even think about it, Rosalinda. And, please, don't say anything inside the firm. I don't want anyone to worry just because my wife has an overactive imagination."

"We'll see." Wendy winked.

Rosalinda wondered how much—if any—of Wendy's story was true. The woman had downed two glasses of scotch in the last half hour. Maybe she was uncomfortable with the snobbish Sweeny Owens crowd. The sole purpose of her "news" might have been to enhance her professional status. In this gathering, employment at a government agency instead of a prestigious firm was definitely blue collar.

CHAPTER 4

September 8, Monday
Maggie

Maggie knew her first day back at the firm would be a bitch. Too many memories of Bryce: the thrill of meeting him, the surprise when he first asked her out, the urgent kisses behind his door when he couldn't get enough of her. The beginning had been so good, and being in the office would bring that all back.

As she rode up to the fiftieth floor of the Metropolitan Bank building, her reflection in the polished elevator doors revealed a woman with dark circles under her eyes and a pallid complexion. Her black hair drained away the color she'd applied to her face that morning. Bryce had described her eyes as emeralds, but this morning they resembled cold, flat jade. Her high cheekbones looked almost skeletal. She sighed, grateful when the elevator doors slid open, erasing her image.

She'd almost escaped the gauntlet of good wishes when Woody Ferguson stepped out of his office.

"Maggie, my dear. How are you?" The tall, heavyset man stepped toward her, arms extended. Rolls of fat threatened to obliterate his plain features.

She raised a hand to fend him off. It wouldn't be the first time the buffoon had tried to get too close. "As well as could be expected. Thank you."

He stepped into her path. Grasping each of her arms, he said, "I'm here for you if you should need anything." He leaned in and planted a kiss on her cheek. "You must be at a loss without a man in the house. I'd be glad to make a house call if you need anything, anything at all."

Maggie jerked out of his arms. "You jackass. Don't you ever touch me again." Anger sizzled through her words like a high voltage current.

"But, Maggie, I was just—"

She marched into her office and slammed the door. Leaning against the hard mahogany slab, she shut her eyes.

The honeyed scent of freesias distracted her from her anger. A towering bouquet of flowers occupied her conference table. She picked up the florist's card. "Good to have you back. Sam."

Sam Forte had sent her flowers? How strange. Thoughtful, but . . . Then she got it. Sam had been Bryce's protégé. He must have known Bryce had ordered flowers for her office every week. Sam was trying to provide a sense of normalcy—as if that would ever be possible again.

She walked to her closet and shrugged off her raincoat. When she opened the door, her spirits plunged. One of Bryce's ties was draped around a hanger. He'd left it there months ago when they'd changed in her office before attending a gala at the Met. Quickly, she slipped her coat on a hanger and closed the door.

She treasured her view of Central Park, but, this morning, heavy dark clouds crowded the sky while sheets of rain slapped the windows. A discordant chorus of bleating horns rose from the snarled traffic on the street below.

Maggie sat down at her desk. Her gaze was drawn immediately to Bryce's picture perched on the corner; her chest tightened.

She couldn't bear to look at the photo and couldn't bear to put it in a drawer. Seconds ticked by as she considered where it should go. Finally, she chose the credenza under her hanging bookcases. There, she'd need to make a deliberate effort to see it from her chair.

She turned back to the empty spot on her desk. She studied her shelves for a replacement, but there were precious few personal pictures in her office. Having more than one or two was perceived as unprofessional.

She rejected a photo of the partners taken at their last retreat and a photo of Wade opening the Exchange. She chose a picture of her father wrapping her in a bear hug at law school graduation. Satisfied, she slipped into her chair.

She glanced at the papers on her desk, hoping to find something compelling enough to quiet the static crackling in her brain. That criterion eliminated the foot-high stack of memos and legal periodicals her secretary, Jasmine Brown, had culled from the mail. She passed over the pile of JJQ matters and reached for the Davidoff pleadings. If the firm was still representing him, she wanted in.

A midlevel expediter, Ira Davidoff had bribed an Azerbaijani customs official to get a shipment of drill bits through faster. When a couple of crates turned out to contain rocket launchers used in an attack on U.S. Marines, the feds charged Davidoff with violating the Foreign Corrupt Practices Act and with aiding the enemy. Although the act prohibited bribery of foreign government officials, the Justice Department had rarely enforced it.

Maggie figured the feds were alleging that violation to make their treason charge look better. But she thought both were bogus—especially the aiding the enemy count. The government was using Davidoff as a scapegoat for its bungled war, and she wanted a role in slapping the feds down.

Davidoff had retained Bryce just before they had taken off on vacation. She assumed the firm had offered up another senior partner in his stead. Sweeny Owens had several experienced white-collar crime specialists. The next one down the totem pole after Bryce was Jack Slattery. He came across to clients as hail-fellow-well-met, a regular Joe with a hearty handshake and an earthy sense of humor. Given Ira Davidoff's background, Slattery might well have appealed to him.

However, Maggie found Slattery crude, and Rosalinda had told her the standing joke among female associates was that any woman he hadn't hit on felt she must be a dog. Maggie had never had a problem with him, but her relationship with Bryce had probably immunized her. Slattery certainly had baggage, but she'd be willing to act as his second chair if it meant working on the Davidoff case.

She was reading the Davidoff indictment when she heard a brisk double knock on her door.

"Come in."

The muscles in her neck tightened. Not a sympathy call, she hoped. She did *not* want to talk about what had happened in Chile. People weren't deliberately ghoulish, but it always came up. The knot in her shoulders loosened when Sam opened the door.

"It's good to see you back in the office." He had a wide smile and lively dark eyes, but their warmth was offset by the jut of his square jaw and the half-inch scar interrupting his left eyebrow.

"Thanks—and thanks for the flowers. They're lovely. A real pick-me-up."

"No biggie." He shrugged. Even in a boxy Brooks Brothers suit, the strength of his shoulders and chest was unmistakable. "Speaking of a pick-me-up, I was wondering what you're doing for exercise nowadays. Want to go for a run sometime and get some endorphins flowing?"

Sam knew she had been in the habit of running with Bryce. It seemed she would be the beneficiary of Sam's devotion to him. How genuinely nice—not a word she'd apply to all her partners.

"When do you usually run?" Maggie asked.

"In the mornings. Could you be ready by five thirty or six?"

"That wouldn't be a problem, but I don't want to impose. I don't know if I can keep up with you." The man had been an Olympic athlete not so many years ago. And, of course, he was four or five years younger. Since Bryce's death, age had taken on much greater significance.

"Let's give it a try. I'll stop by your building tomorrow morning at six."

A single perfunctory rap sounded, and the door swung open.

Erling Anderson stepped into the room. With a quick glance at Sam, he said, "I'm sorry to interrupt, but I wanted to see how Maggie's doing."

"I need to get going." Sam headed for the door.

Maggie's spine straightened. "Andy, how nice of you to come by." More than nice. Unprecedented, actually. Partners were summoned to the office of the firm chairman by his assistant, Regina Lord. He never just dropped in.

Andy slid his small, pinched body into one of her guest chairs. His movement was efficient, almost surreptitious.

"I'm so sorry I wasn't able to attend Bryce's memorial. Senator O'Toole required my presence at the convention. I hope Mrs. Lord conveyed my condolences."

"She did. Thank you."

"Excellent." He paused, recrossed his legs. "Maggie, I'm concerned about you. Are you ready to be back in the office?"

"Yes, I think so. With Bryce and Wade . . . gone, the folks at JJQ are going to need me more than ever. Besides, work will be a good distraction."

"I wish all our partners had that level of commitment to the firm."

"Thanks, but the truth is I enjoy my practice. That makes it easy."

"You can say that, but you're really remarkable. You're a model for *any* partner, and I don't mean just female partners." He smiled as if he thought he had given her a profound compliment.

"We're all the same, aren't we? You didn't mean to suggest there was a different, lesser standard for female partners?"

Andy lifted a hand as if to brush away her concern. "Absolutely not. But you raise an interesting point, one I've been giving a lot of thought to recently."

"Which is?"

"Whether we treat our male and female lawyers equally. That's certainly the firm's aspiration, but I want to be certain we're succeeding."

"You mean equal advancement opportunities, equal pay for equal work?"

"Yes, but more than that. While I'm loath to believe such a thing might be going on at Sweeny Owens, I want to be certain there's no sexual harassment here. Recently, I heard some very disturbing tales coming out of other law firms. I absolutely will not tolerate such things at Sweeny Owens."

She leaned back against her chair. "I'm glad to know you're concerned about these issues." She resisted the temptation to add "finally." Andy's focus had never been the happiness of the firm's worker bees. What he cared about was profits per partner, and, short of a class action, they wouldn't be dented by damages paid for harassment or discrimination. Then she got it: he was trying on the role of statesman, preparing to be attorney general.

"I'm more than concerned," he said. "It's time for action. I'm convening a Gender Equity Committee to investigate the treatment of women at the firm. I'd like you to serve on it."

"Unfortunately, I'll be very busy with JJQ."

"The work of this committee is of such import to the firm, I hope you'll stretch to accommodate it."

He stared at her soberly. Although folds of sagging skin and swollen pouches shrouded his eyes, they remained powerful, unsettling. The dark brown irises were barely distinguishable from the pupils.

He said, "The reason I feel so deeply you belong on the committee is because you're such a strong partner. If the group determines women have been disadvantaged, no one can say you supported that conclusion to excuse your own poor performance."

"That's very kind, but it implies I'm somehow representative of the women at the firm, that women's interests are monolithic. But we can't be corralled into a neat category that's easily dealt with."

"Surely you'd agree all women are potentially subject to sexual harassment and gender discrimination?"

"As women become more senior, men can be subject to the same problems. Of course, so can gays."

"Interesting theoretically, but, in reality, those problems are relatively rare." He drew his dark eyebrows together, an expression that emphasized their contrast with his shock of white hair. "Unless I'm missing something, you're a perfect representative of the firm's women."

"A significant percentage of those women either have children or want to have children. They have issues around pregnancy and child care impacting their path to partnership. I can't represent those women."

"Nonsense. Use that powerful mind of yours. Just imagine yourself in their shoes."

"Truthfully, Andy, I don't understand why these women think they're entitled to different treatment because they've chosen to have kids. As some of the young male partners have pointed out, *they* aren't eligible for paid leave to write a novel or polish their golf game. Their argument makes sense to me."

"Don't worry about it. The committee isn't going to delve into those issues. Perhaps it should, but for now its focus is to be sexual harassment and discrimination."

"Aside from discrimination as a result of pregnancy and child care?"

"Exactly."

She'd scored a point but kept her expression neutral. She knew she should at least appear to consider his request seriously. "Tell me more about this committee. What precisely will it do?"

Andy talked about conducting interviews, drafting a detailed policy, maybe hiring a diversity consultant. He sounded energetic, but he couldn't do anything too drastic without creating the appearance he'd been lax in the past.

She said, "Let's go back to square one—the interviews. Do you really expect women to cite chapter and verse about being put down or pressured for sex?"

"That's certainly my hope. How else can we determine what's going on and correct the situation?"

She shook her head. "Women won't give the committee this information for the same reason they haven't already complained to Bull Holbrooke: they don't want to get in trouble."

"You know women who've been wronged but won't complain?" His voice sounded tight, as if it came from high up in his throat. "I don't understand."

"Every woman at the firm has made an enormous commitment to her career. No matter how egregious the discrimination or harassment, she won't come forward out of fear of antagonizing the offender or being branded a troublemaker."

"My heavens. I never thought of it that way." He clicked his tongue. "We'll do everything we can to reassure them there'll be no repercussions. But your insight demonstrates why you'd be so valuable on the committee. The firm needs you, Maggie."

At best, it sounded like a typical firm committee: a show of concern with minimal, if any, results—except raising unrealistic expectations. On the other hand, it was hard to buck Andy.

Despite the firm's nominal governance structure, he alone had command, the power willingly given to him when he had completed his service as counsel to President Kinsey. The partners had been so eager for his return, they'd offered to rename the firm Sweeny, Owens, Boyle & Anderson. He had modestly declined but demanded virtual control as "Chairman and Chief Executive Officer." She'd been an associate at the time and never understood why men who'd practiced with him for thirty years were so smitten. Still, she recognized his authority.

She said, "Who else would serve on the committee?"

"I've asked Jack Slattery and Bull Holbrooke to act as co-chairs and—"

"Wait. Jack Slattery? I, uh, don't see Jack as someone who's sensitive to these issues."

"The partnership isn't brimming with men who are. That's the very point of the committee. Moreover, I hope his experience on the committee will be educational. I've appointed Jack to take Bryce's place as managing partner to handle the firm's daily affairs. If Senator O'Toole asks me to serve in his cabinet, the firm will need a new chairman. Jack may well be that person. It's imperative he become sensitized to women's concerns."

She swallowed hard. "Do you know that Jack has a reputation for making off-color jokes and, um, remarks on women's looks? There are also rumors of affairs, but I have no direct knowledge."

"What I *know* is that Jack is a tremendous business generator and has brought in many high-profile matters to help establish the firm as a leader in white-collar crime."

Maggie had to agree. Even those outside the legal community had recognized his ability to charm juries. *Time* had profiled him as "Jurors' Joe Six-Pack."

"Granted, but the positions you're talking about require much more. Diplomacy, tact, sensitivity . . . dignity."

Andy said, "Bryce had those qualities in spades, but we've both lost him. Jack is a distant second, but he has strengths—not least of which is client generation. If I go back into government service, the firm will need a man like Jack. This is your chance to train him, to teach him how to deal with women appropriately. Will you do it?"

Damn.

She was screwed either way. Jack Slattery would become firm chairman. Her only real option was to join the committee and try like hell to beat some sense into him.

CHAPTER 5

September 8, Monday
Maggie

Sunny Star-Perez tapped on Maggie's door.

"Ready for lunch? Oh, what gorgeous flowers!" She sniffed the bouquet before slipping into one of the chairs in front of Maggie's desk. "How are you holding up?"

"I'm here."

"Yeah, but how does it *feel*?"

Leave it to Sunny, the daughter of touchy-feely flower children, to go right for the emotion. No preamble, no small talk, just, "How do you feel?" As if Maggie could capture it in a phrase or a sentence.

"About as well as you could expect." She gathered up her papers, tapped them into a neat stack, and set them to one side. "Are you hungry? I'm starving." A gross exaggeration, but it would cut short Sunny's attempted psychoanalysis.

Sunny was a terrific lawyer, but she looked more like a therapist than a partner at a Wall Street firm. Her style hadn't changed much since Maggie had been assigned to mentor her eleven years ago: no makeup, long straight hair, pudgy body, and shapeless clothes. She'd be attractive if she lost twenty pounds and made an effort. She could lighten her mousy brown hair and cut it in a stylish bob. And her coarse features could be camouflaged with some blusher and contour cream.

But Maggie suspected Sunny's mother had been as relentless about the *un*importance of appearances as Maggie's mother had been about their importance. Growing up, Maggie had been barraged by reminders to pull back her shoulders, stick out her tits, suck in her gut, and wiggle her ass. Sometimes she admired Sunny's freedom from makeup and primping. The everlasting pressure to look glamorous was tedious. And what did any of it matter in the end? They were all just fodder for worms and maggots. Thank God Bryce's casket—

"Maggie? Are you okay?"

Crap. Sunny had caught her drifting. "Yeah, sure. Let's go."

They were meeting Ginger at Smith & Wollensky. Ginger had decreed Maggie needed to put some "meat on her bones" and chosen the restaurant accordingly. After three sodden blocks, they were inside the bustling steak house, handing over their wet umbrellas and damp raincoats.

Ginger waited at their table. She stood to hug Maggie, then held her at arm's length. "You look like a wraith. I'm ordering you a ribeye steak and two baked potatoes."

"Come on." The words' sandpaper rasp sounded angrier than Maggie intended, but she didn't need to be reminded of the wreck she saw in the mirror. "I don't look any different now than I did when I saw you two days ago."

"You mean when you were wearing sweats big enough to fit Bill Clinton? Seriously, you're beginning to look anorexic."

Sunny said, "Maybe it's just because she's next to me," and gave a wry chuckle.

"Oh, you're fine." Ginger flapped her hand. "A little chub isn't so bad."

"But I'm trying to take it off." She paused, a smile teasing the corners of her mouth. "I don't need to be carrying any extra weight when I'm pregnant."

Ginger said, "What? Does that mean you *are* pregnant or you're *planning* to get pregnant?"

"José and I are trying. I figure I want to be as healthy as possible when it happens."

"That's great," Maggie said. "I always wanted kids, but Bryce didn't. I even had to agree to that in our prenup."

"Oh, my God! How could you ever have signed that away?" Sunny said.

"Part of me thought I could change his mind. And if I couldn't . . . well, I knew I loved him, loved my work. A baby was an unknown. I bought into his argument that I couldn't do it all. At least not well."

"Ginger has done it."

"Yeah, but I did it at my own firm."

"I'm thinking of going part time," Sunny said. "That should help a lot."

"At Sweeny Owens?" Maggie asked. "It's never allowed a partner to do that. Associates, yes, but not partners. In Andy's words, a 'part-time partner is an oxymoron.' The firm has to be the highest priority in a partner's life."

"Spoken by a man who saves his affection for bulldogs," Ginger said. "You don't—"

"I've heard he secretly lavishes it on others." Maggie rolled her eyes.

"Rumors." Ginger shrugged. "I want to know if you buy into Andy's thesis."

"Well, Bryce and I always treated the firm that way, but I suppose it depends on what you think being a partner means."

"If you look at the economic realities instead of names on embossed letterhead, Sweeny Owens has very few true partners," Ginger said.

Sunny groaned. "You mean, after working like a dog for ten years, I'm not really a partner? If that's true, I'm going to need a drink." She looked at the ancient, squat waiter standing by her side.

"Not if you want to lose weight," Ginger said.

After the waiter disappeared with their orders, Ginger said, "Sorry about that. Being a mother makes me bossy sometimes."

"Bullshit. You were always bossy." Maggie poked Ginger in the ribs. "Maybe the firm is ready to do something about Sunny's issue. Andy has formed a Gender Equity Committee."

Sunny said, "That's great."

Ginger waved a hand dismissively. "Big deal. It's a public relations effort in anticipation of his nomination. Nothing's going to change."

"Not if I have anything to say about it. Andy leaned on me to serve on the committee. I expect to see some real, meaningful changes." *Starting with Jack Slattery's behavior.*

"You think?" Skepticism shaded Ginger's words. "Tell me more about this committee."

After Maggie laid out what she'd learned from Andy, Ginger said, "Be careful. Especially about the interviews. Efforts like this can turn into a exercise in identifying would-be plaintiffs and paying them off, maybe even firing them, before they can make a stink. With Andy hoping for confirmation hearings in a few months, the timing looks suspect to me."

"Son of a bitch!" Maggie felt as if she'd been had.

"Would Andy and Bull really do that?" Sunny asked. "I mean, Andy especially. He always seems so . . . so proper, like the preacher laying down the rules."

Ginger shook her head with exaggerated dismay. "Good thing you're a freaking legal genius because you sure don't have street sense. Haven't you figured out yet, the big boys play by a different set of rules?"

Maggie said, "I've got my own rule. Any woman who makes a complaint to the Gender Equity Committee will be treated fairly. The big guy may have invited me onto his playing field, but I'm not buying into his game plan."

CHAPTER 6

September 10, Wednesday
Maggie

Maggie pressed her forearms against the limestone wall of her building to stretch her hamstrings. She was looking forward to her workout with Sam—or at least she had been until she'd pulled on her nylon running shorts. Her legs weren't bad for a woman over twenty. Actually, they were good, thanks to her years of running. But the backs of her thighs showed traces of cellulite. She'd switched to longer black compression shorts.

That left only one thing to worry about: could she keep up with him? He was in fantastic shape. And, as with everything else in her life, her exercise regime had gone to hell since Bryce died.

A deep voice behind her rumbled, "I'd run by here every morning to see that view."

She glanced over her shoulder at Sam's roguish grin and confirmed he was joking. After his divorce, he could have any lovely young thing he wanted, and, based on Bryce's telling, he did.

"If you're trying to pick up the spirits of a widow lady, you're succeeding." She started to run so she could set the pace. She crossed Fifth Avenue, then asked, "Which way?"

"I don't care. You choose."

"Okay, how about we go up past the Met, turn at the Great Lawn, and cross back to this side at Belvedere Castle?"

"Sure."

Other than mundane observations about the weather, neither one spoke until they'd passed the Met. Sam might be the strong, silent type, but she wanted more in a running companion than a detached bodyguard. As an Olympic gold medalist in boxing, he filled the protector role, but she wanted to get to know him. Their contacts had been tangential, largely based on his relationship with Bryce.

She said, "How'd you get started boxing?"

"When I was young, I was always fighting and getting the shit kicked out of me. My pa said I should learn to do it right."

"You met that goal. Ever think about turning pro?"

"Think about it? Sure. But not for long." He screwed up one side of his face. "It's a shitty world. The fighters are just meat for the promoters."

Maggie bit her lip. As if a man could ever really know what it's like to be treated as a piece of meat.

"I made money from the endorsements and then got out."

"Must have been fun seeing yourself on a Wheaties box. Save one to show your kids?"

"My ma put some away, but they're pretty stale by now." His laugh was abrupt with a hard edge.

They ran in silence, the awkward pause of people learning each other's sensitivities.

He said, "You're setting a pretty good pace here for someone who says she hasn't run much lately."

"Just hoping to keep up with you. Guess you cover about three more inches than I do with every stride."

He looked at her skeptically. "Doubt Maggie Mahoney will be satisfied with just keeping up."

"What's that supposed to mean?"

"I have a friend at Damson & Darby who negotiated against you. He says you're a ball breaker."

"A ball breaker? Wonder why he said that?" She drenched her words with acid.

"'Cause you always came up with the perfect counter to his arguments. If your client gave up a point he shouldn't have, you'd find a way to get it back."

"If that's being a ball breaker, it's something to be proud of." She huffed, "Men relate everything to their genitals."

"You got that one right, Maggie May. Look, I've got to be in the office at nine. Let's slow down. I'll take you back to your place."

"You don't need to." She waved off his offer. "I'll be fine."

"I insist. If I take a lady out, I see her home."

"Do you think a ball breaker can be a lady?" The word *lady* put her teeth on edge. For years it had been used to keep women in their place. A "lady" wouldn't rock the boat or make a fuss.

"Never met one who wasn't."

Maybe he was using "lady" as synonymous with woman. Maggie decided to save the lecture on sexist language for another run—assuming there'd be one.

CHAPTER 7

September 12, Friday
Maggie

Maggie's intercom buzzed. Jasmine said, "Mr. Quigley is on your line."

Maggie's pulse kicked up a notch. This was her first contact with JJQ since Bryce's death. She hoped Kent had a fast-paced deal to distract her.

"Ms. Mahoney?" a female voice asked.

"Yes." She swiveled her chair to look out at Central Park. The summer's heat had seared the trees and shrubs, leaving their leaves limp and dull. She scanned for a hint of yellow or red to signal the arrival of fall's welcome cooling.

"I have Mr. Kent Quigley for you." The line clicked.

"Maggie, I wanted to get to you before the press picks up the news."

The news? She sat up straighter, trying to focus closely. It always took her a second to key into Kent's staccato delivery.

No wasted words. No wasted time. No wasted emotions. She'd thought she was tired of condolences, but it would have been nice to hear some acknowledgment of Bryce's death.

"What news is that?"

"We're moving our legal work to Cabot, Crump and Lowell."

She felt as if she'd just stepped through a rotten board. "But why? Sweeny Owens has represented JJQ for years, given you excellent—"

"That was based on Wade's relationship with Bryce. Quinton is our general counsel now. He prefers Spencer Lodge at Cabot Crump. Strongly."

"But—"

"Sorry. We've made up our minds. Quinton will call about the transition."

"I wish—" Her wish went unheard. He'd hung up.

Her mind screeched, vacillating from disbelief to anger to panic and back again. JJQ had been one of the firm's most important clients, and it had slipped through her fingers.

Quinton Quigley, the boy wonder, had been named general counsel. He was six years out of law school and his uncle was letting him pick outside counsel. *Son of a bitch!*

Her detractors in the firm would seize on this as evidence she'd made partner because of Bryce. They'd relish the news and ramp up their criticisms, broadcasting their insults far and wide. Andy might call her a "model partner," but, to the others, she was just a woman who'd slept her way to the top. A "young honey," a "tasty number." And those were some of the nicer descriptions.

And if that weren't bad enough, losing JJQ's work meant her billable hours would plummet. She'd have to find something else, a new client maybe. But if she did—no, *when* she did—it would prove she hadn't needed Bryce to succeed.

She sucked in a deep breath, tried to metabolize the disaster, and started making a business development plan. She'd never had problems keeping busy before; she'd always been too busy. A few phone calls, a few lunches, and she'd be billing seventy hours a week again. At least she hoped so. She'd call Ed Heaton and Joe Wasserstein and Richard Fuld. No, Fuld had gone down with Lehman.

Shit. She was too stressed to think clearly.

What she needed right now was chocolate and a sympathetic ear. Her first stop would be the vending machines; the second, Len's office.

She knocked on his door, turned the handle.

"Hey, Len, got a minute?"

"Depends." He pretended to study the can she was holding. "Is that a Dr Pepper?"

"I come bearing gifts. Your favorite." He loved the sweet cherry cola, but the only machine in the office that stocked it was on her floor.

"Okay. I've got a conference call in half an hour, but come on in." He grabbed a two-foot-high mountain of documents from the seat of a chair and shifted them carefully to the carpet. Mounds of paper dwarfed his minimalist furniture and created a maze that covered most of the floor. The paper, the dove gray upholstery, and the taupe carpet had transformed the room into a study in neutral tones.

She checked the chair for ink stains, then lowered herself onto the seat.

"So, what's up?" He opened his soda with a pop and a bubbling fizz.

She sighed and filled him in on her conversation with Quigley. With his sagging jaw and pinched forehead, he looked as flummoxed as she felt. "He's moving the business? All of it?"

"That's what he said."

"What are you going to do?"

A simple, but sweeping, question. It encompassed not only what she was going to do in the literal sense—the tasks she would record on her time sheet every six minutes—but, more than that, the fundamental problem of replacing JJQ.

"After Bryce died, I thought I'd have a chance to prove I deserve to be a partner on my own merits. Belonging to a firm like Sweeny Owens means a lot to me." Surprised to feel her throat catch when she described her feelings for the firm, she paused, coughed. "I know some people think I made partner because of my relationship with him."

"That's bullshit. Besides, JJQ was a client before you arrived, obviously based on Bryce's relationship with Wade. They're both dead, the client walks. Not your fault. Bring in your own clients. That'll show the doubters."

"All that matters to the firm is the bottom line. I could bring in fifty new clients, but, if their revenue doesn't equal what the firm got from JJQ, I'll still be seen as a screw-up."

"So what? You don't have to buy into it."

"I guess." She shrugged. "I just hope the press doesn't pick up on JJQ's decision. I can see myself on the cover of the *American Lawyer*: 'Loser of the Year.'"

"Doubt it. But think about the possibility of the *Law Journal* picking it up."

She groaned. She needed to figure out who in hell Spencer Lodge was.

CHAPTER 8

September 16, Tuesday
Maggie

JJQ Replaces Sweeny Owens With Cabot Crump

NEW YORK LAW JOURNAL – Cabot, Crump and Lowell announced it has been substituted for Sweeny, Owens & Boyle as legal counsel for Johnson, Jones & Quigley, one of the country's leading private equity firms. In the past year JJQ has completed transactions valued in excess of 15 billion dollars. Sweeny Owens represented JJQ in each of those acquisitions and many others in preceding years.

When asked about the substitution of counsel, Quinton Quigley V, general counsel of JJQ, said, "JJQ is at the cutting edge of private equity transactions and needs lawyers like Spencer Lodge who are able to think outside the box to find solutions to our legal problems."

Many insiders in the legal community had expected Margaret Mahoney of Sweeny Owens to succeed her late husband, Bryce Chandler, as partner-in-charge of the firm's relationship with JJQ. Ms. Mahoney had no comment on the change.

The *Law Journal* trembled in Maggie's hands. Goddamn Quinton had made her look like an incompetent. She blew out a long breath between pursed lips. *Don't get mad; get even.*

The person who could do it for her was just a phone call away.

Ginger said, "Well, if it isn't JJQ's former counsel—the one who can't 'think outside the box.'"

"Yeah, that's me all right." Maggie sniffed. "Quinton really stuck it to me."

"Indeed he did. I told you Cabot Crump would trumpet the news, but, damn, they even put out a press release. So who is this paragon who's replacing you?"

"A sixth-year associate at Cabot Crump."

"Six years out? That's impossible."

"Not when you consider the fact that Quinton Quigley and Spencer Lodge were both lifers at Buckley School. One went to Princeton, the other Yale, but they graduated from Harvard Law together."

"You're well and truly screwed."

"No kidding. And our PR director declined to give more than a 'no comment' response. He thought it was 'unseemly' to mix it up."

"What a spineless idiot."

"I was wondering if you might mention the old school tie to your connections in the press. Your selective leaks have put the fear of God in several nasty defendants. Would you like to turn the screw on Quinton?"

She chuckled. "Sure. I'm happy to leak the story of two little boys who met in kindergarten and are now doing deals together. I can almost see the headline: 'Buckley Boys Capitalize on Sandbox Connection.'"

"Great. Maybe when Kent Quigley finds out what's behind Quinton's decision, he'll overrule him. A long shot, but . . ."

"Long shot? Sweetie, it's a Hail Mary. Don't get your hopes up. Masters of the Universe rarely change their minds—even when they know they're wrong."

CHAPTER 9

September 16, Tuesday
Rosalinda

Rosalinda squinted to read Len's scribbled comments in the margin of her draft. Two quick knocks sounded on her door. "Come in."

Travis Benally swaggered in with the slight bounce and dip in his walk she associated with jocks. Despite her efforts to chill him out, he still kept dropping by her office.

She saw him check out the empty desk shoehorned into the other side of the small office. With her office mate gone, he'd chew her ear forever.

"Where's your roomie? Gone home so early?"

"Early? It's after seven."

"Listen to Travis. If you want to get ahead in this place, you come in early and stay late. Wherever you're going—even if it's to the john—you walk fast like you're doing something important."

"That's the secret to success at the firm? Walk fast?" She chuckled.

He sauntered to her desk and planted a hip on the corner. *Ay, Dios.* He was almost in her lap. With his thighs spread wide, he was showing off his package. As if she cared.

She looked down at the papers on her desk, glanced at her watch. Maybe he'd get the hint.

"I can tell you're busy."

"Very."

He didn't budge. "I just wanted you to know I told Buddy Clark what a great job you did on the Allied Financial case. You know he's on the Associate Review Committee."

"Thanks."

"Always happy to help you out. You must know that, girl." He smiled and lowered his voice to a purr. "If you want, I'll tell you all of Travis's secrets to success. All you gotta do is go out to dinner with me."

"I have to finish this motion tonight." She picked up a stack of papers. "But thanks for putting in the good word."

"Well, at least I'm glad to see you're taking Travis's advice to heart." He slid off her desk and took her chin in his hand. "You think about my offer, pretty lady." She jerked her head back.

"It's nice of you to want to help me, but . . ." *Leave me alone, Bozo.* No, she couldn't say that. "But it would kind of feel like cheating. I need to figure it out on my own."

He bounced his way back to her door. "If you change your mind, my door is always open."

She thought, *yeah, that and your fly,* but said, "Thanks." She looked at the papers in her hand and held her breath until she heard the door click shut behind him.

What was it going to take to get rid of him? If she had to, she would make a complaint to Bull Holbrooke, the partner responsible for the firm's relations with employees. But maybe that was escalating it too much. She didn't want to look like a baby who couldn't handle her own problems. Besides, being a complainer wasn't *anyone's* secret to success.

But there had to be some way short of death or castration to get him to stop.

CHAPTER 10

September 18, Thursday
Maggie

Despite the story on Quinton and his playmate Spencer that Ginger had leaked to *Page Six*, Kent Quigley hadn't reversed his decision. Maggie still nursed her anger but had accepted that she needed to reconstruct her career.

She tried to set up lunch dates with prospective clients but several dealmakers put her off until the turmoil on Wall Street calmed. She heard a number of variations on, "Love to see you again, but I'm chained to my desk until the dust settles." A couple had penciled her into their calendars, but the time between making her case to them and being retained would be protracted. She needed billable hours *now*.

The most likely prospect was the Davidoff case, and she'd scheduled an appointment with Jack Slattery. Because of Maggie's experience with domestic bribery, Bryce had introduced her to the client. He was a decent guy with four kids who was getting hosed by the system. She warmed to the idea of helping a real person, instead of her usual client: a fictional legal entity.

As she stood in her dressing room Thursday morning, Maggie vacillated about her outfit. She thought of dressing sedately in widow's weeds but didn't want to play on Bryce's death. Instead, she chose a red suit, its jacket cut close to the body and a matching flip skirt that stopped above her knees. After doing her hair and makeup, she studied the final product in her three-way mirror: not bad. Maybe not up to her old fashionista standards, but better than the skeletal zombie who'd skulked back to the firm after Bryce's death.

She leashed her ambition until ten thirty when she headed toward Jack's office. Bryce's former office. More than an office. A suite really. One of the two at the firm that included an internal conference room and private bath. She'd heard it had been totally redecorated.

But just walking down the corridor stirred up old feelings. She remembered the first time she'd crept along the hallway hoping to steal a glimpse of Sweeny Owens's superstar. Her heart had pounded like a jackhammer. When they started dating, she felt—

No. She wasn't going there. Nothing to be served by dredging up those memories. This was a new situation, a new day.

She paused in the open doorway. Jack had transformed Bryce's vintage modern showcase into his vision of patrician elegance. Early American antiques dominated. On the far wall, a sofa upholstered in cream and blue striped silk balanced on feet carved to resemble dogs' paws. Above it, a pair of desiccated oils depicted fleeing foxes and malicious hounds. Two cherry guest chairs with the profile of a harp worked into their backrests faced a massive mahogany desk.

Sam and Jack stood in front of the desk. Jabbing a sheet of paper in Jack's direction, Sam said, "Andy's hitting us up for money big time. If we're already maxed out on our contributions to O'Toole, he expects us to give to his 538. Calls it 'Freedom First.'"

"What can I tell you, champ? Sounds like a good idea to me." He gave a short bark of a laugh.

Slattery was tall with a thick neck and a mop of auburn hair flecked with gray. Maggie suspected his parade-rest posture was an attempt to preserve the appearance of an athlete's build, but middle-aged spread had started to set in. His even features were unremarkable with the exception of a thick brush moustache below a reddish nose. When he saw Maggie, a gap-toothed grin spread across his face. "Well, if it isn't JJQ's former lawyer."

She blinked. It wasn't exactly the reception she'd hoped for. "Kind of you to mention it."

"Hey, I'm just kidding." He put up his big hands in a stop sign. "But it must hurt like hell to get creamed by the *Law Journal*."

"Not so much the *Law Journal* as my former client, Quinton Quigley."

Sam said, "He sounds like a schmuck. Could be you're better off without him."

"Whether I am or not, he's gone." She lifted her hands in surrender. "I've got an appointment to talk to Jack about greener pastures."

"All right. I'll let you get to it." Sam headed to the door. "When you're done, stop by next door. I want to talk about our training schedule for the week."

"Will do."

Slattery walked to his chair, dropped into it, propped his feet on the desktop. "So, *Ms.* Mahoney, what I can do for you today?"

"I want to help on the Davidoff case. I met him when he interviewed Bryce. I've—"

"Unfortunately, the poor slob's stuck with me now."

"Stuck with you? He's lucky to have you. Bryce thought you were a terrific lawyer. He said he regretted you two were so close in seniority that you never had the chance to work together." True enough, but Bryce also had found Jack a boor.

"Too late now." He sounded almost cheery.

"At least it's not too late for us to work together. I've had experience with domestic bribery and kickback prosecutions that should be helpful."

"Sam and I have it covered. We may add one or two other lawyers, but nobody at your level of seniority. Don't want to run up the bill, you know?"

"Ira would appreciate your concern for the bottom line, but, given the stakes, I'm not sure he'd agree. If Ira wants to assert his right to speedy trial, you'll need all the help you can get. What does the timing look like?"

"Bryce's death stopped the clock so we have about sixty days to go."

"That's going to be tight. You might want to think about having Sam take the lead on the treason charge, I could handle the bribery, get a young partner or senior associate to manage discovery, and you could be at the helm, coordinating it all."

He was stone-faced. "Interesting."

"To tell the truth, Jack, I'm looking for work." She flashed her million-megawatt smile, the one that earned comparisons to Julia Roberts.

He looked at his watch. "Tell you what. Let's get together over a drink and see what we can work out. Does next Wednesday work for you? I'll meet you at the Monkey Bar at six o'clock."

She frowned. "The Monkey Bar?" She pictured the glamorous interior of the Monkey Bar, a place she associated more with celebrities than business meetings. She would have guessed Jack favored the raucous atmosphere of P.J. Clarke's. But maybe he thought the din at P.J.'s would interfere with a serious discussion. Or, more likely, he was planning on making a pass.

CHAPTER 11

September 23, Tuesday
Maggie

Maggie and Sam entered the park at Engineers' Gate. The summer snapdragons and petunias that had bloomed so brightly earlier that month had already been replaced by gold and rust chrysanthemums, beautiful reminders that time was slipping by.

She'd had virtually no charged hours that month, and the firm's willingness to cut her slack would expire. How soon, she didn't know, but she was determined to fill her time sheets with more than vague notations about professional education and attempts at client development.

"What's happening on Davidoff?" she asked.

"Jack's talking about going to Azerbaijan, do some boots-on-the-ground research."

"I'd like to work on the case, but going there wouldn't be my first choice."

He gave her a lazy grin. "Good decision. I'm afraid my escort services don't extend that far."

"*Escort services*? So I'm reduced to having a gigolo?"

"Maggie May, most men would pay for the privilege of running with you."

She cuffed his arm. "You're full of shit, but you make me feel good."

He made her feel alive again. She had begun to remember she was a beautiful woman. Bryce had relished the story of a client who had asked if she were a stripper Bryce had sent to law school so he could have a double trophy wife. But hearing she was attractive was different from feeling she was attractive. Sam made her feel attractive for the first time in years.

Sam asked, "What did Jack say about you getting a piece of Davidoff?"

"Don't think he wants me."

Sam's head bobbed back in an elaborate double take. "Doesn't make sense. We can really use the help if we are going to stay on track for speedy trial. Ira wants to clear his name as soon as possible." He scowled at her. "You sure Jack doesn't want you on the case?"

"His first response was a clear no. Said he didn't want to run up the bill given my seniority. He agreed to think about it. We're having drinks tomorrow to talk about it."

"Drinks?"

"Yeah, at the Monkey Bar. Why? Is Jack on the wagon?"

"No. Not exactly."

"Then what exactly?"

He stopped at a water fountain, took a long swallow. "Want some?"

"No, I'm okay."

He started running again.

"You didn't answer my question," she said.

"It's, uh, just that . . . Jack can be . . . sometimes women think Jack is flirting with them. I doubt if he'll do that with you."

"Why?"

"Because your husband just died."

"Of course." How could she be so stupid? It was a fact, albeit one she was ambivalent about. "I hope you're right."

CHAPTER 12

September 23, Tuesday
Maggie

When Maggie walked toward Jack's office a few hours later, she told herself to approach the first meeting of the Gender Equity Committee with a constructive attitude. It was a possible avenue for improvement of women's status at the firm. Andy had at least one other agenda: educating Jack. He probably also wanted to create a record as a feminist sympathizer for his confirmation hearings. But there was no reason all three objectives couldn't be realized. And, if there was a fourth goal—eliminating women with complaints—she'd block it even if she had to throw her body in front of the train to do so.

Her good intentions began to dissolve when she opened the door and spotted Joanna Ambler, Kristin Oswald, and Bull Holbrooke bunched together on one side of the conference table.

Bull's practice and his sympathies lay with management.

Joanna, the firm's first woman partner, had never demonstrated any concern or affinity for its female lawyers. Despite the eventual inclusion of a dozen women in the partnership, Joanna held herself apart as the Queen Bee.

Then there was Kristin, a woman partner who specialized in defending clients charged with gender bias and sexual harassment. A walking embodiment of the term "sellout." During her cynical moments, Maggie suspected Kristin had chosen her career path to punish more attractive women. Short and stick-thin, she worked hard at beauty, but nothing could compensate for her strong square jaw, heavy brow, and small deep-set eyes.

Jack occupied the head of the table. His original Duncan Phyfe table, to be precise. After her first visit to his office, Maggie had researched his furniture. Google answered her style questions, and the firm grapevine reported Jack had paid through the nose to secure museum-quality pieces.

Brilliant sunlight reflecting off the mahogany hutch drew Maggie's attention to the breakfast buffet: coffee, a tray of fresh fruit, and a basket of pastries. The coffee's dark, rich scent beckoned her.

Len walked in and joined her at the sideboard. "How goes the hunt for clients?"

"Shitty."

"Yeah, well, the economy's shitty."

"True."

She placed her plate on the table and pulled out a chair with a delicately carved back. Len sat down beside her.

Jack addressed the group. "Thanks for agreeing to serve on this committee. I realize it's asking a lot on top of your other responsibilities, but it's a high priority for Andy . . . as it should be for all partners, of course. Our committee will conduct interviews to—"

Maggie said, "Excuse me for interrupting, Jack, but could we take a step back? I gather each of us was approached individually to serve on this committee. Now that we're together, could you articulate the committee's goals and methodology?"

"Sure. The committee will investigate the treatment of women at the firm by conducting interviews and, if problems are discovered, recommend appropriate remedial action."

"What kind of action?" she asked.

"Regardless of what we discover, the Management Committee will adopt a more detailed policy prohibiting discrimination and harassment. Other steps might include bringing in a consultant to hold sensitivity training sessions."

"That's it?" Maggie asked. "It sounds like a PR effort rather than tackling real problems."

Bull said, "Jack was speaking of our overall approach. If the interviews reveal incidents of harassment or discrimination, the bad actor will be dealt with."

Len asked, "How?"

Bull shrugged. "Depends on what he did. At a minimum, he'd be orally counseled to change his behavior. Maybe the incident gets written up in his personnel file; maybe he's put on probation. Worst case, he gets kicked out."

"Sounds right," Len said.

Jack smiled. "I guess your wife has educated you on this stuff. She works for the EEOC, doesn't she?"

"She does."

Bull leaned forward. "Did your wife ever tell you which Wall Street firm the EEOC is investigating?"

Maggie said, "What? The EEOC is investigating a Wall Street firm? For what?"

Len raised a hand to tamp back her question and muttered, "Sexual harassment. Tell you later." To the group, he said, "No. She's not working on it. And if she were, she wouldn't name names."

"Well, let me know if you hear anything. Maybe she talks in her sleep." Bull forced a chuckle, the sound somewhere between choking and coughing.

"Now, getting back to the work of our committee," Jack said. "With the exception of Bull and me, each of you will be conducting interviews to determine what problems women have encountered and how widespread the problems are. Bull—"

"Wait a minute," Len said. "If you guys get a pass, why don't I?"

"Our goal is to get the women's complaints out on the table during the interviews," said Bull. "They might not be willing to cite chapter and verse with us."

"What about me? Am I testosterone-challenged or what?"

Jack said, "As chair of the Committee on Associates, you already know lots of the female associates. It's my sense they'll feel more comfortable talking to you than they would to Bull and me."

Len sighed. "Whatever. Guess it's okay."

"Thank you," said Jack. "Moving along. Bull has come up with a list of female associates to be interviewed."

"A list?" Maggie said. "Why not all of them? At least all the female associates in our domestic offices."

"*All* of them? My land, that would be four or five hundred," Joanna said. A frown disturbed her cameo-perfect features framed by a short platinum bob. "I didn't sign up for that." She had a honeyed Southern drawl that turned *I* into *Aah*.

"Of course not," Bull said. "That's why I've come up with fifty-six women." He passed a thin stack of paper to each member of the committee. "The list is on the last page. You'll see there's a cross-section of departments, offices, and seniority levels."

"What basis did you use to select these individuals?" Maggie asked.

"Just wanted to ensure we had a representative sample. We can add more if you want, but each of you already has fourteen interviews."

Papers rustled. Glances were exchanged.

Kristin said, "Looks all right to me."

"What do you think, Len?" Maggie asked. "You probably know the associates better than any of us."

"Fourteen interviews sounds like plenty."

Bull said, "You all right with it, Joanna?" She nodded. "Good. The list has two attachments. One is your script for the interviews. It's important that you don't deviate from it. The goal is to generate comparable results. Also there's a memo that each interviewee will receive to explain the process."

He made a trip to the sideboard while the others paged through the document. At first it seemed straightforward: definitions of harassment and discrimination along with questions about the conduct of partners, senior associates, and clients.

Bull returned to the table, and Maggie thought she saw Jack wince as the other man lowered his enormous frame into the antique chair. Bull stood six foot eight and weighed an easy three hundred and fifty—all of it now supported by four thin wooden legs. Despite his size, Bull's features managed to be too large for his head. Thick glasses flecked with dandruff magnified his bovine brown eyes. His long bulbous nose sat above an overly wide mouth.

She and Bull had started at the firm within days of each other but had never been close. Barely more than acquaintances. She'd never liked him. Probably the inevitable result of sixty-four associates competing for scarce partnership slots. Ten long years later,

only her name and Bull's were included in the engraved partnership announcements. He'd taken the spot that should have been
Ginger's, but Ginger had quickly embraced the notion of starting
a firm of her own to help women. Her enormous trust fund had
made Ginger's decision easier.

And now . . . done was done. Maggie's gaze went back to
Bull's memo.

"What's this?" she asked. "This question about whether the
woman has encountered sexual harassment in some setting other
than the firm?"

"It might be relevant," Bull answered.

"How?"

"It goes to whether the interviewee is someone who's easily
offended. If she has a complaint about her treatment at the firm,
the answer to this question puts the complaint in context."

Maggie turned to Jack. "We should eliminate the question.
First, the significance of prior harassment may be that the woman
is attractive and gets unwanted attention. I've been sexually harassed a number of times. The only relevance of the prior harassment is I have less tolerance for the jackasses who follow." Hearing the angry roughness of her voice, she made an effort to soften
her tone.

"Second, it may be unpleasant or embarrassing for the woman
to relive prior harassment. Third"—she glared at Bull—"it smacks
of blaming the victim."

Bull heaved a sigh. "Look, it could be that the woman is more
sensitive because it's happened before, more likely to take offense
at a small slight."

"So, small slights are okay?" She sniffed. "And, as to your point
that prior harassment may make a woman more sensitive, I remind you of the principle of the eggshell plaintiff: you take your
victims as you find them, overly sensitive or not."

Jack laughed. "Glad my partners are such zealous advocates."

Maggie leaned across the table toward him. "This question turns the interview process into a fishing expedition. It's like he's looking for defenses to harassment claims: she's overly sensitive or she gets hit on so often she must invite it."

Bull thumped the table with a shovel-sized hand. "Don't be ridiculous. It's a valid inquiry."

Jack looked at Kristin. "What does our other expert on employment law have to say?"

"Well . . . I have to say . . . I think Maggie's got the better argument." She squinched one side of her face and glanced at Bull. "Sorry."

Relieved, Maggie took a deep breath. "So the question goes?"

"Point Maggie," Jack said.

"Fine." Bull muttered. "Let's get on with this. Anything else?"

No one spoke.

"Excellent." Jack pushed his chair back from the table. "My secretary will contact you to schedule our next meeting."

The others stood and headed for the door.

Jack said, "Just a minute, Maggie. I need to talk with you about something else." He gestured toward a chair.

What now? Was he going to chide her for arguing with Bull? Tough noogies. She wasn't anybody's rubber stamp. She remained standing, hoping to cut the conversation short.

"Andy asked me to follow up on the situation with JJQ. What have you found to replace that business?"

"As yet, nothing. I've had some preliminary discussions, but—"

"The Partnership Compensation Committee will be meeting in a month to make its preliminary recommendations for next year's draw. You'll need something concrete by then."

She stifled the impulse to point out how totally insensitive this was. "Is the issue billable hours or business generation . . . or both?"

"For now, billable hours. The committee will be lenient in the short term about business generation, but they'll be looking for that next year."

"As to billables, I shouldn't have a problem if I work on the Davidoff case."

He lowered his eyebrows and constricted his features as if he were trying to pass a kidney stone. "Maggie, you need to understand I'm in a hard position. Right now, I'm talking to you as managing partner. Tomorrow, I'll be talking to you as the partner-in-charge of Davidoff. Today's conversation is to put you on notice."

Put me on notice? That was harsh. "Okay, I get it. Let's just discuss Davidoff now."

"Can't. I've got to go to court."

"Well, then, I look forward to our conversation tomorrow."

CHAPTER 13

September 24, Wednesday
Maggie

Maggie's spirits lifted as she scanned the New Business Memo. Len had opened a file to represent Southworth Industries in its acquisition of Titan Manufacturing. She'd read about the deal in the *Journal* that morning. Titan's technology meshed very nicely with that of Southworth's Globex subsidiary. So nicely that Len would surely need help with the antitrust review while he hammered out the acquisition agreement. An instant cure for low billables.

Within five minutes, she'd delivered a Dr Pepper to Len and was sitting in front of his desk.

"Tell me about the Southworth deal. How did you get the business? I thought Gideon Downe had Southworth in its pocket?"

"Did, until Southworth's general counsel found out his kid hadn't even been invited to interview there. Kid's at NYU, decent grades, on law review. Stupid, stupid move."

"Beyond stupid. Idiotic. But how did you connect with them?"

"I represented a company Southworth acquired last year. General counsel of Southworth liked what he saw across the table. Hired me."

"Way to go, Len, my man!" She grinned, then steadied herself for the hard part. "But this deal with Titan has some hair on it. The guys at Justice aren't going to like it. I could help you smoke it by them."

"Thanks...but that won't work."

Damn. "Oh, okay. So who's going to do the antitrust work?"

"Yeah ... well, I haven't lined anybody up yet." He inspected the top of his Dr Pepper.

Her heart did a somersault. Len was her best friend at the firm. What the hell was going on? "What about me?"

Rubbing his forehead, he huffed out a long breath. A minute passed before he lifted his head. His brown eyes were tight with an emotion that looked like shame.

"'Cause I'll get a raft of crap at home." He screwed up one corner of his mouth. "Wendy is insanely jealous of you. Always has been. If she knew I'd asked you to work with me, she'd go ballistic."

"Oh ... I didn't realize." Her mind raced, trying to figure out how she'd gotten on the wrong side of Wendy. She didn't like the woman, but she'd tried to hide it when she was around her. "I'm sorry. I mean, what did I do?"

"Nothing—beyond being beautiful, bright, and wildly successful."

"*That's* what I did wrong?"

"Look. Maybe jealous is the wrong word. Guess it's envy. You could call it *Venus envy.*" He glanced expectantly at Maggie but she couldn't muster a smile. "Okay. Not funny, but what can I do? Wendy is insecure and . . ." He voice trailed off.

"Hey, don't sweat it. Having a happy marriage is a lot more important than my billable hours."

"Hunh. Not sure how happy my marriage is going to be if O'Toole gets elected."

"Why's that?"

He chewed his lower lip, then shrugged. "Andy swore me to secrecy, but it's killing me."

"What? Come on. You can't stop now."

"Andy wants to recommend me to be an SEC commissioner."

"You're kidding me!" She closed her mouth. She shouldn't look too amazed. Len was a good friend, but short on experience for a position like that.

"Nope. Andy called me into his office to ask if I was interested, if it would be possible for my family to relocate. That kind of stuff."

"That's great, but isn't it a little premature? The election's six weeks away. Not to mention the fact Andy hasn't been appointed himself."

"Gonna happen. I can feel it."

"How does Wendy feel about it?"

Len raised his hand, waggled the sides up and down. "Once I told her about the firm's severance package for partners going into government service, she was better about it."

"Can she keep working for the EEOC out of the DC office?"

"Should be able to. We talked about it." He sighed. "You know, she could help me nail this position if she wanted, but she's hanging tough."

"What do you mean?"

"Andy asked what she knew about the EEOC investigating a major law firm. Wants to know what's going on so Sweeny Owens can avoid the same pitfalls. I asked Wendy. She gave me chapter and verse on what the bad guy did, but not the name of the firm."

"Maybe he already knows the name of the firm."

"What?"

"Come on, Len. Take the needle out of your arm. Maybe Andy's afraid Sweeny Owens *is* the firm being investigated. He could be trying to get an early warning through Wendy."

"Yeah." His face drooped. "I was afraid that's what he was up to. But. . . I'd love to be a commissioner."

"Of course you would and someday you could be. You're a great securities lawyer, but you're short on experience right now. I think Andy's using the prospect to get information."

"Really?" He squinted with the disappointment of an investor watching the Dow plummet seven hundred points.

"Sure. It's like he's using the Gender Equity Committee. Do you honestly think it's legit?"

"Well—"

"Especially given Bull's refusal to explain how he selected the women. Representative sample, my ass! He's either looking to find out who's willing to complain and fire them or who's willing to spin a fairy tale and put them on display."

He sagged against the back of his chair. "What are we going to do?"

"Look at your list of interviewees. Do you know if any of them have legitimate beefs?"

He pulled open a file drawer, extracted Bull's memo.

"Don't know them well enough to have a guess. Anybody on your list?"

"I suspect I have a minimum of one unhappy associate. I'm meeting with her later this week."

CHAPTER 14

September 24, Wednesday
Maggie

Stepping into the Monkey Bar, Maggie appreciated its recent face-lift. Wall-to-wall murals of Jazz Age New York City notables had replaced its faded movie-set glamour from the 1930s. The red leather booths and soft, indirect lighting looked comfortable but a bit too sultry for a business meeting—at least one with Jack Slattery.

Slattery chatted with the bartender as the small wiry man poured whiskey into an ice-filled tumbler.

Maggie plastered on a smile and joined them. Standing, Slattery placed a hand on the small of her back. She caught herself before she flinched. He steered her toward a banquette tucked in a corner, followed her into the booth, and slid along the bench until their hips were almost touching.

She asked, "How does it feel to be managing partner?" The

question was part of her strategy for the meeting: pay homage, flatter, and close the deal.

After hearing his long-winded reply, analyzing a position he'd held for barely a month, Maggie went for the blarney. "Bryce and I never talked about his successor, but I'm sure he would approve of your selection."

"Bryce Chandler approve of a dolt like me?"

"What do you mean? He thought highly of you." She hoped her smile didn't look as rancid as it tasted.

"I was one of the first lateral partners at Sweeny Owens. Bryce didn't make any secret of his reservations about transforming a lowlife who'd worked his way up in the DA's office into a partner. Worse, I went to law school at night while I was walking a beat. Didn't sit well with a double Harvard like him. But I guess his standards changed over time." He underscored that observation by giving her the fisheye.

Her stomach spiraled. He was either alluding to her lack of Ivy League credentials or her lack of blue blood like the first Mrs. Chandler, she who was practically conceived on the Mayflower. Nothing to be gained by getting into those topics.

"Whatever misimpression Bryce may have had was erased after working with you. Remember how he sang your praises for your profile in the *American Lawyer*?"

Jack hiked a shoulder. "Yeah, he made the right noises."

"And he meant them." Trying to resurrect her strategy, she said, "You know, I was on your team for the Petrotrans case. I was just a young associate, one of the research drones, so you've probably forgotten."

"Sorry, but there were over thirty lawyers."

"I can still see you delivering your closing argument to the jury. You hit just the right tone with them—not too technical, not too simplistic. I've been hoping for a chance to work with you again. Maybe Davidoff will be my opportunity. What's happening on it?"

"We've got a big hearing coming up. Sam's going to be arguing a motion to dismiss the treason charge."

"How does it look?"

"We've got a pretty good shot. The case has been assigned to George Gibbs. He's a flaming liberal."

"That'll help a lot on the treason charge. But he may be more sympathetic to the government on the bribery. I can imagine him getting righteous about saving foreigners from the immorality of U.S. corporations."

"Yeah, you're right. We've got a ways to go on that count."

"Have you or Sam done a close reading of the Foreign Corrupt Practices Act? I think what Davidoff did may fall into one of the permitted exceptions."

"Sunny's working on that."

"Sunny?"

"Yeah. Sunny's billing rate is probably half yours. Course, she's only half as cute, but she'll do." He served up a lecherous grin.

"Look, I'm the best lawyer to handle the issue. Given the stakes, I can't believe Davidoff is worried about the bill. After all, his employer is indemnifying him."

"Logic Logistics? They tanked, filed bankruptcy a month ago. Davidoff will never see a dime out of them. He's definitely paying attention to the bill. I mean the guy may be sitting out the rest of his life in jail. He's worried about having enough for his family." His delivery was flat, almost indifferent.

The son of a bitch was not letting her into the case, no way, no how.

"Well, if Sunny wants to bounce ideas off someone, you can send her to me. I'd started to think about the bribery issues for Bryce."

"Look, we've been talking law and law firms too long," Jack said, brushing his palms across the tabletop as if to clear away the topics. "I want to get to know you better. How about some dinner?"

Get to know her better? He knew she was a lawyer who'd been dumped by her principal client, a lawyer who needed billable hours. And he'd just shafted her. "I appreciate the invitation, but I'm bushed. I'll see you in the office tomorrow."

"Come on now, Maggie. You don't have to hurry home to an empty apartment. There's a lot more we can talk about than work." He slid his hand to the back of her neck.

She ducked away from his fingers. Nothing was worth letting him touch her.

"Actually, I'm quite used to being alone by now."

"That's a shame, a pretty lady like you."

"I'm too tired to stay." *And be jerked around any more*, she thought. She slid out of the banquette. "I'd appreciate your considering what I can do for your clients. See you in the office."

CHAPTER 15

THE NEW YORK TIMES OP-ED
Even Lawyers Must Obey the Law
by Micah Levin

Yesterday the Equal Employment Opportunity Commission announced an initiative to attack what it views as persistent problems of sexual harassment and discrimination in the legal community.

Perhaps the EEOC will succeed where private plaintiffs have failed. Significant individual damage awards have thus far failed to deter sexual harassment in law firms.

When a secretary was awarded more than
$7 million as a result of a partner's crude
gropings and bawdy remarks, many were
shocked. The partner was employed by Baker & McKenzie, the world's largest law firm.
Despite having thousands of supposedly
smart lawyers, this law firm failed to act on
its own evidence of the partner's repeated
misconduct toward the plaintiff and other
women.

When the verdict was delivered in 1994,
commentators predicted the sizable award
would incent law firms to obey federal and
state laws prohibiting sexual harassment.
However, the Baker & McKenzie decision
failed to achieve its predicted deterrent effect.

The most egregious example of this failure occurred a decade later at Holland &
Knight, a 1,200-person law firm, where, in
response to complaints by female associates, an internal investigation resulted in the
reprimand of a senior partner for sexually
charged conduct. Progress, you might say.
But the women had reason to protest again
six months later when the offending partner
was promoted to third-in-command.

Given the failure of the pocketbook to mo-
tivate lawyers to change their behavior, it's

time to consider their motivation in persisting in predatory behavior toward females.

Some suggest the seeming tolerance of firm administration for this conduct arises from a lack of awareness of the daily goings-on among the rank and file. Others attribute it to misplaced trust that legal professionals will behave more prudently than employees in other industries.

Both these explanations fail in the face of persistent sexual harassment in private law firms. The true reason is hubris.

Lawyers pride themselves on their knowledge of how to execute end runs around legal constraints. Harassing lawyers are certain that, if challenged, their unsurpassed trial tactics will prevail in a courtroom.

The EEOC has commenced its initiative with an investigation of one of Wall Street's oldest firms. It is yet to be seen whether these brilliant attorneys are capable of learning that they, too, are subject to the law.

CHAPTER 16

September 25, Thursday
Maggie

The intensity of Indian summer surprised Maggie. At 7:00 a.m., the pavement radiated heat. By noon, the spires of St. Patrick's Cathedral would wilt. The plus side of the weather was that Sam wasn't wearing a T-shirt. His six-pack abs and perfect pecs were a sight to behold. Determined not to mimic guys who'd stared at her chest, she looked away from his sculpted torso.

He asked, "Did you see the op-ed piece in today's *Times*?"

"Yeah. Bet it ruffled some feathers. Andy's probably praying O'Toole doesn't see it."

"Think it's us?"

"Possible. The firm's got enough crap going on to deserve it."

"Do you really think we're worse than other Wall Street shops?"

"Hard to say. They all worship the almighty buck. Values like compassion and fairness don't even hit the screen."

He cocked an eyebrow. "You sound pissed."

"Yeah, well, I've got Jack Slattery leaning on me to bring in clients and keep my charged hours up."

"And if you don't?"

"My compensation gets cut which, of course, signals to the world I'm a screw-up."

"Just the world of Sweeny Owens."

"Yeah, the world where your worth is determined by how many dollars you're paid."

"That's true of every big law firm."

"It's a goddamn sick system. Feeds on the *American Lawyer* annual profitability rankings. Stupid trade magazine publishes firms' profits per partner and *that* establishes how good the firm is. Not so profitable? Crappy firm. Must be dumb lawyers."

"Sad but true. That's how people take it."

They ran north along the Reservoir for minutes without speaking.

Sam said, "Maybe I could help you prospect for business; go on calls with you. Sometimes guys remember my name from the Olympics and it opens doors."

"You use that to get business?"

"That's how the game's played, specially cold calls. It's the ticket to get the meeting."

She blew out a long breath. "Yeah, I know. You use your medal. I use my looks. We do what it takes. Don't you ever get tired of it?"

"I never liked it. Hate prospecting for clients. Hate kissing up to them once they're in the door."

"Maybe you should work for a nonprofit or be a public defender. Represent people who need you."

"That's what I wanted to do when I got out of law school. My ex wouldn't have it. Her desire to defy convention only went so far."

"What do you mean?"

"Long story short, Sloane was a wealthy WASP. She married me to piss off her parents, but she got squeamish when I talked about being a public defender. I might bring home lice or TB or God-knows-what."

"Sounds like a sweetheart."

"Oh, she was. I thought I had everything I'd dreamed of—hot blonde with class and brains." He shook his head. "It turned into a nightmare."

"How's that?"

"The satisfaction of pissing off her parents only lasted so long. She decided what she really wanted was to climb even higher on the social ladder. Take Brooke Astor's place. For that, she needed a husband with deeper pockets. After shopping herself around, she found one."

"And that's when she left you?"

"Uh-huh."

"Bitch. So who'd she end up with? Does she make *Page Six*?"

He ran his palm down his face. "Let's not go there. Said too much already."

She felt sad Sam had been so badly used, but understood his desire to shut down the topic. "I'm starting to see how hard business generation really is. It's . . . it's kind of a twisted undertaking. You and I are both good lawyers, but what do we use to bring in business? Externalities. Stuff that has nothing to do with how talented we are."

"True."

"What about people who don't have some calling card to get in the door? How do they get business?"

He shrugged. "That's the good part of big firms—institutional clients generating enough work for a dozen partners."

"Sure, but the partner-in-charge of the relationship handpicks the team. What if he doesn't like working with women or blacks or Jews? What if the client says no women? Would the partner honor that?"

"Hope not. Is this something your committee's looking at?"

"No, but probably we should. I've got my first interview this afternoon. Maybe it'll come up."

She looked into his face. She gazed a moment too long and didn't see a small rock on the path in front of her. When her foot landed on it, she stumbled. He grabbed her arm, steadying her until she regained her footing. His grip felt warm and strong. "Thanks," she said and stepped away. "You know, I'm going to head back to the apartment. I'm frustrated and hot and clumsy. Not fit company."

"Hey, nobody's perfect. See you tomorrow morning. Maybe you'll fill me in on your interview. Unless it's just girl talk." He winked.

Her response was a grimace and a dismissive wave. She wasn't totally convinced Sam's sexist remarks were teasing. Chances were he said things just to get a rise out of her—at least she hoped that was it.

CHAPTER 17

Maggie leafed through the black vinyl notebook Jasmine had set up for her work on the Gender Equity Committee. She reviewed Bull's handouts and the excerpts she'd photocopied from a treatise on employment discrimination law.

Given Nancy Holstein's reputation as the go-to girl for hookups, Maggie had initially concluded it was unlikely she'd have complaints about sexual harassment. But then she realized her analysis was shortsighted and judgmental. With Nancy's notoriety, she might well have more problems with harassment than other women at the firm. And she was as entitled to say no as anyone else.

Maggie tapped on Nancy's door at the appointed hour. Nancy opened it, and, to Maggie's astonishment, they were wearing the same two-piece dress.

"Oh, my God!" Nancy said. She covered her face with her hands.

Maggie chuckled. "This is like that feature in the magazine: 'Who wore it better?'"

Michael Kors had shown the short-sleeved black outfit with a wide black belt and black pumps. That was how Maggie wore it today—albeit not in a size zero.

Whatever size Nancy was wearing, it was a size smaller than it should have been. And she had substituted a big red belt and high red boots over black tights.

Smiling, Maggie stepped into the room. "I'll bet it's important for an entertainment lawyer to fit in with her clients. They'd see me as an old fart."

"I wouldn't say that."

"I would, and it's okay. Different strokes. My clients are corporate types. While yours . . ." Maggie sat in one of the firm's standard-issue guest chairs upholstered in brown and beige tweed, then gazed around the room. Framed posters of rock star Sancta dominated two walls. A miniature pink plastic Jacuzzi and four bikini-clad dolls decorated Nancy's credenza.

Maggie pointed to it. "Are they supposed to be the Sweet Tarts?"

"You know them?" Nancy chose a nearby chair.

"My goddaughters adore them. I'm afraid I can't say as much."

"Understandable. I'm more of a Sancta fan." She glanced at a poster of a woman hitchhiking, naked but for her high heels.

"I hear you're virtually the partner-in-charge of that relationship."

"In everything but name."

"How did that happen?"

"Barry Carleton made one too many crude cracks about her—within hearing range, the asshole. Her manager threatened to take her business elsewhere if Sancta ever had to deal with him again." Nancy tossed her head, sending a heavy curtain of blonde hair across her shoulders. "I'm the only one she wants to work with."

"Good for you. That's a real coup. She's a big client."

"More in reputation than billings. She's good for between five hundred to eight hundred thousand a year—which would be freaking phat if it all ended up in my pocket, but that's not how it works unless . . ." Nancy lifted a shoulder. "Well, it just doesn't."

"Unless what?"

"Look, Maggie, we don't really know each other. I mean, what, we've made nice at a few firm events? Now I'm supposed to bare my soul to you 'cause we got paired up for this BS committee? No offense, but you're part of the establishment."

"The establishment? You mean because I'm a partner?"

Nancy screwed up her mouth. "Yeah." She paused. "No. It's more than that. It's like, well, you don't have that much to do with the other women here. Not in general anyway. You've got your pets like Sunny and Rosalinda but . . . I mean, being married to Bryce Chandler and all, you come across sometimes like you're on the old boys' team."

The accusation scraped Maggie's heart. Sweet Jesus, had she become another Joanna Ambler? That wasn't how she thought of herself but there had to be something behind Nancy's complaint for her to have the brass to make it.

"I'm sorry to hear that. If that's the case, I apologize. I do." She went silent and carefully considered her next words. "I believe, deeply believe, that women should be free from harassment and discrimination. I hope my work on the committee can change things here. But if women aren't willing to tell me what's going on, I can't help."

"Right." Nancy's voice had a zombie flatness.

"Would you prefer to be interviewed by someone else on the committee? Joanna Ambler or Kristin Oswald?"

Nancy snorted. "That'd be a step in the wrong direction."

"Maybe Len Wang?"

"Nah. I butted heads with his wife at a firm event. She was carrying on about how obscene Sancta is and I . . ." Nancy flapped her hand. "You don't need to know, but I doubt he'd be sympathetic."

"Maybe you'd prefer not to participate in an interview. This is your partnership year. Reticence is understandable."

Nancy looked away, then rose from behind her desk. She walked to a small table holding a pink plastic carafe and assorted bright cups. "Would you like some coffee?"

"No, thanks. I'm fine."

Carrying a steaming mug adorned with Sancta's face, Nancy eased back into her chair.

"Let's talk." She sipped her coffee. "I've worked like a dog for almost ten years and I've got bubkes to show for it. I'll probably get screwed over in the partnership decisions. But, if I go down, I'm going to go down swinging."

"Thank you." Maggie exhaled, surprised to realize she'd been holding her breath. "What did you hear in your last review?"

"The usual bullshit. 'It's a very competitive year. Blah-blah-blah. Keep doin' what you're doin'. Try to broaden your client base, but it's great you're keeping Sancta happy.' Ford didn't say I'd make partner, but he didn't say I wouldn't either." She blew a raspberry. "Being at Sancta's beck and call twenty-four hours a day makes it hard to take on new clients—especially when the big guys won't let me near them."

That sounded ominous. Maggie opened her notebook and scribbled a few words. "What's going on?"

"Our department is about hand-holding and schmoozing. Yeah, you gotta be a good lawyer, but it's a much more personal relationship than representing some corporation and making nice with the general counsel.

"A lot of that so-called bonding goes on outside the office, specifically in strip clubs. The partners who are, *of course*, all guys, routinely take clients to strip clubs and rent a private room for the evening. Ford MacLeod's secretary told me that one night his tab ran over a hundred thousand dollars."

"My God! How do they spend so much money?" An image of a naked woman kneeling in front of a man in a suit flashed through Maggie's mind. "Never mind. I can guess."

"Right." The word zinged with the razor-edge of sarcasm. "And then there are weekend junkets to Las Vegas. First a private jet, then luxury suites, and, of course, hookers. Excuse me. 'Entertainers.'"

"And you're not invited?"

"Never. I asked MacLeod about it once. He said the clients wouldn't feel comfortable 'interacting' with the 'entertainers' if I were there."

"I bet the partners wouldn't either."

"Yeah. I might run into their wives at some firm event and say the wrong thing."

"Pricks," Maggie muttered. "Look, this raises several issues. One is whether strip clubs are appropriate locations for client entertainment. Other departments do it, too, but it seems much more prevalent here. Another issue is firm reimbursement for such outrageous amounts. I had no idea what it costs. But what seems to be most important to you is that you're excluded."

"Exactly."

"What about male associates? Are they invited?"

"Of course. And Cinderella here stays home. Usually doing some dog-shit assignment like writing a memo to clients about the latest development in digital music distribution."

"So, in addition to more client contact, you'd say male associates get better assignments?"

"Abso-fucking-lutely. Female associates are stuck in their offices doing research while the guys are working with clients or negotiating deals. Not always, mind you. But way too often for it to be luck of the draw."

Maggie sighed. "You've given me a lot to think about." And research. How much of what Nancy had said was true? How much was self-serving exaggeration? And what about the notion Maggie was part of the establishment? Shit. "I'm sorry you're having a bad time."

"Yeah, me too." She shrugged. "But, like they say, life is hard, then you die."

"What about sexual harassment? Is that a problem for you?"

Nancy hooted. "You mean do I harass guys or do they harass me?"

"The latter."

"Nah. That's one thing I can't complain about."

"Good." Maggie closed her notebook. "If there's anything else you'd like to talk to me about, just give me a call."

"Thanks."

As she reached the door, Maggie turned. "It was nice to talk with you. I mean *really* talk. I appreciate your honesty. This place has gotten so big, I rarely meet people out of my practice area." She paused. "And I haven't reached out as much as I should."

"Yeah, well, that's history. I'm glad you're doing this committee. Maybe you can change things."

"If the women we interview are as frank as you, that's guaranteed."

Maggie kicked herself as she walked to the elevator. Guaranteed? The only thing she could guarantee was that the firm would change or she would leave. No more being part of the "establishment."

CHAPTER 18

September 25, Thursday
Maggie

Maggie sat at her desk and watched the sky take on a red glow. She wished Bryce were still alive. She didn't really miss Bryce himself so much as she missed having someone to talk to. If he were still alive, they'd be getting ready to run in the park. It was the one time of day she could count on having his attention. Or had been, until he'd started wearing a Bluetooth.

She'd gathered some juicy tidbits today, but had no one to share them with. Actually, they were more than tidbits. They were clues to what Andy was up to on the Gender Equity Committee. She thought she knew what they meant, but Ginger could definitely tell her where they fit in. Maggie dialed her direct line.

"Got time for a drink before reporting to the home front?"

"No such luck. I'm late as it is."

"Unh-unh-unh. You're going to miss some good dirt."

"No fair! You're being a tease."

"Sure you won't change your mind?"

"I really can't. At least give me a morsel. Have pity on me. I'm going home to dress and undress Barbie and Ken fifteen times." Ginger sighed. "I'm going to kill my mother-in-law for buying them. The dolls are bad enough, but the outfits. Damn."

"All right, this will give you something to smile about as you undress Barbie. Ford MacLeod spent over a hundred thousand bucks at a strip club in one night. He—"

"Ford? The head of the Media Department, the guy with the twitchy eye? You gotta be putting me on."

"Can't you see him with his face buried between some stripper's breasts while she's giving him a lap dance? Well, you wouldn't see him exactly—just his bald dome."

Ginger giggled. "Not a pretty picture."

"Here's a question for you, Ms. Plaintiff's Counsel. If female associates were deliberately excluded from such highbrow client entertainment, could they allege discrimination? Say the lack of client contact hurt their partnership prospects?"

"They could *allege* anything. But, yeah, I'd take the case—and try it in the court of public opinion. It's time firms like Sweeny Owens got slammed. Got a client for me?"

"What? And have you sue me as a member of the partnership? I don't think so." Although, if Nancy got passed over for partnership, some plaintiff's attorney would be suing all the partners. And *that* was probably why Nancy was one of the Gender Equity Committee's interviewees. Bull wanted to know just how pissed off she really was.

"Maggie, it's time for you to come over from the dark side."

"Yeah, right."

"I'm serious. Think about working with me."

"No offense, sweetie, but that would be like moving from Trump Tower to Levittown."

"Maybe, but I have the luxury of having principles. Think about it."

"Later. I've had all the change I can handle for a while."

⌑⌑⌑⌑⌑

Late that night Maggie abandoned her futile efforts to sleep. She poured a tall glass of pomegranate juice spiked with Grand Marnier. At least half the concoction was good for her.

She trudged to the breakfast nook and lowered herself into a molded metal chair. Another of Bryce's cold but stylish selections. She should get rid of all that crap and start over, but she didn't have the energy for it. Not now.

Now, she needed to pay attention to Nancy, to Bull, to Jack, to Andy…The list went on and on. She lowered her head and buried her face in her hands. Then kicked herself in the butt for feeling overwhelmed. There was nothing she couldn't handle. She just needed to determine her response to each problem. Identify the solutions one by one.

The first solution that jumped to mind was leaving the firm and escaping its nonsense. She thought about her conversation with Ginger. Why had she automatically rejected the notion of resigning from Sweeny Owens?

It didn't take long for the answer: leaving it to work with Ginger would mean abandoning a dream.

A Wall Street firm with its status and wealth had been her goal as she'd slogged through law school. Getting an offer from Sweeny Owens, the best of all Wall Street firms, was the first step. Partnership had taken ten more years of working sixteen-hour days, seven days a week. Seeing the brilliant glow of her name on the partnership announcement had made it all worthwhile.

She sucked in a deep breath. This was too important a decision to make out of anger, even cold considered anger. And there was always the chance that the firm would do the right thing by its female lawyers, that her conclusions about Andy and Jack and Bull were wrong, that . . . that some part of the dream was true.

No decision was possible until she'd gotten to the bottom of things, starting with Nancy's complaints. The strip club situation infuriated Maggie: female associates excluded from client contacts while the firm shouldered exorbitant expenses. Those issues were clearly within the purview of the committee. Andy and Jack would want to avoid the question of whether strip clubs victimized their performers. But the cost and the exclusionary effect were problems that couldn't wait until the committee's next meeting.

CHAPTER 19

September 29, Monday
Maggie

Maggie's first priority was determining whether Nancy's claims about strip club entertainment were true. She got the firm controller on the line. First he tried to bluster his way around the topic. Eventually, however, he allowed that the gist of what Nancy had said was correct, although he refused to name names.

Next, she wangled an appointment with Andy. Meeting with him jumped the chain of command, but she couldn't imagine convincing a sexist pig like Jack Slattery to ban strip club entertainment. Andy's assistant, Regina Lord, ushered her into his office as he finished a telephone conversation.

Andy put his hand over the mouthpiece. "Almost done." He gestured toward one of his guest chairs. The party on the other end was so loud, he might have been hiding behind Andy's chair.

Maggie tried to ignore the conversation but every now and then the word "senator," spoken in cigarette-roughened drawl, blasted into her consciousness.

Maggie gazed around the room, then decided to study the portrait of Andy's Grand Champion bulldog, Mountbatten. A lifelong bachelor, Andy lavished his affection on his dogs, and Mountbatten had won Best in Show at Westminster the year before. The painting was framed in gilt laurel garlands, a lavish touch but consistent with the ormolu and gilded bronze detail of the office's Louis XVI décor. It was over the top but understandable for a man who'd dodged his family's calling in the coal mines.

Andy said, "Yes, Howdy, I fully understand the importance of the vote."

Maggie's suspicion was confirmed. The caller was Howdy Pickens, Senator O'Toole's chief of staff, a porky, red-faced good old boy rumored to be as pushy and abrasive as he was loud.

"I will call Representative McCarter immediately. I know. I know. Having suspended his campaign to deal with the crisis, the senator needs to deliver. Understood." Andy replaced the handset and made a quick note.

When he turned to her, she said, "Thank you for making time for me. I can tell it's a busy day for you."

"That's how it is with political campaigns. And now with the financial crisis, everything is turned upside down." He gave his head a small, stiff shake. "But I take it you're here on firm business."

"Yes, as part of my work on the Gender Equity Committee, I want to discuss the practice of partners entertaining clients in strip clubs. It is absolutely appalling. Not at all consistent with your commitment to parity for women. At a minimum, the Management Committee needs to stop reimbursing such enormous expenses. More than that, I believe it should outlaw entertaining clients at strip clubs, regardless of who picks up the tab."

Andy folded his hands in front of his face as if in prayer and leaned his forehead against his thumbs. When he lifted his head, pink splotches appeared high on his cheeks.

"The Management Committee considered this very issue last year and declined to take action."

"*What?* You mean the exclusionary effect, the expense—it's all *okay?*"

"Not okay, but . . . a sensitive topic with strong feelings on both sides. The committee decided it was best left to the discretion of each partner."

"Wait. You're saying each partner has the discretion to spend a hundred thousand dollars or more *in a night* for client entertainment—whether strippers or . . . or a string quartet—and get reimbursed?"

"Partners must trust one another to exercise good judgment. That's the essence of a partnership, after all."

"Did the committee understand the disproportionate negative impact this practice has on women?"

"That point was raised."

"And ignored." She snorted. "Of course, there are no women on the committee."

"That's a legitimate concern, one that Kristin Oswald has raised with me as well. It's possible we may include a woman this year."

"If that happens, I hope it's someone who's willing to advocate women's issues."

Maggie paused when she heard her own words. Weeks ago, she hadn't believed "women's issues" existed. She'd thought women were all different, not a uniform class. But the last month had opened her eyes.

Andy's saccharine smile was anything but reassuring. "Indeed."

"It is the responsibility of each partner, especially the partners on the Gender Equity Committee, to see to it our female lawyers are treated fairly," said Maggie.

"Of course. Now, if you don't mind, I need to make a call."

Maggie silently vowed she, by God, would live up to her responsibility. Starting today, that would include being up to speed on the laws on sexual harassment and discrimination. No more relying on Ginger's off-the-cuff advice.

Maggie marched to the elevator and punched the floor for the firm library. She'd use her time plowing through statutes, case law, and treatises. Andy might have envisioned the Gender Equity Committee as a PR showcase, but she was going to see to it that it had teeth—long, jagged shark teeth, to bite the sanctimonious old boys in the butt.

CHAPTER 20

Maggie opened her office door and was greeted by the dissonance of three women speaking simultaneously. Her secretary, Jasmine, looked furious; Woody Ferguson's new secretary, Lily Ching, looked teary; and Heather Weaver, another secretary from down the hall, looked embarrassed.

"Mind if I join you?" Maggie asked with a grin.

"I'm sorry," Jasmine said. "Lily was really upset and needed to talk to someone. She didn't want Woody to hear so we came in here. Maybe now you're here, you can tell her what to do." Blinking her dark eyes, Jasmine jammed her glasses up on her nose with two fingers. Her jaws were clenched so tightly, ridges appeared under her mahogany cheeks. Her wiry body seemed to swell with rage.

Maggie crossed the carpet to her desk and slipped into her chair. "I'm not sure I can 'tell her what to do,' but I'll certainly try to help."

Lily flushed. "No. It's okay. I don't want to make trouble."

"Girl, you need to talk to Maggie. She'll get this straightened out," Jasmine said.

"Well, maybe." Lily spoke in a childlike, wispy voice. "If it's not inconvenient."

"Lily, why don't you have a seat? Jasmine and Heather, I think it's best if you go back to your desks and cover the phones. Okay?"

Mumbling their agreement, the two women left. Lily perched nervously on the edge of a chair. She was a real beauty, with large oval eyes and long black hair, but her slender body seemed to almost vibrate. Deliberately, she lowered her hands to her lap as if they would anchor her to the chair. Her fingers were wrapped around a long, narrow, velvet-covered box.

"So, what's going on?"

"It's Mr. Ferguson. He called me into his office this morning and told me to shut the door and take a seat. When I did, he came out from behind his desk and gave me this box." As she extended it toward Maggie, it trembled. "He said it was a present to celebrate my working with him for a month."

The satin-lined box held a gold chain with a single pearl pendant. The whole thing looked fake: a gold-plated chain with a glass blob at the end.

Maggie said, "I suspect you're not here because of his, uh, seeming generosity."

"God, no. Not at all. I told him I couldn't take it, but he insisted on putting it on me. He lifted up my hair and ran his fingers along my neck." She grimaced. "It really creeped me out." She rubbed the back of her neck with her palm as if to wipe away any trace of him.

"I kept saying that I couldn't take it, that I didn't want it, but he wouldn't listen. I stood up and reached behind me to take it off, but he stepped in front of me and . . ." She swallowed hard.

"He ran his hands down the chain and then put them on my breasts."

Maggie winced. "That's awful. Really disgusting. I'm so sorry."

Lily looked down at her hands as they wrestled with each other in her lap. "It's not just that. He said if I *took care of him*, he'd be a great boss, make sure I got a big raise, let me come in late, take long lunches, whatever I wanted." She lifted her face. "I told him I didn't want any of that. I just want to be a regular secretary and he could have his damn necklace back."

"Good for you! I bet that knocked him back on his heels."

"I don't know if it did or not. He said he'd be out of the office until late this afternoon and that I should think it over." She sighed. "I shouldn't have taken the job with him, but I needed the work. I mean, he was weird even in my interview."

"Like what?"

"He asked things like if I could get pregnant, if I had any sexual fantasies. Then at the end of the interview he flexed—you know, his bicep—and asked me to feel his 'guns.'"

"He is such a jackass!" Maggie said, then paused to figure out the best way to help Lily. Getting emotional wasn't it. "Are you working late tonight?"

Lily shook her head vaguely as if she didn't quite understand the question. "I wasn't planning on it. I mean, do you need help with something?"

"No, I just wanted to wait until you were gone for the day and then talk to Woody. With your permission, I'll speak to him about his need to treat you with respect. Is that okay with you?"

"You'd do that for me? I mean, a partner standing up for a secretary?"

Maggie didn't like the sound of that. "Of course I will. Do I have your permission?"

"Yeah, sure. But I don't want to get fired because I complained. I need the work and the benefits are good, too. With the economy being so crazy, it could be hard to get another job."

"Don't worry. You won't get fired for talking to me. Mr. Ferguson needs to be educated on appropriate workplace conduct. Okay?"

Standing, Lily managed a small smile. "Okay."

Maggie lifted the box. "Do you want me to give this back to him?"

"For sure. I don't ever want to see it again."

Someone tapped on the door and edged it open. Sunny looked in. "Sorry, I can come back later." Her tone was bleak.

"No, we're done here," Maggie said.

Lily said, "Thanks so much, Ms. Mahoney."

"Glad to help. Let me know if you have any more problems."

▣▣▣▣▣

The door clicked shut as Sunny slumped into the chair Lily had vacated.

Maggie said, "What's going on?"

"Guy troubles." With a sigh, she swung a handful of hair over her shoulder, studied it carefully, then meticulously nipped a split end between her fingernails.

"Is it Jack Slattery? Did that dickhead come on to you?"

"He's *not* a dickhead. Besides, isn't that sexist?" Sunny glared at her.

"Oh, please. If he hasn't come on to you yet, he will. So be warned. He came on to me the other night."

That got Sunny's attention. "Jack? I know there are rumors, but he's never less than professional with me—not that I'm much of a test." She offered a crooked, self-effacing smile.

Maggie clicked her tongue. "Sunny, don't talk about yourself that way. You're perfectly . . . pleasant looking. And, besides, I doubt appearance matters much to jerks like him. It's about power, not sex appeal.

"He's a pig, through and through. *You* may want to discount the rumors but I'm convinced they're true. I have it on very good authority he was screwing his secretary the whole time his wife was having chemo. Cheating is vile anytime, but to do it when your spouse is hurting . . . That's a capital offense."

"Nope." Sunny turned her head from side to side. "Unless you heard it from him or the secretary, it's not good enough authority for me. He's incredibly nice to me. Working with him is the only thing that's going right in my life now."

Maggie sagged deeper into her chair. "Well, then, what's going wrong in your life? Is it José?"

"It's . . . You remember we were trying to get pregnant?" Maggie nodded. "José's sperm is defective, misshapen, the doctor says. Bottom line, he's infertile."

"Oh, I'm so sorry. That must be hard for both of you."

"Very hard. We both want kids. We talked about having four or five."

"How about donor insemination or adoption? You can still have a baby."

"That would be okay with me, but it's a huge issue for him. He says crazy things like he's not a man anymore and I deserve a real husband." She rubbed her forehead with her palm. "I've told him again and again I still love him, but he just pulls away. I don't know what to do."

"You need to be patient. How long have you known?"

"A few weeks. But it seems like every day he gets sadder and farther away from me. Last night he wouldn't sleep in our bed. He said he belonged in the guest room."

"You can't let this drive you apart. You two love each other."

Sunny and José were the one truly happy couple she knew. If they couldn't make marriage work, what chance was there she could ever have a happy marriage herself? "A marriage counselor might be able to help. Have you tried that? Maybe your doctor could even recommend one. Someone familiar with infertility."

"I got a name, but José won't go. His says the problem's not in his head."

"Maybe you could go by yourself."

"But I'm okay about his infertility. Besides, I'm real busy. Jack keeps coming up with more and more stuff for me to do."

"Sunny, listen to me. *Make time to see the therapist.*" She spoke slowly with a pause after each word. "You'll probably feel better, and you might get some idea of how to help José."

Sunny sniffled. "You know, when I was growing up, my mother went from one guy to another. I always told myself, I'd find the right man and stay with him forever. It kills me that this is driving us apart."

"José needs your support and full attention right now. Do you have vacation days?"

"Yeah, but Jack is really depending on me."

"Do what's best for you and José. Don't worry about Slattery, or about Davidoff. You're not indispensable, no one is—at least not on a case. You've got a great marriage. Make it a priority."

"When you put it that way . . . Yeah, you're right. My marriage *is* a priority."

"I usually am." Maggie chuckled, hoping to see a smile. "Go back to your office and call the therapist. Think about the rest. Okay?"

"Okay." Sunny bobbed her head, but her face remained solemn.

After Sunny closed the door, Maggie exhaled deeply. Being a partner meant dealing with legal problems no associate, no matter how capable, could solve. That she was used to. But personal problems were something else. She'd been handed three difficult situations in the last twenty-four hours.

In truth, only Sunny's problem was purely personal. Both Nancy and Lily were being mistreated, but they damn well had legal remedies.

⊞ ⊞ ⊞ ⊞ ⊞

Maggie waited until the secretaries left for the day before she tackled Woody. He would need time to cool down before he saw Lily again.

When she opened his door, he beamed at her. "Maggie, my dear, how nice of you to stop by. Have a seat, have a seat." Her rude rejection of him had seemingly been forgotten.

He rose from behind his desk and gestured to a wingback chair upholstered in the Ferguson tartan. He chose a matching chair on the other side of a round oak table, topped with a brass lamp made from a hunting horn.

"It's so nice to have you visit. To what do I owe this pleasure?"

"I'm here on behalf of your secretary. She—"

"Lily? You're here on *her* behalf?"

She slid the box across the table. "Yes. She was quite upset today when you put this pendant on her and—"

"A gift? She was upset by a gift? That's ridiculous."

"If you'd let me finish a sentence, you'd understand."

"By all means."

"Your putting the pendant around her neck and fondling her—"

"*Fondling her*? She gave you the wrong impression. My hands may have brushed her as I was putting on the necklace, but it was inadvertent. Totally innocent."

"Woody, cut the crap. You had a hand on each breast. That wasn't inadvertent."

His face flushed. "Any . . . any contact with her was purely accidental. She's lying if she says otherwise."

Maggie resisted the impulse to tell him he was a pervert. Name-calling wouldn't help Lily. "In addition to what happened today, you've made comments she understandably found distressing, like asking about her sexual fantasies and whether she could get pregnant."

"And you've come to talk to me as her champion?" He grunted. "You should know you're defending an incompetent twit who couldn't find her buttocks with both hands."

"Why would you give her a present if she was incompetent?"

"Why . . . I wanted to build her self-esteem. Encourage her. The gift was inconsequential." He flicked his hand.

"Yeah, I thought it was a fake," she scoffed. "Her competence or incompetence doesn't matter. She is another human being who deserves respect. And if that isn't reason enough, there's something called Title VII which would impose liability on you, me, and all the partners in this firm for your blatant harassment of her."

Woody tsked and shook his head, his jowls quivering. "How ironic having a strumpet call me on the carpet for sex inside the firm."

"*What* did you call me?" Her voice was raw and hot with anger.

"You heard me. I could also call you the woman who earned her partnership on her back."

"That is totally untrue. Only someone who didn't know what happened could possibly say that."

Woody sneered. "I know what happened. You arrived at Sweeny Owens determined to become a partner any way you could. Seducing Bryce Chandler was a handy shortcut."

"Bullshit! Whenever the litigation partners reviewed associates, Bryce left the room."

"Please. Spare me the righteous indignation."

"No." She spit out the word. "The bar was higher for me

than anyone else because the firm tried so hard to avoid letting my relationship with Bryce effect my evaluation. For ten years, I had nothing but the highest praise on my work. I made partner because I'm a damn good lawyer—not because I was married to Bryce."

"We all live by our rationalizations," he said airily.

"How do you rationalize being such a sexist pig?"

His ruddy face darkened. "This conversation is over. Leave."

"In a minute." She rose slowly from the chair, placed a hand on the table, and loomed over him. "The firm is adopting a detailed policy prohibiting sexual harassment. Violators will be disciplined. You are my number one candidate."

"You're fooling yourself if you think Andy will come after me. I handle the estates of many prominent New Yorkers, heirs of the Four Hundred." He lifted his hands as if showing her the open pages of the social register. "Besides, I'm no different than most of the other partners. He won't single me out."

"Don't count on it." She pivoted and marched out of his office. Her words may have sounded ominous, but Woody could be right. Andy's commitment to the firm's women was questionable, but, until he was sitting in the attorney general's office, she still had leverage.

CHAPTER 21

October 1, Wednesday
Maggie

Maggie decided to take advantage of Bull's reputation for arriving early. By Manhattan standards, that could mean 8:45. But she wanted to be certain to catch him before clients preempted his time. She appeared at his office at eight.

To her surprise, his assistant, Kim McSwain, already sat at her desk. The woman's long maroon hair tumbled over her shoulders, drawing attention to the ample cleavage displayed in a tight scoop neck sweater. Inappropriate for the office, but then so was her makeup, apparently applied with a spatula and crayons.

Glancing at the closed door, Maggie asked, "Is he in?"

"Yeah, but he's on the phone. You want he should call you later?"

"Do you know how long he'll be?"

"Shouldn't be long. It's his wife. I mean, what can she have to say? Bull just walked outta the house an hour ago. Jeez." She rolled her eyes and twisted the side of her mouth. The expression turned a plump thirtysomething into a hag.

"Okay. I'll wait." Maggie leaned against the wall outside his office.

In a few minutes, the secretary said, "He's off now."

Maggie opened the door. Even at this early hour, Bull looked rumpled. His collar was unbuttoned, his tie was loose, and his shirtsleeves had been rolled up to reveal thick, fleshy forearms heavily matted with black hair.

"Bull, I need to talk to you about a problem one of the secretaries brought to me."

Without waiting for an invitation, she shut the door and lowered herself into an enormous leather club chair. Within seconds, she regretted closing the door. The room reeked of stale cigar smoke, but, with his secretary in earshot, she really didn't have a choice.

She described Lily's problems with Woody.

"Tell Lily she has to make a complaint to me directly."

"Why? She talked to me. That should be enough. It may be intimidating for her to—"

"Nope. She's gotta see me. It's in the firm's interest—and your interest as a partner—that we limit the number of individuals who can receive notice on the firm's behalf."

Maggie drummed her fingers on the arms of the chair, took what was intended to be a deep calming breath. "Okay. I get the idea, but has this approach ever been tested in court? The firm is a general partnership and notice to one should be notice to all."

He leaned back in his chair and clasped his hands across his gut. "Never been tested, but there's no point in giving away a potential defense. It may work, it may not. But it's how we do it."

"So it doesn't matter to you that the culprit is Woody Ferguson, a man known for hitting on women? The man whose karaoke performance at the Tax Department retreat two years ago included the announcement he was looking for a woman who could suck the chrome off a trailer hitch? I'm sure you got notice of that when it happened."

"No point getting into ancient history. If he's done something improper to his secretary, the firm will address it." He looked at his watch. "I don't have any more time for this. I gotta be in court. Just tell her to talk to me."

"Why don't you go see her?" Maggie put her hands on the arms of the deep chair to push herself out of it. "It preserves your notice argument but takes some of the intimidation away."

"What am I going to do? Interview her in the hall outside Woody's office?"

"You could use my office."

"Tell her to talk to me. If that doesn't work, then we can consider alternatives."

"We don't want her resorting to the *alternative* of going to a reporter or her own lawyer, do we?"

"Of course not. You tell her to see me. If she's upset, she'll come to me before she does anything like that. You know, the only thing most of these women want is to be heard by their employer. Hear someone say, 'Sorry this happened. He was a bad boy.' And you're doing that."

"Bull, think about what you just said. You're trivializing her complaint." She clicked her tongue and sighed. "The stated purpose of the Gender Equity Committee was to understand women's problems with the goal of improving the status quo. Your approach to this situation is totally antithetical. What's going on?"

"Nothing. I don't know what you're talking about."

"Either the firm is committed to helping women or it isn't. Based on this conversation with the firm's employment counsel, I'd say it isn't—which makes the committee a sham."

"Look, there's nothing I'd like better than to wring Woody's neck, but I can't. What I'm doing is by the book. You gotta take my word for that. Come on; I'm your partner after all. We're in this together." Bull looked at his watch again. "Maggie, I'm sorry, but I really gotta go. Let's give it a day or two. See if she comes to me. If not, we'll talk again."

She wasn't happy leaving it that way, but she agreed. She'd get Lily to talk to Bull if she had to drag her to his office by her hair.

⬛⬛⬛⬛⬛

Maggie was still steaming about her conversation with Bull when she got off the elevator. She approached Lily's carrel and invited the secretary into her office.

Maggie sat beside Lily in the other chair in front of her desk. "How are you doing today?"

"Me? Oh, I'm okay."

"Is Woody behaving himself?"

"I haven't seen him this morning."

"I talked to him after you left yesterday, but I don't think I got through." Now there was an understatement. "This morning I spoke to Bull Holbrooke, the partner-in-charge of . . . this kind of thing. If you explain the problem to him, I think he can help."

Lily looked away. "I don't know about that."

"Believe me, it's the best thing to do. Bull can make sure Woody backs off."

"I don't want people to think I'm a troublemaker."

"Talking to Bull won't jeopardize your job. You're within your rights to complain."

"Maybe not." She paused. "Maybe Mr. Ferguson thinks I'm fair game because I slept with Roger Demos, you know, the new associate down the hall."

"That—"

She hung her head. "I didn't mean to. I don't even like him that much. It's just that I got drunk and we did it. When I told Roger I didn't want to see him again, he got mad and told everybody I'd had sex with him. Maybe that's why Mr. Ferguson is so . . . you know."

"Even if he told Woody—which I very much doubt—that doesn't give him the right to harass you. You've told Woody no and he has to accept that answer." Maggie put her hand on Lily's arm. "You should talk to Bull. He agrees you don't have to put up with any nonsense from Woody."

"Yeah, well . . ." She hiked a shoulder. "I've asked Personnel for a transfer. Whoever I get *has* to be better than Mr. Ferguson."

"It's your decision. Just let me know if I can do anything to help."

"Sure." Lily slipped out of the chair. "I appreciate what you did."

⌸ ⌸ ⌸ ⌸ ⌸

Maggie spent the rest of the morning kicking herself for not pushing Bull harder. She should have asked how his notice protocol would play out with harassment allegations made in the committee interviews. Granted Lily wasn't part of that process, but would his answer have been different if she had been? Would he require an associate who griped about harassment in an interview to make an appointment with him to complain formally? Maggie would nail his ass but good at the next committee meeting. First, she'd ask him—.

A knock on the door interrupted her scheming.

"Hey, Maggie May, got a minute for me?" It was Sam.

"Of course. Anything for my running partner."

He perched on the padded arm of a chair facing her desk. She looked at his face. Rough-hewn but handsome, all masculine angles and edges.

"So, is this visit business or pleasure?"

"Seeing you is always a pleasure, *cara*." He touched his heart.

"You're full of it, Forte." She chuckled. "Now that you've brightened my otherwise hideous day, what can I do in return?"

"That bad, huh? Want to talk about it? We could run after work."

"Thanks, but I'm still recovering from this morning's workout." She decided to take a chance. "Want to have dinner?"

"I'd like to, but I can't. Ira and I are celebrating."

"Celebrating? You got the treason charge dismissed?"

"Gone like a cool breeze." Sam smiled as if he'd won the New York City Marathon.

"Great! That was totally spurious. What did Judge Gibbs say? I hope he reamed the prosecutor for filing it in the first place."

"You mean besides saying he was *dismayed* by the abuse of prosecutorial discretion?" Sam grinned. "So now I'm starting to think about the other charge. If you're not going to be working on the case—which I think is a travesty—maybe you'll share your experience on domestic bribery prosecutions with me."

"Glad to. I don't suppose you've gained any insight into why Jack is freezing me out?"

"I could guess, but . . ."

"Okay, guess," she said.

"Well, it's probably no secret Jack's got a big ego."

"Name one guy around here who doesn't." She lifted her eyebrows. "Fine. I'll stipulate Jack has a big ego. But what does that have to do with me and the Davidoff case?"

"Jack bitches endlessly that he was treated like a second-class citizen when he joined the firm even though he came in as a partner. Bryce was one of the prime culprits. You're on his shit list by virtue of having been married to Bryce."

"Second-class citizen? We're all second-class citizens compared to Andy, Bryce, and the handful of white guys on the Management Committee. But Jack jumped that chasm a couple of years ago."

"Yeah, I was surprised when he went on the Management Committee. Never figured out how he made it into Andy's graces. No offense, but Bryce seemed like more of a kindred spirit—full of refinement and restraint."

"That describes him to a T."

Sam paused, then shot her a hard glance. "Was he always like that? I mean, I worked with him a lot, but he was always all business. Couldn't have been a fun guy to be married to."

She forced a laugh. "What? It's not enough you're my running partner and bodyguard? Now you want to be my psychoanalyst, too?"

He shrugged. "No. It's just that you're not like that. You're fun, spontaneous. You're . . . different."

"I'd like to think so. But it seems like Jack can't see me as anything other than Bryce's wife."

"His loss. He's missing the good stuff."

CHAPTER 22

October 1, Wednesday
Sunny Star-Perez

The windows on the western wall of Jack's office admitted light warmed by the sunset. Its rays kindled a red glow on his antique mahogany furniture. As Sunny stepped into the room, the grandfather clock chimed seven times. The golden minute hand pointed at the corresponding Roman numeral and beyond it to a painting of a castle tucked in the corner of the clock face. The hour hand pointed to a semicircular fox hunting scene displayed above the face.

Nasty, but at least it fit in with the rest of the office. Jack had several paintings of old-fashioned riders in breeches and top hats chasing helpless wild animals. She hated looking at them. Better he should have battle scenes where at least both sides were armed.

"Sunny, I really like working with you. Not least among your *many* virtues is promptness. I can always count on you to be on time."

"Thanks." She bobbed her head, uncomfortable with his praise—or anyone else's for that matter. She slipped into a carved wooden armchair in front of his desk, propped a yellow legal pad on her lap, and poised a pen over the paper. "I heard Sam got the treason charge knocked out this morning. That's great."

"Yeah, he did a fantastic job. Now all we have to deal with is the bribery charge. The info I get in Ordubad about the customs agent and his habit of shaking down shippers will be key. I'd been planning on asking Travis to go with me, but I'm not sure he's got the skill set I need." He frowned.

"What are you looking for?"

"Primarily someone with good people skills. I mean that in two ways. The ability to put people at ease and the ability to tell if someone is lying."

"That makes sense."

"Here's how I see it going down. I'm going to do all the interviews myself with backup to watch for nonverbal reactions. You know, signs of lying. But if the person who does that affects the dynamic of the interview itself, then all bets are off."

"What are you worried Travis might do?"

He sighed. "Look, this conversation is one partner to another, right? We're equals."

"We're both partners. I don't know about equals. You're the managing partner, after all."

"Ah, the hell with that. We're equals." He dismissed her comment. "Travis could be a problem because he's black or mixed race—whatever he calls himself. As far as I can tell, there aren't many, if any, black Azerbaijanis. At a minimum, having him in the room would be a distraction. At worst, it could turn the witnesses against me."

An unpleasant reality, but Jack was probably right.

"So I was thinking maybe you could come in his place. How about it?"

"Me?" Her voice cracked. "Isn't it a Muslim country? I can't imagine a woman would be very well received."

"Because you'd be in a subordinate position, it would work fine. You'll be ignored as inconsequential. Look, I know Azerbaijan is a dump. It's not like I'm offering you a plum assignment, but you could be a big help. Whaddya think?"

It might be fun—an adventure and a chance to get away from José's moping. "Sure, if that's what you want."

"Sunny, you are one hell of a team player." He gave her that wide, delighted grin that made him look almost boyish. "I'll have my secretary make the travel arrangements." Then his smile suddenly disappeared, replaced by something that looked like paternal concern. "This isn't going to give you any problems at home is it?"

"No, of course not." Jack surprised her with his consideration. She couldn't ever remember any other partner asking if travel would inconvenience her family.

CHAPTER 23

October 2, Thursday
Erling "Andy" Anderson

Andy heard the click as Mrs. Lord transferred the call to his direct line. "Erling Anderson here."

"Yes, Mr. Anderson. This is Micah Levin. I'm a reporter with the *New York Times*."

"I don't believe we've spoken before, Mr. Levin. I understand you've taken over the legal beat from Adam Liptak." *And written that blasphemous op-ed piece on law firms.* Andy wedged the phone in the crook of his neck, grabbed a notepad, and reached for his fountain pen roll. He chose the Caran d'Ache Mille et Une Nuits. "What can I do for you today?"

"Mr. Anderson, I've heard persistent rumors that Sweeny, Owens & Boyle is about to be sued by the EEOC for sexual harassment. Has it contacted the firm?"

The pen's cap fell from Andy's fingers. "Certainly not. And there is no pending suit. As you said, it's a rumor, nothing more."

"When you say 'no pending suit,' you mean no action has been commenced by a governmental agency or by one or more individual plaintiffs? Is that right?"

"That is correct."

"Are you also telling me no action has been threatened?"

"That is exactly what I am telling you." Andy's stomach burned.

"I understand the firm has formed a committee to review its treatment of women. Was this done in response to complaints by female employees?"

"No. Absolutely not. We have received no such complaints." *Not formally.* "It was done to be proactive, to prevent such problems from arising here. Sweeny Owens is committed to treating all its lawyers fairly and with respect."

"Thank you for your time, Mr. Anderson."

Andy resisted the temptation to ask where the reporter had heard these rumors. He knew he'd never reveal his sources. The only way to deal with the inquiry was a flat, absolute, unconditional denial. And the subtle threat of an action for libel.

"Your paper is recognized around the world for its careful journalism. I have denied the scurrilous rumors you've heard. I would be most disappointed to read an article republishing these unfounded allegations."

"I understand your point. As you say, we're careful journalists. Good day, Mr. Anderson."

◘ ◘ ◘ ◘ ◘

Andy buzzed Mrs. Lord on the intercom. "Did you speak to Bull directly or to his secretary? What's taking him so long?"

"Mr. Anderson, it's only been——. Oh, here he is now. I'll send him in."

"Hey, Andy, what's up?" Bull loped across the room and slumped into the nearest chair.

"What's up is that I just got a phone call from a reporter asking about rumors the firm was about to be sued for sexual harassment. This reporter was the author of that ridiculous piece in the *Times* about lawyers obeying the law."

Bull stared at him like a well-trained dog. "Tell me everything he said."

Andy repeated the conversation.

Behind his heavy black glasses, Bull blinked his eyes. "He's looking for confirmation before he writes anything up."

"Tell me something I *don't* know." Andy slid open his desk drawer. It contained a Limoges cobalt and gold box. He lifted the lid and picked up two pink Pepto-Bismol tablets.

Bull said, "His source isn't a plaintiff's lawyer. If it were, the lawyer would have shown him a draft complaint. Levin would have mentioned that to rattle you. And it's not the EEOC. That's not how they operate."

"What do you mean?"

"In the beginning of an investigation, they make nice. They save the tough-guy tactics for later."

Andy said, "I spoke to Len Wang about the SEC as you suggested. He confirmed that the EEOC is in fact investigating a law firm, but couldn't supply the name of the target. He did give me a description of the conduct involved, but that was it."

"What did he say prompted the investigation?"

"Some cretinous partner who routinely asks women to touch his muscles."

"Can you tell me anything else?"

Andy pursed his lips. This was so distasteful. "Additionally, he camps out in female associates' offices and chats them up about their clothes, exercise regimes, their love life. Even their method of contraception."

Bull cleared his throat. "We might have a situation somewhat like that." He shared Lily's complaint.

"It's uncomfortably close," Andy said. "What did Woody have to say for himself?"

Bull looked away, shifted his bulk in the chair, returned his gaze to Andy's face. He expounded on the technicalities of legal notice and blamed the woman for not coming to him herself.

"So you've spoken to *neither* Woody *nor* the secretary?" Andy clicked his tongue at the boob's intransigence. Surely Bull understood the stakes. A suit, even an investigation, if publicized, could ruin his prospects as attorney general. "You need to seek her out. If she's unhappy, assuage her. She could be the one."

"I doubt it. This only happened a few days ago. The rumor about the EEOC started at Bryce's funeral."

"Let's hope you're right." Andy swept his fingertips across his lips. "So who do you think this reporter's source is?"

"I have no freaking idea. It could be anybody from the would-be plaintiff herself to her secretary to her sister. Anybody."

Anybody. The limitless possibilities were appalling. "What's the status of the two women we discussed earlier?"

"I haven't heard anything more about Rosalinda."

"And Nancy Holstein? What about her?"

"The reporter said 'sexual harassment,' right?"

"Correct."

"Then it's not her. She'd have a real uphill battle making that claim."

"Why?"

Bull smiled broadly, showing his enormous yellow teeth. "You don't know? She's . . . very free with her favors to put it kindly. She shares them so freely, it would be more defensible for a guy to keep asking."

"So, we have an imminent plaintiff and no idea who she is."
An anonymous bête noire lurking in the shadows.

"That's about the size of it."

"What about Jack Slattery? Any scuttlebutt on him?"

"Nothing more than the usual gripes about his being overly friendly, talking too much about women's looks. The kind of stuff he's been pulling for years."

Andy sighed. "I do hope you can persuade him to change his ways."

"I think what he hears on the committee will smarten him up."

"I certainly hope so, and, if the committee serves its purpose, I'll be leaving him a clean slate." Andy steepled his fingers. "Check out Woody."

"Right." Bull nodded. "You know, there is another way to identify our possible plaintiffs."

"Which is?"

"We infiltrate with secret operatives."

"You've been reading too many spy novels. Don't waste my time."

"Look, maybe I said it the wrong way, but it could work. How about this? We'll hire—"

Andy jerked his hand up, palm out. "Do as you think best, but I don't want to know about it. Understand?" He hoped his instructions were sufficient to achieve plausible deniability.

"Got it." Bull bared his revolting teeth in a conspiratorial grin.

CHAPTER 24

October 2, Thursday
Maggie

Maggie was finally getting a chance to make her pitch to Ed Heaton, one of her best prospects for new business. The year before, Heaton & Liddle had partnered with JJQ to acquire a Texas utility. Sweeny Owens had acted as lead counsel. Ed had complimented the firm's work even while grousing about his share of its fees. She wasn't sure how committed he was to Cooper, Smith & Wainwright, the law firm he often used, but she knew she wouldn't get any of his work if she didn't go after it.

She and Ed chatted pleasantly enough over the entrée. She'd decided to hold the pitch until dessert. If he wasn't receptive, she could pay the bill and head out. As she pretended to ponder the menu, she told herself she wasn't requesting a personal favor. Sweeny Owens was a sterling firm that would superbly represent any client. Sure, she'd be one of the lawyers doing the work, but she wasn't really asking for herself. She was asking for the firm.

With the waiter standing at her shoulder, she ordered the raspberry ginger sorbet. The sunlight pouring in through the restaurant's two-story glass façade made her feel optimistic.

"No dessert for me. Just an espresso."

She looked across the table at Ed. Tall with a barrel chest and silver hair, he reminded her of her father. But Ed had a killer instinct that ran wide and deep. Brilliant and ruthless, he seized every advantage and squeezed every possible penny out of a deal.

"Ed, I really enjoyed working with you last year. I hope you'll think of us as you look at other acquisitions." Tucking her hair behind her ear, she smiled.

"I'd like that, too." He sipped his espresso.

Bingo! She tried to conceal her excitement. "Great."

"But unless we're partnering with JJQ or JJQ has passed on the deal, wouldn't you be conflicted out?"

She studied his face. It was like testing a frozen lake before stepping on it. Was he clueless or was he pimping her? Either way, she had to play it out.

"The firm's relationship with JJQ grew out of Bryce's relationship with Wade. Now that they're both . . ." She looked down at the white napery and blinked. Maybe she could muster sympathy as a bereaved widow. She didn't want to think she was manipulative and reminded herself she was in fact a widow. "They're both dead, so JJQ is planning on moving its legal work."

"Really?" Ed arched his eyebrows in exaggerated surprise. "That's too bad, but I've got to say we're real pleased with Ron Goldman at Cooper Smith. A hell of a guy. You know we climbed Denali together this summer."

"Wow." She tried to look appropriately impressed. "How high is that?"

"Twenty thousand feet. The highest peak on the North American continent. That's six for me."

"Six?"

"The highest peaks on six continents. I'm going after Everest in the spring."

"Is Ron going, too?"

"You betcha. But it'll only be his third. He just got into climbing a couple of years ago." He chuckled. "I got to say that boy is game."

"Amazing." *What some people would do to suck up to clients.* She plastered on her widest grin. "I can see it's going to be hard to change your loyalties, but, if Ron is ever conflicted out, I hope you'll think of us."

"Of course." He drained his small white espresso cup. "It's been good to see you, but I've got to get back to the office." He glanced around for their waiter who was out of sight. "Well, I guess this was on your nickel anyway. I'm going to head out and let you handle the check."

"No problem. Hope to hear from you soon."

Getting shot down by Ed was a real loss. Her list of prospects was shrinking by the day, and it was more and more likely she'd get her compensation cut. Her concern wasn't money; it was *standing,* the regard of her partners—most of whom would assume that the committee had made the correct decision.

On her way back to the office she consoled herself with a purchase of Teuscher truffles. Hoping to boost her spirits, she nibbled a chocolate and cruised Barneys' windows. Too bad she couldn't find a client who'd like to do that instead of climbing some freaking mountain.

But maybe she could.

First thing when she got back to the firm, she'd research female general counsels. Hell, they could bond together at a spa!

CHAPTER 25

October 2, Thursday
Rosalinda

Glancing up from her draft, Rosalinda realized her office mate hadn't closed the door when she'd left for the day. *Shit.* With Travis stationed down the hall, he might take it as an invitation to come calling even though she'd told him 'no sale.' She pushed back her chair and headed to the doorway.

Travis beat her to it. He took a step inside the room.

"Hey there, pretty lady. How's it going tonight?"

She marched to the door and grabbed the inner handle.

"Not good. I have a big project due tomorrow. I was—"

"Anything I can help you with?" He took another step into the room.

"No, thanks. I was just going to close the door to shut out distractions." She pushed it forward a few inches.

"You don't want to shut Travis out, now do you?" He pretended to pout.

"As a matter of fact, I do. I really need to work." She nudged the door toward him another inch.

He mugged as if his feelings were hurt. "Oh, baby, you gotta let me in sometime or you won't know what you're missing." He propped a hand on the door frame.

"What I'm missing is the time I need to finish my project." She paused. "Look. I've told you I'm not interested in a relationship. *Please* let it go."

"Baby, you don't want a man who can be scared off so easy now, do you?"

"Travis, leave me alone. I can't say it any plainer."

He chuckled, straightened up. "Just give me a minute here. I got me an itch I need to scratch." He leaned his back against the doorframe, rubbed his spine back and forth, up and down.

The son of a bitch was marking her door as if it were his territory. "Go use your own scratching post. Mine isn't open for business. Now or ever."

"You are one tough lady. That's what I love about you."

Rosalinda saw Harvey Humphrey, an elderly firm messenger in blue blazer and gray slacks, coming up behind Travis. Harvey did an elaborate double take, popping his cloudy blue eyes open and tipping his head back. "Best be careful, Miss Rosalinda. This one looks like he might have fleas."

Rosalinda laughed. Travis flushed and whirled on Harvey.

"Mind your own business, fuckface. This ain't got nothing to do with you."

"Hey, take it easy," Rosalinda said. "He was just making a joke."

"He shouldn't be making jokes about attorneys. He's a peon and he best remember it."

"Travis, you are *way* out of line. You have no call to speak to him like that."

Pouting, Travis turned back to face Rosalinda. "Oh, baby, don't be that way."

"I am most definitely not your baby. Now leave." She lifted an arm and pointed to his office.

Travis shot Harvey a poisonous glare before trudging down the hall.

"Sorry about that, Harvey. He's a jerk."

"'S okay. You're a good lady to stick up for me." He nodded and pushed his mail cart in the opposite direction.

She shut the door and threw the dead bolt.

What in hell was she going to have to do to get rid of Travis?

No matter how clearly she told him she wasn't interested, he wouldn't accept it.

She wasn't sure she wanted to make a long-term commitment to Sweeny Owens, but she wouldn't let that bozo drive her out.

Maggie might be able to give her some advice. She'd always been helpful on professional things and this was professional . . . but personal, too. Maybe she shouldn't go to a partner with this, but lately Maggie seemed more like a friend than a partner. Or like a friend as well as a partner; there was no way to forget the professional gulf.

CHAPTER 26

October 2, Thursday
Maggie

"Maggie, he won't take no for an answer. I don't know what to do." Rosalinda's large dark eyes snapped with fire. "Ten minutes ago I was ready to leave the firm to avoid him, but then I realized that's ass backward."

"Exactly!" Maggie's sigh sizzled with disgust. "He's the one who should be leaving the firm—with Bull's foot planted firmly on his backside."

"I don't know. That seems kinda harsh. I mean, he's killed himself for ten years to make partner. To get kicked out now . . . I don't want to be responsible for that."

"Do you want to be responsible for his doing it to another associate *after* he's a partner?"

"No. Of course not. But he's not a bad guy. He's helped me a lot, even answers questions on cases he's not working on. Maybe it's just some weird chemistry or something he has with me."

Maggie saw the anger in Rosalinda's eyes replaced by confusion; she suspected gratitude was now competing with righteous indignation. "Come on. Weird chemistry? You believe that?"

"I don't know." She looked away.

"Rosalinda, you need help dealing with Travis. It's Bull's job to provide that help." Of course, Bull might do the same thing he did for Lily: nothing.

Rosalinda's gaze returned to Maggie's face. "Can you talk to him? *Please?*"

"If I say no, will you talk to Bull?"

Rosalinda shook her head.

Exactly what Ginger had said would happen: the good girls didn't want to rock the boat. Defense lawyers counted on it.

"All right," Maggie said. "I'll do it. But if I hear he's bothering anyone else, I'll drive a stake through his heart, and, when I'm done, I'll go straight to Bull."

"Thank you." Rosalinda smiled for the first time since she'd walked through the door.

"If you don't need to stay at the office tonight, I'll wait fifteen minutes to give you time to clear out, then I'll go to his office and lay down the law. Does that work for you?"

"It's perfect. Thank you so, so much."

⊡ ⊡ ⊡ ⊡ ⊡

Maggie crossed the threshold to Travis's office, closed the door. "We need to talk."

He offered a wide grin. "My pleasure. Have a seat."

"No, thanks. I won't be long."

"Suit yourself."

"Travis, you need to listen very carefully to what I have to say. Do not interrupt me. Do not try to provide explanations or excuses. Understand?"

Emotions washed over his face: bewilderment, understanding, and, finally, fear. He blinked and the fear was replaced by smug bravado. "Am I allowed to say yes?"

She fixed him with a withering stare. "If you hope to become a partner, those are the last words you will utter until I leave this office."

His smirk disappeared.

"Until an hour ago, I would have said I thought you were a talented lawyer and a good person, the kind of person I'd like to call my partner. Since then, I've heard from Rosalinda how persistent and crude you've been in your attempts to initiate a sexual relationship with—"

"You—"

She put up her hand. "Not one word or I walk out and go directly to Andy's office."

He gave a small, stiff nod.

"You will leave Rosalinda alone. You will not go into her office uninvited. When I say 'office,' I'm including her door, doorway, doorjamb, and threshold." His face reddened. "You will not initiate contact with her. If she says hello, you say hello back. But that is all you will say.

"If I hear you have acted otherwise, I will see to it you never, ever become a partner. If you do become a partner but pursue her again, I will see to it you are expelled from the partnership. Do not doubt I have the will or power to fulfill my promises." She turned and strode out of his office.

Her blood pressure was still elevated by the time she sank into her desk chair. His smirk had set her off, the look of bold assurance that he knew what was coming and could easily bat it away.

The firm was full of smug bastards like Travis and Woody and God-knew-how-many others. As feeble as the Gender Equity Committee was, it might be able to root them out.

And if it failed . . . Well, there was always Ginger's idea: Maggie could join her firm and start working on the side of the angels. Maybe even represent women working at Sweeny Owens. Wouldn't that be sweet!

Now that she'd begun to see through the firm's glittering façade, leaving seemed like less and less a loss. The dream she'd cherished through ten years in the trenches as an associate was looking more like a fantasy.

She rummaged through her files, looking for the most recent brochure for Marshall and Associates. Like most other law firms, Marshall and Associates updated its promotional material annually. Maggie had never done more than flip through it, looking at the photos, but today it deserved greater scrutiny.

CHAPTER 27

October 3, Friday
Maggie

With the temperature in the high thirties, Maggie dressed for the day's run in tights, a long-sleeved top, and a fleece jacket. She angled her legs behind her and was pushing against her building when Sam arrived.

He said, "Maybe we should train for a marathon. You're beginning to look like a serious runner."

"Yeah? It feels like my hamstrings and calves are getting stronger." She stood, checked out the back of her legs. "Bigger, too."

"No begging for compliments." He tousled her hair. "Come on, let's warm up and do some interval work."

They jogged across Fifth Avenue and entered the park. The night's frost had singed the chrysanthemums planted a few weeks earlier. The rich mahogany and gold blossoms that had delighted her in September were now rotting, their glory faded.

Sam said, "Have you heard anything on the Gender Equity Committee about the EEOC investigating Sweeny Owens?"

"Nothing meaningful. I asked Ginger. Ginger Marshall. Remember her?"

"Sure."

"She specializes in employment discrimination. I suspect she's representing the plaintiff but she won't say which law firm. Could be more than one firm under investigation. The op-ed piece suggested as much."

"So one of them could be us?"

"Absolutely. Some things at the firm don't add up."

"Like what?"

"Andy launched the committee the same time he made Jack managing partner. Why give Jack that power if he was honestly concerned about how women are treated?"

"You say 'honestly' as if the committee is just window dressing."

"Or worse."

"What would be worse?"

"Between us?"

"Sure, we're partners."

"Ah . . . I'm beginning to wonder how much that means at Sweeny Owens."

"Yeah, there are the 'real' partners who have Andy's ear and there's everybody else. With Bryce gone, I guess you're one of the great unwashed like the rest of us."

"*Unwashed*! I resent that, Forte. Most mornings you reek of secondhand perfume. There's Miss Black Orchid, Miss Eternity, Miss Euph—"

"All right already! I get your point. How about this? We're *running* partners. Members of the Sweaty Sock Syndicate never divulge what they learn during a workout. Good enough?"

"Good enough. Want to know what's worse? Suppose the committee's real purpose is to ID women having problems so they can be let go or, if facts are bad enough, paid to go away? Then they're gone if the EEOC investigates *and* Andy gets good PR for sensitivity to women's issues."

He squinted at her. "That's pretty paranoid."

"Paranoid with a reason. Or maybe two reasons. First is Andy's ambition to be AG. Using the committee like that would clean up the place."

"And second?"

"Back to Jack. Andy plans on Jack replacing him if he makes AG. But he admitted Jack needs to be educated on women's issues. Andy wants to turn the firm over with a clear conscience— or at least a clear record."

"You could be right, but . . . so what? Clean—"

"*So what?*" Anger tightened her throat; her voice was thin and sharp.

Sam answered, "Think about it. Cleaning up the place is a good thing. Same as Andy leaving with a clear record. I get that you want things to change but the firm is like a hundred and twenty years old. You can't turn the Titanic on a dime."

"The *Titanic*, huh? Interesting analogy. You *really* do not understand what it's like to be a woman at the firm. You're in the privileged class, a white male. Better yet, a jock that the nerds idolize. You . . . you . . ." She stammered with rage.

"*You* need to burn out some of that anger." He spurted ahead of her. "Interval time."

She caught up to him, but couldn't sustain the pace for more than a few minutes. Stepping off the path, she braced her hands on her thighs and gulped in air.

Sam swatted her bottom. "We're alternating sprinting with slow running. Not with stopping. Move it, Maggie May."

"I never knew"—she gasped for oxygen—"you had a vicious side."

Vicious was an exaggeration, but his complacency was a blow. Sam had talked about helping people, becoming a public defender. Apparently, his compassion went only so far. He'd bought into the machine.

He wasn't the man she had thought he was. Another fantasy tarnished.

CHAPTER 28

October 3, Friday
Maggie

Maggie usually felt energized but relaxed after running with Sam. This morning she was on edge. Sam's attitude had stoked her fervor for reform.

She looked at the artfully arranged buffet of fruit and pastry on Jack's gleaming sideboard. A copper pot on his antique table brimmed with mums and cattails. A beautiful setting for the second meeting of the Gender Equity Committee. So beautiful, it might have been staged by a *Forbes* photo stylist for an article titled, "How Gentlemen Assuage Ladies' Concerns."

Jack sat at the head of the table with Bull, Kristin, and Joanna on his left. Maggie and Len were on his right.

Jack said, "Thank you all for being here. I thought a review of our work to date would be in order."

Kristin, Joanna, Len, and Maggie laid out what they had learned. Based on their reports, Maggie thought Nancy Holstein had the most meritorious complaint, but she wasn't the only one who'd been ill-used. The group concluded the firm needed sensitivity training.

"Please try to finish your interviews in the next two weeks," Jack said. "My assistant will contact you to arrange our next meeting."

Maggie said, "Before we break up, I want to report on two instances of harassment that have come to my attention outside the interviews."

"*Two?*" Bull asked.

"Yes. One was the secretary harassed—groped—by a partner. You know about that situation. The other is a very young associate who complained about a senior associate making persistent advances including certain . . . sexual displays."

"Sexual displays?" Joanna said. "What on earth are you suggesting?"

"It's not easy to describe, but he wasn't exposing himself. And I don't think this group needs to get into it because the woman asked me not to use names. As frustrated as she is with the situation, she doesn't want to hurt his career. She asked me to talk to him and I did. Quite forcefully."

"He understands his conduct will not be tolerated, that it jeopardizes whatever partnership prospects he may have?" Jack said.

"I made that perfectly clear. But the reason I raise these cases is to explain my larger concern about the firm's environment. I have to think there are more situations like this going on. I wonder if we're not hearing about outright harassment in the interviews because the women we're talking to are afraid such a complaint would hurt their careers."

Joanna said, "Excellent observation. Complaining could well be perceived as career limiting."

"Shouldn't be," Bull said. "I expressly noted in the memo they got before the interview that their comments would be off the record unless they requested otherwise. We should be getting the straight scoop."

Kristin said, "We *should* be, but Maggie's point is a valid one. There are undoubtedly instances of harassment out there we don't know about.

"If there are enough—on top of the discrimination we heard about today—the firm could be deemed a hostile workplace environment. We need to turn things around as soon as possible."

Jack said, "Bull, what are your recommendations?"

Bull lifted his enormous hands. "Look, we don't want to overreact or send out any public signals we've got problems. After all, we need to be sensitive to Andy's situation. The election's only a month away."

"I have to disagree," Joanna said. "This is a situation that simply cannot be tolerated. It's just baiting trouble. I know for certain Andy wouldn't put his own individual interest ahead of the partners if there's a question of liability." She managed to sound like one of Andy's admirers while sticking it to him. She'd never forgiven him for making her—the first female partnership candidate—put in an extra two years as an associate.

Jack looked around the table. "Bull and I will consult with Andy. We'll reconvene this group to report on our discussions. Bull, if you'll stay, we can call Mrs. Lord to set up a time."

CHAPTER 29

October 9, Thursday
Andy

Andy had been roiled up tighter than a trigger since Jack's phone call about the problems that had surfaced in the Gender Equity Committee. He made a point of looking at his watch as Bull deposited himself in a chair. "Jack is due in five minutes. Give me a quick report. Start with that Holstein woman."

"Nancy has contacted several plaintiff's attorneys about suing us for sexual discrimination. It looks as if she's settled on Georgia Albright."

"Damnation. That woman is a media hound. She'll spread our names all over the news."

"Not if we get Nancy out the door on satisfactory terms before the complaint's filed." Bull showed his horrid yellow grin.

"And how do you suggest we do that?"

"Find her a good in-house position in the entertainment

industry. Plus we give her a payment in lieu of the bonus she'd get at the end of the year."

"Yes. I like that." Andy paused. "Here's what I want you to do. Work with Ford MacLeod. Have him start by asking the partners in her department if any of their clients are looking for an in-house lawyer. If that doesn't work, they should reach out to their counterparts in other firms. Hire a headhunter. Whatever it takes, I want her out of here faster than the flip of a dime. Understand?"

"Yup. Gotcha."

"Do you think Nancy has filed a charge with the EEOC?"

"Doubt it. She didn't mention it in any of her conversations."

"Then who is it? From what Jack told me last night, there's no shortage of candidates."

"I really don't think Sweeny Owens is the target. Like I told you before, the timing on Woody's run-in with his secretary just doesn't jibe with the rumors. Same with this latest complaint about the junior associate and the senior associate."

"Then why in blazes did that reporter call me?"

"A fishing expedition. Maybe his source told him something like 'one of Wall Street's oldest firms.' Naturally, he thought of us."

Mrs. Lord opened the door to admit Jack.

"Have you started without me? Sorry. I didn't realize I was late."

"You haven't missed a thing," Andy said. "I was just asking Bull if he knew anything about the incidents Maggie alluded to in the meeting."

Bull said, "I've learned Woody Ferguson harassed his new secretary. I've—"

"Harassed? In what way?" Jack asked.

Bull sketched out Woody's misconduct and Maggie's report in a few sentences. "I've talked to the woman and Woody. Their version of the facts is remarkably similar. He tried to characterize his actions as 'playful,' but they made her uncomfortable. At her request, Personnel reassigned her to another desk. She seems happy enough there."

"Any hint she's going to sue?" Andy asked.

"No. None whatsoever. She says she likes it here, likes the benefits."

"What about the situation between the two associates?" Jack asked.

"She's probably referring to Rosalinda Morales and Travis Benally," Bull said. "The secretarial grapevine reports Rosalinda's really pissed about his refusal to take no for an answer. Sounds like Maggie gave him a loud and clear cease and desist order."

Andy thought of being grilled at his confirmation hearings as to why the firm didn't have more minority partners. "We've got to do everything we can to help him stay on the reservation."

Bull chuckled. Andy glared at him. His smile disappeared.

"Sorry. Guess that was an unintentional pun."

"What? Yes, of course it was. These matters are extremely serious. The firm needs minority partners. We can't lose him now."

Jack said, "Besides relying on Maggie's reprimand, perhaps I should talk to Stan Bemis. He handles work assignments in Rosalinda's department. I'll tell him to avoid putting them on the same matter."

Andy nodded. "Good idea."

Jack asked, "So, if Woody is removed from the picture, are we in the clear?"

Bull said, "It certainly seems that way."

"What do you think, Andy?" Jack said.

Andy picked up his Mille et Une Nuits pen, rolled it between his fingers, thought of signing Supreme Court pleadings with it. "It's time to ask Woody to resign from the partnership. I want his resignation on my desk by the end of the week. Can you see to that, Bull? Jack will go with you."

The furrows across Jack's forehead deepened. "I'm not sure I should be in on it. This kind of message requires the dignity of the chairman's office. He may feel trivialized if I'm there instead of you."

"Given we're discussing his forced resignation, his feelings are beside the point."

"Well, if that's what you want . . ."

"It is." Andy realized he was clenching the pen. He released his grip and set it on the desk. The barrel's gold overlay had left an impression on his palm. "I appreciate your willingness to do this. You're correct that this is the sort of dirty job the chairman should perform himself. While I think Woody will go quietly, I can't take the risk of being intimately associated with his termination. Not with the election so close."

"Okay, I got it." Jack nodded. "Bull, set up a meeting with Woody for tomorrow morning. Let's get this behind us."

"Can't. I'm in an arbitration."

Jack glanced at Andy. "Do you want me to do it on my own? It's either that or wait until I'm back from Azerbaijan, which won't be until the twentieth."

Andy felt light in the gut. Neither choice was good.

"No. Not alone. There should be another witness. But it can't wait. We don't want to look indecisive."

"Or worse—that by delay we're ratifying his conduct," said Bull.

"Certainly not," Andy responded. "Bull, get the meeting on Woody's calendar for the minute you're done. I'll join you, but I expect you to carry the ball. My role is to be strictly that of a witness."

CHAPTER 30

October 11, Saturday
Sunny

Sunny groaned when she heard a tapping at the door of her hotel room in Ordubad.

Jack said, "Hey, Sunny, I forgot to tell you something about our meeting tomorrow."

She was undressed, ready to jump in the shower. They'd just spent six hours together on a plane from London. Hard to believe he'd forgotten anything.

"Be there in a minute." She looked for a hotel robe, but, of course, there wasn't one. She shoved her arms into her blouse and buttoned it up. Grabbed her skirt and slipped it on. Woozy from the champagne on the flight, she shuffled to the door in her bare feet.

"What's up?" She looked up into his face. Without her heels, she felt like a midget next to him.

"I need to talk to you for a minute. Can I come in?"

"Yeah, sure. Come on in." She stepped backward, swayed a bit.

He frowned. "Sunny, are you okay?" He put his arm around her and walked her to the bed. "Maybe you'd better rest. What I had to say can wait."

She could feel herself blush. How embarrassing to be knocked out by jet lag and a few glasses of champagne. "I'm fine. Really."

"Come on. Sit down." He clasped her shoulders and gently pushed her until she sat on the bed, an ocean of slick red polyester.

"Okay."

He perched next to her. The mattress was soft and she tilted toward him. He looked around the room. "This ain't exactly the Ritz, is it?"

"It's okay." It was large. Windows with sheer white curtains let in the late afternoon light. The dresser and headboard were old and solid, but they gleamed. The room smelled of waxy lemon furniture polish.

"I wanted to take you to a real nice place, but this is the best they got." He grasped her hand. His fingers were warm and smooth.

"It's fine." She looked away. It was weird sitting next to him on the bed, holding hands. Maggie had said he was a lech, but that couldn't be what was going on. Jack was too considerate, too nice to be putting the moves on her. And, besides, why would he want her? He'd go after someone pretty.

Jack lifted her hand, stared at it. "Did I ever tell you what beautiful hands you have?"

She looked down, shook her head.

"Well, you do. Lovely hands with long tapered fingers and such lovely nails. I like it that you don't polish them. They're natural. Just like you."

She didn't know what to say, but she was pleased. She'd always thought her hands and her hair were her best features. Her only good features, in truth.

Jack put his other hand on the crown of her head, combed her hair with his fingers. Her stomach tightened. "You've got the most gorgeous hair. I've wanted to run my fingers through it since the first time I saw you."

She didn't want him to stop. No, that was wrong. She *did* want him to stop. There was José. They shouldn't be doing this. But it felt so good. And he was just touching her hair after all.

"You were sitting at your desk. The sunlight came in the window. When it landed on your hair, it looked like you had a halo. You were wearing a pink blouse. And you had music playing real low. It was 'Come Away with Me.'" He ran his fingers along the nape of her neck and down through her hair again. She got goose bumps.

"So beautiful," he whispered. He brushed her hair to one side with his fingers, leaned over and lightly kissed her neck. She could feel the coarse hair of his mustache.

She groaned. She couldn't help it. But when she heard her voice, she knew she had to stop him.

"No, Jack, we shouldn't." She inched away from him.

"Sunny, please. Just let me touch your hair. Please." He was pleading. How could she say no?

She didn't say anything. He slipped off the bed and kneeled in front of her. He lifted both hands to her hair and combed it again and again with his fingers. It was so soothing. She closed her eyes. If she were a cat, she would be purring.

But then she felt his fingers on the buttons of her blouse. She flinched. Her eyes flew open. "Don't. Just my hair. You promised." She put her hands over his.

"I just want to see you with your hair down over your shoulders." He smiled and lifted his head, his lips now next to her ear. "Please, Sunny." His breath felt like a warm, moist breeze. "I've pictured this in my mind a thousand times. Please, let me have my vision."

Her hands trembled as she lowered them to her lap. She closed her eyes. He slipped the buttons open, pushed the silk down her arms and moaned.

His hands went back to her hair. Gently, slowly, he spread it over her. The strands slid over her bare breasts, making them tingle. As he arranged her hair, his fingers grazed her nipples. She tried to tell herself it was an accident. It happened again and again, but she didn't say anything.

She could feel the wetness between her legs. It had been a long time since José had touched her. She squirmed and swallowed a groan.

Then she felt his lips around her nipple. He drew hard. She gasped. He rolled her other nipple between his thumb and index finger. He pushed himself onto the bed, nudged her backward, pressed up against her. She could feel his erection. He was big and thick. A lot bigger than José.

José!

"No." She opened her eyes and tried to push him away. "Stop."

He did, but remained beside her. "Sunny, I know you want this, too."

She shook her head. "No."

"Tell me the truth." He pushed his hips against hers. She could feel his heat through their clothes.

She bit her lips and looked away.

He lifted her chin until she was looking into his eyes.

"The truth, honey. That's all I want."

She didn't say anything for what seemed like a long time. He just kept looking at her. Finally, she said, "Yes, I do want it, but I'm married. I can't do this to José."

"If José was taking care of you, you wouldn't want this." His voice was husky. He slipped his hand between her legs, felt her wetness, and stroked her.

She was so close, but she didn't want it with him. She said, "Don't," but couldn't hold back a moan of pleasure.

"Sunny, let me do this for you." He kissed her. His hand moved faster. Her body bucked involuntarily. After the waves of pleasure stopped, she twisted her head away.

"Oh, my God," she whispered.

"Was it good, honey?"

"Yeah." She was ashamed, but she had to admit it was.

"Ready to go for number two?"

She heard his zipper.

"What do you mean?"

"Sunny, you can't leave me in this condition." He grabbed her hand and took it to his penis. He lowered his head to kiss her.

"No. I can't. I'm married." She jerked her head away.

"Being married didn't stop you from just havin' the best orgasm of your life."

"I didn't mean to."

"Come on, Sunny, we're both grown-ups."

Her heart hurt. She didn't want to do this. All she could say was, "It's not right."

"You think it's right to leave me like this?" He bumped his erection into her again. "Fair's fair, honey. Now it's my turn." He lifted his mouth to her ear. "Okay?"

It wasn't okay. She didn't want this, but, before she could say anything, he was inside her.

CHAPTER 31

October 13, Monday
Andy

Andy had hoped that Bull's request for an immediate appointment signaled progress, but the oaf's discomfort suggested otherwise. After lowering himself into a chair, Bull began to jiggle his leg as if he were performing some strange, seated dance.

"Nancy Holstein visited me. She complained that sexual discrimination in her department had negatively affected her partnership prospects."

Andy leaned forward. "Is that what she said? Those were her words?"

"That's right."

Andy could feel his pulse jumping in his neck. "I thought we were aiming for an amicable resolution, an in-house position for her."

"I'm still working on that, but . . ." He shook his head. "The good news is she didn't threaten suit. Didn't mention filing a complaint with the EEOC. I think she was just firing a shot across our bow."

"For what purpose?"

"To shake us down. Demand a partnership or a big payoff."

"It seems you've let this situation get away from us. The dynamic would be different if you'd lined up another position for her as I instructed." Andy took a deep breath and told himself money could cure this mess before the confirmation hearings.

"I talked to Ford about it. He said he'd talk to the other partners in the department, but I guess they didn't know of anything."

"*But* nothing. I explicitly said to use a headhunter if necessary. Have you retained one?"

"No, not yet."

Andy tsked. "You've failed abysmally."

Bull look dazed. Andy rapped the top of his desk with his knuckles. "Are you listening?"

He blinked. Thick lenses magnified his eyes. "Yes, of course."

"Start settlement discussions with Nancy. Low-key it, but get her to start talking numbers."

"How high can I go?"

"Check with the controller as to what size payment requires the approval of the Management Committee and stay south of it by a hundred thousand. If I need to get involved, there'll be room to raise the ante."

"Will do."

"And redouble your efforts to find her a position." He leaned back in his chair to signal the meeting was over.

CHAPTER 32

October 13, Monday
Bull Holbrooke

Bull saw his secretary's face light up as he trudged down the hall. Kim always had a smile for him, no matter what.

"Doin' okay, big guy?"

"Not really." He slumped into his desk chair.

Kim closed the door behind her, propped a hip against the edge of his desk, and took one of his hands in hers. "Hey, babe, what is it?"

Just having her near, feeling her touch, smelling her perfume, made him feel better.

"It's Andy. He's treating me like I'm a fuck-up, like this is all my fault." He gave her a play-by-play of his meeting.

"Baby, that ain't right. I'm worried about you." She squeezed his hand. "What's gonna happen when O'Toole gets elected? In a few weeks, all Andy's gonna be thinking about is kissin' Sweeny

Owens good-bye. If the shit hits the fan, Andy will say he didn't know anything and you'll be left holding the bag."

"That's not going to happen."

"Yeah? Tell me why not? Andy treated you like a dog today. He wouldn't piss on you if you was on fire. And the firm has plenty of ACLU types that would lynch you for the stuff you been doin'—all at Andy's request. But he'll deny it, the weasel."

He took off his glasses, rubbed his eyes. His head throbbed. "It's not going to happen. At least I hope not."

She threw her hands in the air. "Shit happens. How does Micah Levin know what's goin' on? Tell me that."

He sure as hell wished he could. He didn't say anything.

Kim said, "Look, there are more people involved in this than you and me. You don't think they could be bought off?"

"Okay, suppose you're right. There's not much I can do about it now except hope Andy doesn't leave me with my butt flapping in the breeze."

"You're wrong there. What if you was to tape your meetings with Andy? You make sure he says stuff that shows he knows what's goin' on. If all hell breaks loose, you're covered no matter what the old bastard does."

"Jeez, Kim, I don't know. I mean, he's the head of the firm. Someday he's gonna be the attorney general."

"I'm just sayin' . . . Come on. You won't use the tapes unless he turns on you. If he does, then making them was right. If he doesn't, you throw them away when this is all over."

He looked at her. Kim might not be refined or educated, but she was street-smart. "I'll think about it."

She kissed his forehead. "That's my guy." She winked and headed for the door.

"You're the best." As she touched the handle, he said, "Get Ford MacLeod on the phone for me, okay?"

"Sure thing."

And, in less than a minute, shit was flowing downhill. "Ford, you need to know Andy is extremely upset you haven't found an in-house position for Nancy yet."

"I'm sorry, Bull. I've been really busy and—"

"Hey, you don't have to apologize to me. It's the big guy who's pissed off. I mean, think about it, Ford. You screwed up her review. I show you how to make it better and what do you do? You drop the goddamn ball." Bull noticed his second line light up, but let Kim handle it. "Now what are you going to do about it?"

"Find her a job."

Bull could picture Ford's eye twitching as if he'd been hit with pepper spray.

"You do that. If you have to promise the client a discount or that you'll work for free, you do that. Whatever it takes, get her out of here."

Bull cut the connection, pleased to have transferred to Ford the anxiety Andy had loaded onto him. Yup. The way to deal with stress was to inflict it on other people.

The intercom buzzed. Kim said, "Beverly called. She wants you to pick up Alistair from lacrosse practice on your way home. Ya know, Bull, that woman has no idea what kinda pressure you're under here. She's as bad as Andy—treatin' you like an errand boy."

Too true, but Kim didn't know that Beverly was a Whitmore. They were all that way. But he wasn't dumb enough to make excuses for his wife to Kim. She was squarely in his corner and he needed to keep her there. If anyone could save him from this mess, she could.

CHAPTER 33

October 14, Tuesday
Maggie

Maggie glanced around the sunlit restaurant. Its pale peach walls and banks of white phalaenopsis orchids instantly lifted her mood. She'd been on edge since Jack Slattery's call this morning reminding her of the upcoming meeting of the Partner Compensation Committee. Her silent protest that his demands were unreasonable hadn't stopped her from feeling inadequate.

She hoped she'd be able to report progress after today's lunch. Barbara Diamond, the general counsel of AstraMed, had quickly accepted Maggie's invitation.

Barbara was a trim blonde in her late fifties with a wide smile that didn't wrinkle her unnaturally smooth eyes and forehead. "I probably shouldn't have accepted your invitation to lunch, but I get so tired of being the only woman in the executive dining

room. I've heard such good things about you, I really wanted to
meet you."

Maggie winced inwardly at Barbara's disclaimer about ac-
cepting the invitation. It didn't bode well, but Maggie had to play
it out. "This could be the first of many luncheons. I really hope
we can work together."

"To be honest, I'd like nothing better, but . . . You do know the
Butcher family controls the company?" Maggie nodded. "Three of
our twelve directors are family members, and the partner at Gideon
Downe who represents the family trust has a seat on the board, too."

"Bill Burkhardt? I figured his seat was based on the trust."

"Yes, but the ties between the family and Gideon Downe go
back further, almost a hundred years. And, if that's not enough, the
managing partner of the firm's New York office is married to one
of the Butcher heirs."

Maggie sagged against her chair. "I can guess where this is going."

"Look. I wish I could send some work your way. You've got
a terrific reputation, and I'd like to do my part and hire other
women. But my hands are tied." She lifted her shoulders.

Maggie tried to mask her disappointment. "So, tell me what it's
like to be the only female executive in a Fortune 200 company."

While Barbara answered, Maggie silently reviewed her ever-
shorter list of prospects. At the bottom was Charles Poynter, a guy
she could call if she got truly desperate. He had never bothered
to hide his sexual interest, even when she was married. A little
harmless flirtation might get him in the door.

But was preserving her compensation really worth it? She
could easily rationalize using her sex appeal given the crap wom-
en routinely had to take from men. Turnabout was fair play and
all that. But it didn't feel right anymore. A compensation cut *could*
signal being a screw-up or it could signal an unwillingness to sac-
rifice certain principles. Or both. She sighed.

CHAPTER 34

October 16, Thursday
Andy

NEW YORK POST
PAGE SIX

WE HEAR . . .

—THAT **Bootsie Huntington Worth** may be following **Woody Ferguson** to his new home at Danzig, Sheetz & Katz. Woody has been helping Bootsie fight off charges she altered the will of her late mother, **Becca Huntington.** Woody bolted from Sweeny, Owens & Boyle, taking many of his blue blood clients with him. Could it be because the EEOC has Sweeny Owens in its sights?

Andy reread the story, dismayed the press had now explicitly linked the rumor of an EEOC investigation to the firm. The O'Toole campaign might pick it up, but, as long as the investigation remained a rumor rather than an actuality, he should be safe. The most immediate consequence of the item would be increasing Nancy Holstein's perception of her leverage in their meeting to "discuss partnership prospects."

That was how she'd characterized the agenda when she'd requested the conference; both of them knew it was a settlement negotiation.

He looked up as she arrived in his office. Her demure outfit was a sure sign she had been prepped by Georgia Albright to demonstrate her effectiveness on the witness stand. With her hair in a ballerina's bun, she looked demure in a simple two-piece white outfit with a high neckline.

They got through the pleasantries quickly enough. Rather than starting with a debate about whether she would become a partner and why not, he decided his remarks would be based on the presumption that both of them knew she wouldn't. Even if Ford MacLeod had mishandled her last review, she'd figured it out by now or she wouldn't be talking to Albright.

"I have some very good news. Our client TechniVerse is looking for an associate general counsel. Ford thinks you'd be well suited for the position."

"I've worked hard for nine years to become a partner. It would be foolhardy to throw that away when I'm so close to my goal."

Apparently, she planned to be difficult.

"Your goal?"

"Becoming a partner, of course."

"See here, Nancy, you've known that wasn't a possibility for some time." From now on, that would be the firm's official position. Her last review had been one-on-one with MacLeod, and, unless she'd somehow recorded it, Andy's version of history would stand.

She pressed a hand to her chest like the shocked heroine in a silent movie. Her lips formed a circle. "I don't know what you mean."

"Ford told you in your last performance review the department wouldn't put your name in for partnership consideration."

"*No*. He never said that. The partnership decisions are only a few months away and this is the first I've heard of it."

Andy produced an extremely skeptical expression, the one he usually reserved for show judges who failed to appreciate his bulldogs' finer points. "Oh, really? There's a memo memorializing the review in your personnel file." Or there would be before the firm produced its contents in litigation. It wouldn't be the first time Andy had played hardball.

"Then it's fiction because he *never* told me that. Not once."

"So you say, but, with Ford's memo in your personnel file, who will believe you?"

"Anyone who knows the employer controls what goes in the file."

"Accusations of that sort are not constructive. Perhaps we have nothing further to discuss."

She produced a handkerchief embroidered with violets and touched the corners of her eyes. It was a wonderful touch, so old-fashioned and innocent. "Could I have a glass of water, please?" Her voice was strangled.

He passed the request along to Mrs. Lord who quickly appeared and gave her a bottle of water. Looking grief-stricken, Nancy took several sips. She'd probably role-played the meeting a dozen times with Albright.

"I don't understand. Everything I've heard from the partners in my department is that I'm on track. They always praise me for managing the relationship with Sancta—something Barry Carleton can't do. The only suggestion for change I've ever heard is to broaden my client base."

"That is certainly an issue. Beyond—"

"But that's so unfair. I'm—"

Andy lifted a hand. "Let me finish. There are many factors that go into partnership decisions. Intellectual capacity, legal talent, client relationships, and, for lack of a better word, gravitas.

"Your intellectual capacity and legal talent are adequate, but not exceptional. You have a strong relationship with one client who generates significant fees but not enough to cover the compensation of a first-year partner. Then there is gravitas, an area in which you fail miserably."

Sniffling, she raised the handkerchief to her nose. "I don't understand what you mean by that."

"Of course you do."

"Honestly, I don't."

There wasn't anything honest about the entire conversation.

"If you insist." He sighed. "In considering partnership candidates, gravitas means dignity, weightiness, a demeanor that commands respect."

"Perhaps in your mind, only white males have sufficient *gravitas*." She spit out the word as if it had soiled her mouth.

"Not at all. As you well know, we have female partners and minority partners. What all our partners, regardless of gender or ethnicity, have that you lack is a dignified demeanor. Your vocabulary, your dress, and your sexual relationships with other firm personnel are all inappropriate. Your bearing is entirely unsuitable for a partner."

Anger blazed in her face. "It's a double standard. Men have become partners despite failing your gravitas criterion."

"Nancy, this decision wasn't easy for the partnership. You have many excellent qualities, which is why we've recommended you for a position with TechniVerse. Your . . . style is much better suited to an entertainment company than a corporate law firm. I know you're disappointed, but you must remember you were one of more than seventy-five associates who joined the firm upon graduation from law school. At the very most, five of them will eventually become partners."

"So I've given Sweeny Owens nine years of my life for nothing?"

"You've received more than three million dollars compensation over that time, not to mention superb training. But we don't want you to feel mistreated." He adopted an avuncular tone. "If you took the position now, you wouldn't be here at bonus time. The firm would be prepared to pay you two hundred and fifty thousand dollars now in lieu of your bonus."

"Yes, but if I became a partner, I'd be earning a multiple of that every year. You're asking me to walk away from lifetime financial security."

"No. That's incorrect. Your alternative is not a partnership."

She offered a brittle smile. "If that's the case, then my alternative is a suit alleging sexual discrimination. The firm's alternative is very unpleasant publicity that might affect your confirmation hearings."

Andy's jaw knotted. "That would be most unfortunate for everyone. I doubt you would enjoy having your many indiscretions made public."

"I make no pretense about who I am. Sweeny Owens, however, pretends to be a paragon of legal probity."

Andy raised his palms in a conciliatory gesture. "There's nothing to be gained by trading accusations. I think the firm could pay you five hundred thousand to ease your transition to TechniVerse."

"If the firm wants a release from me, it will cost a million dollars."

"A million dollars? You do think well of yourself."

"No, I think well of my many friends in the press—the advantage of having been a member of the Media Department for nine years." She paused. "Do we have an agreement?"

"You will release the firm from all claims, known or unknown at this time, and hold your allegations and this settlement confidential?"

"When you say confidential, you mean not disclose it to anyone outside the partnership? Obviously, the partners will know because they'll have to approve it."

She assumed the firm was a democratic institution. How naïve to think the approval of rank and file partners would be needed. While the partnership agreement did require the members of the Management Committee to bless expenditures in excess of five hundred thousand, he didn't plan on asking them. Presenting the settlement to them might delay resolution of Nancy's claim. He wanted her long gone by the time of his confirmation hearings.

"The partnership will be a party to the agreement." A nonresponsive answer but close enough for her purposes.

"Right. So it shouldn't be a problem to carve the partners out of the confidentiality provision."

What partners did she want to tell? She had personal relationships with the Media Law partners, but they'd be reluctant to tell the rest of the firm how much their mismanagement had cost. Who else? She might be sleeping with another partner and want to brag about her coup as pillow talk. But that fellow wouldn't be apt to talk. Andy didn't know where she was going, but he didn't like it. He'd try to brush her back from the plate.

"Nancy, do you want a deal or not? Let's agree on standard confidentiality and other settlement provisions and be done with it."

"Andy, do you want a deal or not? Exclude from the confidentiality prohibition my legal and financial advisers, my physicians and psychological counselors, my immediate family, and the partners. Agreed?"

He paused. "Agreed. Now, if there's nothing else, I have several other pressing matters." He gestured toward the door.

As she left, he realized she was a better attorney than he'd given her credit for. She'd negotiated well, although she'd never have been so successful if his nomination hadn't been on the line.

He lifted the handset to inform Bull of the terms of the settlement. Andy also wanted to quiz him about Nancy's relationships with partners. Something was driving her insistence on carving partners out of the disclosure prohibitions.

◆

CHAPTER 35

October 16, Thursday
Maggie

From her office window Maggie watched the streetlights blink on in the park. She held the phone away from her ear as Ginger hacked.

"Little kids, they give you every goddamn bug that's going around." Her voice was husky and nasal.

"Is that cold real or an attempt to play on my sympathies?"

"Real. Way too real." Ginger sniffled. "Give me another half hour. Promise I'll be there by eight thirty."

"Okay, but I'm starving." She hung up the phone and considered how to kill the time. She couldn't stand to look at another piece of paper. No more research into employment law, prospective clients, or anything else.

She smiled when she thought of a research question that didn't involve fine print: asking Rosalinda about the current dating scene.

Even though her marriage had been troubled, Maggie hadn't given up on the institution. She'd like to find a smart, funny, warm man to settle down with. Have a baby with. She'd always wanted kids, but Bryce adamantly did not. Now she had a second chance.

When Rosalinda answered, Maggie asked, "Are you working on anything pressing or do you have time for some . . . girl talk?" The description sounded cheesy but Maggie didn't know what else to say. "Advice to the lovelorn?" Just trying to put a label on her concerns gave her second thoughts, but Rosalinda was quick to invite her to her office.

Moments later, the elevator doors slid open on Rosalinda's floor and Maggie started down the corridor.

The sound of a man shouting stopped her. She heard a woman's muted replies. Adrenaline flooded her system. She could hear whole sentences now.

"What a fucking stupid mistake! If I hadn't caught it, it could have cost me my partnership."

Maggie turned the corner. Travis Benally loomed over Lily Ching's desk. His hands were balled into fists. His eyes blazed.

Farther down the hall, Rosalinda opened her office door.

Color choked Lily's cheeks. "I didn't make a mistake. *You* did. Your instructions weren't clear." She lifted her chin. "You're lucky to have a great secretary like me."

"Great secretary? *You?*" Travis threatened to explode with anger. "The only thing you're good for is to suck my dick." He yanked open his fly and waved his penis at her.

Lily cringed and twisted her head. "Get away!"

"Travis! Into your office. Now!" Maggie bellowed.

His head snapped in her direction. "Ww-wait. L-let me explain." He stepped toward her.

"Zip yourself up before I call the cops. Get into your office." He pulled up his fly. "Please, Maggie, I can explain."

"Later. Get in your office and close the door. Don't come out until I ask you to. Understand?"

He nodded and shuffled away.

Maggie hustled to Lily's side. She put a hand on her back. "He's gone." She leaned closer. "Are you okay?"

The woman turned toward Maggie. Her face was streaked with tears. "That was . . . awful." Her lips trembled. She sucked in air.

"I have no doubt. It was pretty bad just from the sidelines." She offered a half smile. "Catch your breath. I'm going to get you some water."

"*No*. Don't leave me."

"I'll get it." Rosalinda looked only slightly less shocked than Lily.

Rosalinda returned with two cups of water. She handed one to Lily and put the other on her desk.

Lily finished the first cup. "Thanks. That's better." She fished a tissue out of a drawer, dabbed her face, blew her nose.

Maggie wasn't sure how to help her, but the first step had to be getting her out of the office.

"I'd like Rosalinda to call a car for you. She'll ride with you back to your apartment. Then she can have the car take her home or bring her back here—whatever she wants." Maggie looked at Rosalinda. "Is that all right?"

"Sure. No problem. I'll go call them."

Maggie squeezed Lily's arm. "Stay home tomorrow and rest. I'll talk to Personnel about getting you a new assignment. Don't worry about it, okay?"

Lily nodded and raised her gaze to Maggie's face. Her lips were pressed together so hard they made a white line. She blinked. "It wasn't my fault. His instruct—"

"Don't worry about it. There is absolutely nothing you could have done that would justify his reaction."

Rosalinda returned. "The car will be here in five minutes. Maybe we should go downstairs." Her soft voice had a note of gentle encouragement.

After they disappeared around the corner, Maggie twisted the handle on Travis's door, pushed it open, and took a single step inside.

He was pacing behind his desk. He stopped behind his desk chair and grasped the top with both hands. "Maggie, you have to understand what happened. She—"

"I don't care what she did. There is no possible excuse for your behavior."

He ran a hand over the top of his head. "But it's a criminal matter. She was going to send a privileged document to the prosecutor."

"I don't care if she was sending a death warrant to your mother. As far as I'm concerned, your career here is over."

She pivoted and marched down the corridor. She refused to look over her shoulder but listened for the sound of footsteps. When the elevator doors closed behind her, she exhaled. She'd been holding her breath.

Her heart was still pounding when she stepped out on her floor. She opened her office door and started. Ginger was sitting behind her desk.

Ginger said, "Where have you been? I've been waiting almost half an hour and I'm sick as a dog. I'd still be stuck down in the lobby except the guard remembered me."

"I'm sorry. I got caught in a . . ." She shook her head and a shudder rippled through her body.

"Jesus, what is it? Come on, sit down." Ginger jumped out of the chair. When Maggie finished her story, Ginger said, "Welcome to my world."

"You don't have to see it firsthand."

"No, but I hear the women cry, reliving it again and again. You had the advantage of being there to confront him firsthand— so to speak."

Maggie winced. "It was too awful to joke about."

"You need a drink. Let's go." Ginger grabbed her purse.

"First, I need to go to the john and wash my face and hands. I feel scuzzy. Can you give me a minute?"

"Sure. I'll be here when you're ready." Ginger plopped down again in Maggie's desk chair.

"Good. Trade legal advice for the dinner check?"

"Tonight you get dinner *and* free advice. You deserve it."

CHAPTER 36

October 17, Friday
Andy

The intercom buzzed. Mrs. Lord said, "I have Micah Levin from the *Times* on your line."

"Mr. Anderson, I've received some interesting news about one of your attorneys and wonder if you can confirm it for me."

"From whom did you receive this news?"

"I've agreed to keep the source confidential."

Andy clicked his tongue. "Is your source reliable? Someone in a position to know what's going on inside the firm?"

"Yes."

"So you say."

"My source tells me Travis Benally, a senior associate at the firm, displayed his genitals to his secretary, Lily Ching, because he was distressed by her inadequate performance."

Andy felt a bubble of panic rise in his chest. What on earth was Levin talking about?

"Ridiculous. Your so-called source has an overactive imagination."

"So you're denying it?"

"Yes. It's a total fabrication. Really, you need to be more discriminating."

"Thank you for taking my call, Mr. Anderson."

Thinking he heard a note of amusement in the reporter's voice, Andy said sharply, "Good day," and returned the handset to its cradle.

The intercom sounded again. "Yes? . . . Oh, all right, if she insists. Ask Bull Holbrooke to come to my office immediately. Send him in when he arrives."

Andy fixed Maggie with a critical glare. "Mrs. Lord says you have an urgent need to speak with me. I trust that's so as a number of pressing matters await my attention."

"None as pressing as this." She launched into a description of the scene she'd witnessed the night before.

By the time she'd finished her report, his mouth was dry, his palms damp. "You're sure he exposed himself?"

"Absolutely."

"Good Lord. How awful for her. You, too."

"I plan to call her later this morning and see how she's doing. I think we should give her the rest of the week off and look for an easy assignment for her when she gets back."

"Yes, of course."

"You need to talk to Bull about terminating Travis. Immediately."

"Terminating Travis?" But the firm needed minority partners. *He* needed minority partners. "I'll certainly consult with him."

"You'll consult about terminating Travis, correct?"

"We will do whatever is legally required. Travis is—"

"Legally required?" Her hands bunched into fists. "Are you saying our standards are no higher than those required by law? We are one of the country's leading law firms. A firm that has heralded its interest in gender equity."

"I understand your position. But you must appreciate Travis has rights as well, and, as a minority, he is a highly valued member of our community. We can't act intemperately." Although keeping Travis might prove as difficult as saving a man who'd already stepped off a cliff.

"It would be totally inappropriate to have different, and lower, standards for him because he's a minority." She pushed herself out of the chair. "If this incident doesn't provide sufficient grounds to dismiss Travis, I can produce an associate with complaints about his sexual harassment, actions that included sexual displays."

"You can? Who is it?"

"She prefers to remain anonymous, but she'll come forward if necessary."

"It's important to have all the facts to make the correct decision. Who is it? Has the situation been going on long?"

"As I said, she prefers anonymity."

"Maggie, as firm chairman, I must insist you give me the name."

"I can't do that. My promise to keep her identity secret didn't have an escape clause if you ordered me to breach it."

Andy hoped the brisk tap on the door signaled Bull's arrival. If nothing else, the oaf would spare him from more of Maggie's unpleasantness.

Bull and Maggie muttered each other's name by way of greeting as they passed. Bull pulled the door shut behind him.

ⸯⸯⸯⸯⸯ

Andy said, "Tell me everything you know about the Travis Benally situation."

Frowning, Bull settled slowly into a chair. "What situation?"

"Unlike the *New York Times*, you are apparently unaware of it. Travis exposed himself to a secretary named Lily Ching last night in a fit of pique."

"What?" His oxlike jaw sagged open.

Andy passed along Maggie's details about the incident as well as an accounting of his phone call from Micah Levin.

"Son of a bitch! I'd heard Travis had a short fuse, but I had no idea it would lead to this."

"Well, it has. Now, what do you recommend we do?"

"It's—"

"Does the firm have an alternative except to discharge him?"

"No. No, not really."

Andy glanced at his watch. He had a conference call with Senator O'Toole's campaign manager in ten minutes.

"All right. Three months severance, plus the services of a headhunter. Jack will write him a reference."

"Okay," Bull said. "He'll want to stay in his office. It'll help finding the next job, but it's not a good idea. The firm needs to be seen as acting promptly and decisively."

Andy stared out the window without seeing anything and considered how best to contain the news. Clearly, Travis wouldn't tell a soul. The woman probably would, but she was at home today. She'd have to be dealt with as soon as possible.

Maggie might talk—but shouldn't. It was against the firm's best interests, and she was a partner. She'd need to be cautioned about talking. But that wasn't the entire universe of people who knew. One or more other people knew and had tipped Micah Levin.

"You need to talk to Maggie and this secretary as soon as possible. Find out if anyone else saw Travis do it. If not, one of them must be the leak, directly or indirectly."

"I doubt it was the secretary. She's probably still shell-shocked. Could be Maggie. She's getting more and more strident on these issues, but she's so in-your-face, I don't see her using the press to pressure us."

"*Someone* talked. I expect you to find out who it was."

"I'll do my best, but you may have more luck talking to Maggie. She and I have been butting heads lately. She wouldn't give me the sweat off her balls." The dullard snorted as if he'd uttered a clever witticism.

Andy did not need one more thing to deal with. "Take the experience as a cautionary lesson. You're much less useful to me if you alienate people, especially one of the firm's most powerful women."

"I'm sorry, but, I promise you, she's not going to give me anything."

"Oh, for heaven's sake. I'll talk to her. Now, as to the woman—"

"You do realize this is the same secretary Woody harassed?"

"Damnation! That's why her name sounded so familiar." Andy could feel his gut burning. "We'll give her a very generous settlement. In return, she'll agree to an ironclad confidentiality agreement."

"What do you want to do about Travis?"

"I thought we resolved that."

"Can he use his office while he's looking for a job?"

"Find him a desk somewhere on the support floors. Stick him in accounting or HR or the mail room. I don't care where; just get him out of sight."

Andy slid open his desk drawer and reached for the Limoges box. "Now, if that's all, I have an important call scheduled in a few minutes." Lifting the lid, he picked up two pink tablets.

He'd get an ulcer if Bull didn't stop the leaks. The blockhead needed to identify the quisling immediately.

CHAPTER 37

October 17, Friday
Maggie

When Maggie returned from Andy's office, she found Rosalinda waiting. Her eyes were surrounded by blue-black shadows, her body radiated nervous energy. Like Maggie, she'd probably had trouble sleeping.

"I really need to talk to you," Rosalinda said.

"Sure." Avoiding the barrier imposed by her desk, Maggie eased into the chair next to Rosalinda.

"I feel so bad about last night. If I'd listened to what you said about going to Bull, it would never have happened."

"No. Travis was so crazed, he wouldn't have remembered a caution from Bull."

"But it's just like you said. Imagine how I'd feel if Travis did it to another associate. Worse, he picked on a secretary." She sniffed.

Maggie patted her arm. "Hey, take it easy. It's not your fault. It's . . . it's this place. Women have been systemically discriminated against and harassed, and we've put up with it." She shook her head. "I guess we rationalize it as the price of playing with the big boys."

"Well, it's wrong. It has to stop."

"You're preaching to the converted, but I don't know how to make that happen."

"What if the firm got sued? Then they'd stop."

"Sued? If the circumstances were embarrassing enough, if the plaintiff got enough money, *maybe* that would do it."

"I remember meeting a friend of yours who does this stuff on the plaintiff's side. Her name was Ginger . . ."

"Marshall. Ginger Marshall."

"Maybe she'd represent me."

Maggie studied the younger woman. "You should think about it carefully. There are lots of negatives."

"So, your friend can tell me about them, then I'll decide. Will you give me her number?"

"I will, on the condition that you wait a couple of weeks before calling her. Last night was appalling. I don't want you making decisions until the shock has worn off. Will you do that?"

She screwed up one corner of her mouth, paused. "Okay, but I'm not going to change my mind."

After Rosalinda left, Maggie moved behind her desk, a beautiful French antique with double pedestals in burr walnut, set off by ebonized trim and an inset black leather writing surface. The desk had been the first item she'd purchased with her decorating allowance when she'd made partner. She had been thrilled and awed to be invited inside the exclusive community.

But the drive to become partner had somehow blinded her. She'd been so fixed on her own career path, she'd ignored what was going on around her. It wasn't so long ago she'd told Andy women's concerns weren't monolithic. What an idiot she'd been. Sure, there were differences, but, when men pulled stunts like Travis and Woody had, their interests damn well became monolithic.

A sharp knock pulled her back to the present.

"Come in."

Andy stepped into her office and closed the door behind him. He offered a cloying smile. "Maggie, I felt bad when I realized I hadn't asked about your own response to the incident with Travis. You've certainly been through the wringer these last few months."

The man who'd instructed Jack to put her on notice about her charged hours suddenly was concerned about her mental health? Unlikely. "I'm a big girl. I'll be fine."

"I suppose it's the kind of thing it would help to discuss."

"You mean with a therapist?" Touchy-feely was way out of character for Andy.

"That, or someone who'd experienced the same thing."

"I suppose."

"Did anyone else see what Travis did?"

Did he suspect Maggie had invented the episode? "Lily Ching unquestionably did."

"Yes, of course. I meant to ask if anyone other than you or Lily witnessed it."

"Why do you ask?"

"Naturally, I'd be as concerned about that person's psychological well-being as I am about yours."

"I appreciate your solicitude."

He paused, flattened his lips, narrowed his gaze. "Should I extend it to anyone else who might have seen the vile display?"

"No, I don't think so." Whatever he was after, she wasn't going to give it to him.

"Very good. You'll be relieved to know that I've concluded
Travis must be discharged. While I'm here, I wanted to mention
the importance of keeping this whole business confidential. As a
partner, I'm sure you agree."

"I understand." She understood Andy wanted to protect himself.

He hovered at her door as if deciding if he should say more.
He cleared his throat. "Do let me know if you get any inquiries
from the press."

"The press? I don't expect that, but I'll let you know."

After he walked out, she realized she should have asked Andy
if *he* had gotten a call from a reporter. The scrutiny of the press
might be exactly the motivation Sweeny Owens needed to clean
up its act.

CHAPTER 38

Maggie's morning coffee was still hot when Sunny stepped into her office. She looked wretched, with dark plum-colored circles around her eyes and several swollen zits or bugbites on her face. But, on the upside, she looked ten pounds thinner.

"Sunny! When did you get back from Azerbaijan?"

"Late last night." Her tone was flat.

"Long flight, I guess."

After dropping into a chair, Sunny said, "Long flight, long shitty trip."

"Sounds like it was pretty bad." Maggie took a swallow of her double espresso latté dosed with two packets of raw sugar. She'd had trouble sleeping since the episode with Travis.

"Bad? It was a total bummer. It was . . . you won't believe what Jack did."

"That bastard's capable of anything. What did he do?"

Sunny looked away. "Jack and I . . . w-we had . . . we had sex while we were in Azerbaijan. It was . . . I don't know how to explain it." She lifted a shoulder; a tear rolled down her cheek. "I guess it was consensual or that's what Jack would say, but it didn't feel that way to me."

"My God! Sunny, I'm so sorry. What happened?" Maggie grabbed some tissues from her drawer and walked around the desk to sit next to her. "Here." She pressed the tissues into her friend's hand. Sunny swiped her eyes.

"I was kinda drunk. He kept ordering champagne on the plane, and, after we checked into the hotel, he came to my room. He claimed he needed to talk about our meeting the next day." She sucked in a long, shuddering breath. "Then he . . . I don't know, manipulated me, I guess. Gave me compliments. Said how beautiful my hair was and my hands. He started, uh, touching me. He was so persistent and I tried to say no." She lifted her head and glanced quickly at Maggie. "I really *did* say no—"

"That son of a bitch! He is such a goddamn sleaze. Did he overpower you physically?"

"No, I can't say that. Not physically. It was like psychological power. I mean, here he is the managing partner and all along he's been praising my work. So, I'm flattered that way and impressed that someone as important as him is attracted to me and . . . then he kept pressuring me to have sex. I told him no, that I was married, but then he'd say he could tell I really wanted it. But I didn't." Her gaze dropped to the ball of damp tissues she was busily shredding. "It was so nasty."

Maggie said, "More than nasty. It was date rape—not that you were on a date, but he was an acquaintance who psychologically coerced you into having sex."

"I don't know. I mean, I let him touch me . . . you know." Blushing, she pointed to her crotch.

"Consent to petting isn't consent to penetration. Didn't you learn that in criminal law?"

"Yeah, I guess so, but what difference does it make? I wasn't going to call the Ordubad cops."

Maggie cupped Sunny's chin in her hand and gently lifted her head. "It makes a hell of a lot of difference. It means you didn't consent to intercourse with Slattery. I think that matters to you. I'm sure it would matter to José."

"José?" Her voice went high and thin with terror. "You don't think I should tell him, did you?"

"No, I don't. The only one that kind of confession helps is the sinner."

"It's tearing me up inside. I keep thinking about José finding out. I would *never* tell him on purpose. It would kill him. But I worry about saying something in my sleep or his noticing, you know, like physically, I've had sex with someone else."

"Wait a minute. That sounds like it's still going on."

"After the first time, there was no turning back. Jack said if I didn't have sex with him again, he'd tell Andy I was doing a miserable job on the case. I know I'm just a disposable baby partner. It's not like I have a client base or anything."

"That's bullshit. Don't worry about it. Do you think Slattery will pursue you now that you're back?"

"God, I hope not. We just got in last night but he said stuff on the plane about how we could do it in his office or go to a hotel or . . . I told him it was over. I said, 'What happened in Azerbaijan, stays in Azerbaijan and *stops* in Azerbaijan.'" She sniffed. "Like it was something to joke about, but it isn't. It's awful. I can't keep doing it even if it means getting kicked out of the firm."

"That is not going to happen. Even if Slattery carried through on his threat, I'd tell Andy you've done great work. I'm sure Sam and other partners would say the same."

"I don't know what to do. Jack won't accept no from me. I say the words but he ignores them. Maybe he needs to hear it from someone with more clout like Andy or . . . I don't know, maybe Bull."

Maggie leaned back in her chair, considered her friend. She'd always been Sunny's mentor. Maggie's heart told her to champion Sunny now, to go to Andy and ask that he come down hard on Slattery, an outcome long overdue. But Sunny *was* a partner. She needed to take responsibility for herself. More importantly, she needed to assert herself, to stand up to Slattery.

"You need to stand up for yourself, be your own advocate."

"I can't."

"*Yes, you can*, and, by doing it, I think you'll feel better about yourself and what happened in Azerbaijan."

"But what if he won't listen?"

"Do you think he'll try to overpower you physically?"

"No. Not really."

"Then you'll be okay. He won't be stupid enough to go after you. If he did, it would backfire. People would see through it. If he tries to do it, then you can involve Bull and firm management. But, first, you need to stand up for yourself. That's important." She put her arm around Sunny's shoulder. "I know you can do it."

Sunny squeezed her eyes shut and bit her lip. After a moment she exhaled deeply and looked at Maggie. "Okay. I will."

"Good. Come back and tell me how things are going. I want to help you but you need to help yourself."

As Maggie watched her friend trudge out the door, she considered her advice. No doubt she'd drawn the right conclusion for Sunny. But Sunny wasn't the only party in interest.

Slattery was involved, too. And because he was a partner—hell, the managing partner—so was Sweeny Owens. The episode in Azerbaijan perfectly illustrated why he shouldn't have a position of power inside the firm. In fact, what he'd done merited disciplinary action, if not expulsion from the partnership. If Maggie took Sunny's complaint to Andy, he'd have to act. Personally, Maggie would love to see Slattery kicked out on his ass, but she doubted Andy had the stomach for that. Stripping him of his managerial authority would be the minimum response necessary. Andy would probably have the backbone for that.

She shook her head as she tried to parse the competing interests. Sunny would be best served by resolving this on her own with Slattery. If, after she'd done that, she wanted to make a formal complaint, she could—but it would be her decision. The firm would be best served by someone, anyone, informing Andy immediately what had happened and letting him punish Slattery. Slattery's interest would be best served—.

Hell, she didn't give a damn about what was best for him.

So, the choice was between Sunny and the firm. That seemed easy except the firm was more than Andy. It was made up of partners who'd be liable for Slattery's harassment if he inflicted it on someone willing to file a complaint. More than that, the firm had to consider the women he would hit on in the future. They deserved to be protected from him.

Maggie could take the story Sunny had told her to Andy in confidence and protect the partners and female employees. But that didn't feel right.

A few years ago, Andy had said the firm had to be the highest priority in a partner's life. Maggie had never before felt she had to choose. Now . . .

Her mind balked at making the selection.

CHAPTER 39

October 22, Wednesday
Sunny

When two days passed without hearing from Jack, Sunny began to believe he'd accepted her refusal to continue their affair. "Affair" made it sound almost romantic, and Jack had tried to dress it up that way in Azerbaijan—giving her presents and sending flowers to her room. But the correct description was adultery. And it was over.

Wednesday morning Jack sent an e-mail requesting she review the attached transcripts of their first three interviews and meet with him at six that evening. Nothing personal. Just a straightforward work assignment. That part was good, but a meeting after business hours could mean he wanted privacy. Or it could mean nothing. Some partners didn't make time for associates until after they were done dealing with clients. Jack had no discernible pattern.

When she entered his office, he gave her a perfunctory smile. "Let's sit at the conference table so we can both look at the transcripts. I made a few notes on my copy."

So far, so good. He sat at the head of the rectangular table; she took a chair at the side. Deliberately, she passed over the chair closest to him and chose the second one down.

He said, "So what's your take on Hajiyev's interview? Notice anything that didn't pop out at you while it was going on?"

She felt herself unclench. It was a business meeting.

After rehashing the interviews for over an hour, Jack excused himself to go to the "little boys' room," as he called it, even though he was the only "boy" who used the private bathroom attached to his office. When he returned, he circled past the door to the corridor, closed it, and pushed the lock.

Click.

Her mind screamed. *He wants sex.*

Jack walked to her side, kissed her cheek. "I've—"

"Don't." She pushed her chair back from the table and stood up. "It's over."

"Oh, come on now, don't be that way. We had a good time in Ordubad, and it doesn't have to stop there." He tried to put his arms around her.

She swatted at his hands. "*Don't.* I'm telling you I don't want this. Leave me alone." Her heart hammered.

"Sunny, sweetheart, we've talked about this. I know you're saying these things to soothe your conscience. You really do want—"

"No, I mean it."

"I get it. You need to say this so you won't feel guilty. And to help you with that, I'm going to remind you that, if you keep up this foolishness, your career will suffer. You don't want that, so just be a good girl. Go along and you'll get along." He leaned into her for a kiss.

Moving away, she said, "No. I won't have sex again and . . . and I don't believe you'll try to hurt my career. If you give me a bad performance review, it will stick out. The other partners I work with like my work. If you say something way negative, people will wonder why."

"Sunny, Sunny, Sunny." His voice was a singsong. "You're being naïve. I'm the managing partner. I don't have to weigh in at review sessions. I'm one third of the compensation committee. All I have to do is express reservations in that setting and your compensation gets reduced. When that happens, the partners will see you as a screw-up, someone not to be trusted. You'll stop getting good assignments, then your hours will go down. In three years, you'll be out of here with no place to go. You don't want that, now do you?" He tugged the end of a strand of hair.

If she didn't have sex with him, he'd ruin her career. She had worked so incredibly hard for ten years to make partner and now he was going to take it away from her. She fought her tears, took several shaky breaths. "Why me? Why are you doing this to me? I know I'm not attractive. Why don't you pick on someone else, someone pretty?"

"Baby, you're beautiful to me."

More of his manipulative bullshit. Surely in time he'd lose interest in her, find someone else. But how much time? She couldn't keep betraying José. It boiled down to a choice between her marriage or her career. Given how badly José was dealing with his infertility, her affair with Jack would inevitably end their marriage if he found out.

Her answer to Jack had to be no. But was there a way for her to say it that at least appeased him?

"Jack, you have the ability to make me choose between the two things I value most in the world—my marriage and my career. I see that now. I didn't understand how much power you

have as managing partner. You really have my fate in your hands."
She clasped her palm across her mouth. The truth of the words
made her nauseous. "Give me some time. I need to think." She
stepped toward the door.

"Do what you gotta do, but don't take too long. Big Dick
and the twins miss you." He patted the front of his trousers. "Just
remember they won't take no for an answer."

CHAPTER 40

October 22, Wednesday
Maggie

Perched on the edge of a cowhide chair in Maggie's study, Sunny drained a bottle of Pellegrino. "I'm sorry to barge in, but I couldn't go straight home to José after talking to Jack. I *couldn't . . .*"

Sunny's words tumbled out faster and faster as she replayed her conversation with Slattery. Repelled by her account, Maggie nestled into the corner of her suede chaise. Her study with its Western art and cowboy décor had been her refuge, a place where the good guys always won. Now Slattery's evil permeated the room.

Sunny said, "So, no matter what I do, I lose."

"Only if you play by his rules."

"What do you mean? He's the managing partner. What other rules are there?"

"Andy's. Slattery may be the managing partner, but it's Andy's firm. We all know that. Andy would be horrified by Slattery's threats."

"You think? I don't believe he cares about anything but leaving Sweeny Owens with a clean record and getting confirmed."

"Even if you're right, you can play that to your advantage. Andy doesn't want to be dogged by rumors he tolerated sexual harassment—especially not by his handpicked successor."

"So you're saying I have to leak what happened in Ordubad? I can't. It would get back to José."

"No. Not at all." Sunny was so panicked she wasn't thinking straight. "I'm not talking about you leaking it. Make a complaint. Take it to Bull or, better yet, to Andy himself. Whoever you start with, at the end of the day, Andy will have to deal with it. He can't risk inaction with the possibility you could come forward at his confirmation hearings."

"*Are you nuts?* I would never do that. Bad enough if José found it, but going public with it would humiliate him."

Maggie scooched to the end of the chaise, took Sunny's hands. "Listen to me. You're forgetting Andy doesn't know how desperate you are to keep this quiet. Think about it: he will be even more desperate to hush this up than you are. It'd kill him in his confirmation hearings. He'll do whatever it takes to bury this."

"Like what?"

"Like removing Slattery as managing partner. That's the minimum. With conduct this egregious, I think he has to kick him out of the firm entirely. Either way, he's neutralized. He can't touch you."

"Yeah, I get it." Sunny's shoulders sagged as her tension eased. "That's the answer. So, who should I go to?"

"Andy. Definitely Andy. First of all, you want to catch him unprepared, get his immediate reaction. Second, Bull can't do anything without Andy's approval so no point in going through the whole litany with him and letting him prep Andy."

"It's not going to be an easy conversation no matter who I go to."

"It'll be easier with Andy. He's . . . I don't know, almost chaste. He won't go for the seamy details."

"There's something to be grateful for."

"So you'll go to him?"

"What choice do I have?"

CHAPTER 41

October 24, Friday
Andy

Andy glanced at his watch as the young partner slipped into a guest chair. Sunny Star-Perez, a plump, ill-kempt woman, seemed an unlikely bearer of "sensitive, personal information critical to the firm's reputation." Nevertheless, that had been how she'd justified her urgent request for a meeting to Mrs. Lord. Mrs. Lord's deep faith in the unimportance of junior partners, coupled with her dislike of pushy women, had caused her to put Sunny off for a day. Now Sunny sat before Andy to reveal her knowledge in the ten minutes Mrs. Lord allotted to her.

"Thank you for seeing me."

Those were the last pleasant words she spoke. By the time she'd poured out her tale, Andy's mind crackled with anger at Slattery.

"Oh, my dear, I am so sorry. It must have been distressing for you."

She nodded. "It was. I mean, it *is*. Really, it's worse now because Jack wants to keep having sex even though we're back."

"You mean it happened more than once in Azerbaijan?"

"Oh, yeah. And now Jack says that if I won't keep doing it, he's going to ruin my career. He's—"

"What? He actually said that?" Slattery's temerity was breathtaking.

"He went into detail. Said he was one third of the compensation committee and he'd see to it that my compensation was cut. He said, after that happened, senior partners wouldn't want to work with me and then my hours would go down, and, within three years, I'd be kicked out of the firm with no place to go. That was how he put it."

"How did you leave it with him?"

"He gave me the ultimatum Wednesday night. I told him I needed to think, that he was making me choose between my husband and my career. I won't give up either one. He can't extort sex from me. It's against the law." She lifted her chin but a slight tremor belied her confidence.

"You've done the right thing in coming to me. I will deal with Mr. Slattery." Andy envisioned a scalpel, the only tool that could definitively curb Jack Slattery's libido.

"Good." Sunny slid forward on the chair, but paused. "Just to be clear. You're telling me I can refuse further sexual contact with Jack and my career will not suffer. Right?"

"I certainly am. Now, that isn't to say you may not encounter some other obstacle to escalating compensation like . . . client dissatisfaction, but, I can assure you, refusing Jack Slattery will be irrelevant in your future evaluations."

"Thank you."

"One more thing, Sunny. I suggest you absent yourself from the office during the next week to avoid further contact with Slattery until I have had time to sort this through."

As soon as the door closed behind her, Andy asked Mrs. Lord to summon Bull, but was dismayed to learn Bull was driving his son about to look at colleges. Ridiculous. The child's mother should have been doing that and Bull should be in the office pulling his oar.

He had to settle for Mrs. Lord telling Bull's secretary to have him report at 9:00 a.m. Monday. Andy hoped no other catastrophe occurred before then.

CHAPTER 42

October 27, Monday
Andy

Andy couldn't fathom Bull's cheery demeanor. The lummox fairly tap-danced across the Aubusson carpet, unaware of the crisis that had arisen during his absence.

Bull lodged himself in a chair. "You want some good news?"

"Yes. That would be a refreshing change."

"I've identified the leak." He offered his fright mask of a grin.

"Excellent. Who is it?"

"Maggie Mahoney."

Andy's head bobbed back. "Maggie? Are you certain? That seems quite unlikely."

"No doubt about it. We got her on tape telling Micah Levin about Travis and Lily."

"When? I visited her specifically to caution her not to talk about that incident."

"Same night it happened. Remember, Levin got to you before she did? You didn't try to muzzle her until after she'd already spilled the beans."

"Are you sure it's her? Did you listen to the tape?"

"When I got in this morning, I got the report from our operatives. Next thing I did was listen to the tape."

"Does it sound like her?"

"Sounds like a woman with a bad cold. But it's definitely from her extension. The call was made a few minutes after nine, which would have been right after it happened. Who else is going to be using her phone at that time of night?"

"But why would she do that?"

"Like I told you before, she's been coming on strong in the Gender Equity Committee."

"But still, to put the firm in a position of ridicule . . ." *To endanger my appointment.* He drooped against his chair. "She must be stopped before she does more damage."

"You're going to have to confront her. Tell her if she does it again, she'll be expelled from the partnership."

"Yes, unquestionably." Andy rubbed his temples with his fingers. "On to other unpleasantness. I scheduled this meeting to inform you Jack Slattery has commenced an affair with Sunny."

"What? *Sunny?* But she's a dog."

Andy clicked his tongue. "Surely the motivation for such acts is multifaceted."

"Yeah, you're right. It just surprises me. So tell me what happened."

Andy set forth the unpleasant particulars.

"Assuming what she says is true, Slattery's in deep shit. But, before we get into discipline, we should talk to him. Get his side of the story."

"Yes, of course." Andy paused, steepled his fingers as he considered whether he should participate in the interview. Better to be at a remove. He could shape his response after he heard Slattery's answer. "You should met with him as soon as possible. Let me know how it goes."

CHAPTER 43

October 27, Monday
Maggie

When Mrs. Lord called to "invite" Maggie to join Andy in his office at her "earliest convenience," Maggie sensed trouble but couldn't pinpoint the source. It would take an impending train wreck to divert Andy from O'Toole's presidential campaign this close to Election Day.

As she slipped into Andy's guest chair, she realized she'd forgotten he kept the temperature at eighty degrees year round. Her quilted LaCroix jacket added polish, authority—and warmth.

"There's a very important matter we need to discuss." He sounded as edgy as she felt.

"Indeed. And what is that?"

"Would you agree that, as a partner, you owe a fiduciary duty to me and every other partner in this firm?"

"Of course."

"Would you also agree that leaking unfavorable information about the firm to the press would violate this duty?"

"It would depend on the circumstances, but, in theory, yes. What are you alluding to?"

"Your telling the *Times* about Travis's confrontation with his secretary."

"I have no idea what you're talking about."

"Oh, really? I have it on good authority that you called Micah Levin from your office the same night it happened."

"Don't be ridiculous. If the reporter said that, he's covering up his real source. Who told you it was me?"

"I'm not at liberty to disclose my source."

"Whoever it is, is wrong."

"They are, most assuredly, right. That's all I'm going to say about the matter except to warn you, if this *ever* happens again, you will be expelled from the partnership."

"Expelled? On what evidence? I resent the accusation and demand the right to confront my accuser."

"Don't be ridiculous. This isn't a criminal matter. It's a matter between partners. Strictly civil."

She stood. "I will contest in a most *uncivil* manner any attempt to expel me based on a false accusation. I will sue you for slander if you repeat this monstrous lie."

❑❑❑❑❑

Len looked up as Maggie marched into his office and banged the door shut. "That's not a happy face."

"Understatement of the century." She plopped down into a chair and gave him a play-by-play of her meeting with Andy. Finished, she squeezed her eyes shut and huffed out a breath. "I am so angry at that bastard. He was absolutely righteous accusing me of telling the press about Travis's weenie-wagging!"

"Why accuse you?"

"I have no freaking idea." She paused, rubbed her forehead with her fingertips. "He said I'd called from my office. Why would he mention where I called from? I could have called from home or from my cell, unless—." Her eyes flashed.

"Your line was tapped. Son of a bitch!" Len sounded pissed. "Somebody called the reporter from your office. Must be it."

"Yeah, somebody named Ginger Marshall. She was there when I got back from nailing Travis. We talked. Then I went to the bathroom. She's got great connections to the press. She must have called while I was away."

Len tipped his head to one side like a dog trying to decipher a sound. "But you're smiling?"

"Hey, Ginger's my best friend in the world, and, if anybody has a right to stick it to the firm, it's her."

"Yeah, but using your phone implicates you."

"She didn't know my phone was bugged. And, besides, maybe it was good she used it. Now I know about the wiretap."

"Who do you think hired the techs to do it? Bull?"

"Absolutely Bull. Andy says jump, Bull asks how high."

"What are you going to do?"

"For now, nothing beyond being careful what I say on the phone. Although I could have a little fun with it, plant some disinformation." She stood and shot him a devilish grin. "Maybe put in a call to you, letting you know Ginger has been hired by one of our associates to sue the firm. That'd get them chasing their tails."

"You're bad!"

"Hey, even better, I could say Ginger is representing Bull's secretary."

"His secretary?"

"Yeah. Kim what's-her-name. They've been having an affair

for years. One time when Ginger was still with the firm, she needed to talk to him so she tapped on his door and opened it. There was Kim on her knees, giving him a blow job."

"Bet that's the last time they forgot to lock the door."

"No kidding. And Ginger was such a good scout, she never mentioned it to anyone at the firm except me. A year later, Bull made partner and Ginger was passed over."

"That sucks."

"Yeah, and Kim does too." She chuckled.

CHAPTER 44

October 29, Wednesday
Andy

With a smug smile, Bull sank into the chair facing Andy's desk. "No matter how long I do this, people still surprise me. Human nature, I guess."

"I gather from your expression you've been pleasantly surprised."

"Oh, yeah. I talked to Slattery about Sunny. He says he never laid a hand on her. He—"

"What?" Andy wondered if he had misunderstood. The cacophony of rush hour traffic seemed to grow louder every day. The sound of blaring horns, rumbling diesel engines, and whooping sirens filled the room.

"That's what he said. I expected him to cop to having a consensual affair with her. But he says nothing happened between them."

"How does he explain her accusation?"

"He says she came on to him, but he turned her down. Told me she was so ugly, he wouldn't screw her with my dick!" Bull laughed, a snorting bray. "He says her accusation is the revenge of a woman scorned."

Although greatly relieved, Andy did not find the situation amusing. "Slattery has a way of dragging everything into the gutter with him. What do you make of the conflicting accounts?"

"I think she's telling the truth. I don't see Sunny embarrassing herself by making a false claim. She's got to know she's not much to look at."

"But, in the face of his denial, we do nothing?"

"A little more than nothing. I go back to Sunny, tell her what Jack said, tell her we can't discipline him in the absence of proof, but we'll exclude him from her evaluations and compensation review. I'll also recommend that she not take any more assignments from him. He'll have to find a replacement on the Davidoff case."

"Yes, I like that result. In essence, it satisfies her concern but spares him. Very good." It also spared Andy from a very painful, and possibly dangerous, confrontation with Slattery. Additionally, it offered another plus: work for Maggie Mahoney. "As to Davidoff, tell Slattery to use Maggie instead of Sunny. That way she'll have more to think about than the Gender Equity Committee."

CHAPTER 45

October 31, Friday
Maggie

After a single perfunctory rap, the door to Maggie's office swung open. The visitor didn't wait for an invitation; Slattery strutted in like the cock of the walk. "Well, Ms. Mahoney, you're about to get your wish granted."

"I am? Does that you make you my fairy godfather?"

He laughed sharply, but his chortle sounded more like indignation than amusement. "Me? That's a good one. I've never been accused of being light in the loafers."

"True, more like Don Juan or the Sheik of Araby." She offered an acid smile.

"Aren't you the clever one? Don't believe everything you hear."

"Thanks for the sage advice. Glad I can look to the managing partner for wisdom. But we digress. What glad tidings do you have for me?"

"I'm here to solve your problem with charged hours. You do remember that problem?"

"Yes, you had the foresight and compassion to warn me about the issue."

"But nothing's changed?"

"Not yet." She refused to grovel, to describe the calls and meetings with prospective clients that hadn't yet borne fruit.

"Here's the solution. You're replacing Sunny Star-Perez on the Davidoff case. Andy has pulled her off on another matter."

"Me? Won't the client be put off by my billing rate?"

"Don't worry about it. After Sam got the treason charge dismissed, the client's totally sold on the firm."

Maggie plastered on a happy expression. "Great. I look forward to it."

"Don't get too happy about it. I need you to spend the weekend reading the transcripts of the interviews Sunny and I did in Azerbaijan."

"No problem."

"Make sure you get through all of them by Monday morning. You and I may be heading back there next week to take another crack at some of the witnesses." He paused inside the doorway. "They're all lying pieces of shit so prepare yourself."

Prepare herself? If she had to travel with Jack Slattery, she'd prepare herself with a Beretta Bobcat.

CHAPTER 46

November 2, Sunday
Sunny

Sunny was so relieved when Maggie opened the penthouse door, she almost peed her pants right there. "Maggie, you are absolutely the best to let me come over so early on a Sunday." Before peeling off her coat and scarf, she plopped a brown paper bag on the glass-topped metal table in the foyer.

"No problem. I was thinking about going for a run, but, other than that, I don't have much on my agenda besides work. What's up?"

Sunny grabbed the bag. "I got to go the bathroom real bad. Tell you when I get back."

"Okay. Meet you in the kitchen. I'll make some coffee."

The guest bathroom had a bizarre, decorator-on-drugs look: minimalist white fixtures and black walls.

God. This was not how she had visualized this moment. It was supposed to be exciting and romantic and . . . She squeezed her eyes shut and sighed. *Just do it. Get it over with.*

Her hands shook as she ripped open the box. She glanced at the instructions, took the top off the tester, and laid it on the counter along with the collection cup. She squatted over the toilet. Groaning in relief, she released the pressure on her bladder and caught some urine in the cup.

After she put herself back together, she dipped the stick and waited for the results to materialize. *Please, please, please, let it be negative.*

Desperate for a distraction, she looked around for a magazine but the immaculate room contained nothing so prosaic. She studied the results window on the stick but it was blank. *Too early.* This was the time to plead with God and maybe even bargain, but she'd never really learned any prayers. She closed her eyes and repeated a dozen times, *Please, God, make the test negative.*

She looked at the stick again: pregnant.

It can't be. It can't be. The test must be wrong.

She jerked the top off the other box, dipped the stick in urine. After three minutes, the result was the same. Goddamn Jack Slattery had gotten her pregnant.

Maggie tapped lightly on the door. "Hey, Sunny, are you okay?"

She sniffed back her tears. "Yeah, I'll be right out. Sorry."

Sunny trudged into the kitchen and sat at the table, a weird glass-topped sculpture kind of thing.

Maggie placed a mug of coffee in front of her and sat down. "Hey, what happened to the bagels?"

"Bagels?" Crap, she should have brought some, but she was so preoccupied, she didn't even think about food.

"Never mind. I thought that's what you had in the bag." She pushed back her chair. "I have some yogurt or whole wheat bread if you want. I may even have some bagels in the freezer."

"No, thanks. Coffee's fine."

"You look exhausted. Did you get any sleep last night?"

Sunny shook her head and stared into the steaming cup.

"I'm sorry." Maggie's voice softened. She laid her hand on Sunny's arm. "You have been royally jerked around by Slattery. After coercing you into sex, then the bastard denies it, denies anything ever happened at all. He is truly a piece of work."

"You'll get no argument from me."

"Sure you don't want something to eat? I have some chocolate-dipped biscotti hiding on the top shelf in the pantry."

"No, thanks anyway. I'm not hungry."

They stared silently at the tabletop and shared a dead, heavy pause. Sunny kicked herself for being so feeble. She needed Maggie's help but she couldn't get the words out. It was as if her tongue were stapled to the roof of her mouth.

She exhaled and said, "I have good news and bad news."

"Okay." Maggie juiced the word. "You're batting five hundred. What's the good news?"

"I can prove Jack is lying about what happened in Azerbaijan."

"You can? That's great."

"Not really. That's the bad news. I'm pregnant."

Maggie winced. "No. Oh, Sunny, how awful. Jack's baby?"

"Nobody else's but. José and I haven't had sex in months."

"You're sure you're pregnant?"

"Oh, yeah. That's what was in the paper bag. Two home pregnancy kits. Positive and positive."

"Shit."

"My sentiments exactly."

"What are you going to do?"

Sunny had asked herself that question at least a thousand times since she'd missed her period. She believed in a woman's right to choose but abortion was a choice she had never, ever thought she would make for herself or for her baby. *Her* baby. She couldn't think of it that way. The thing growing inside her was Jack's. Not hers.

"What *can* I do?" The words wobbled as she fought back tears. "I can't pass it off as José's. That would be low. And, even if I were willing to do it—which I'm not—the timing's wrong. Plus, there's the fact that José is a small dark-skinned Latino and Jack is a hulking red-headed Irishman."

"That's all true, but you could tell José what happened. He loves you. In time he'd understand."

"Doubtful. And, even if he did—which is a huge, huge stretch—that doesn't mean he'd want to raise the kid as his own. The child of the man who raped his wife? I don't think so."

"You could tell him. Give him that choice."

"The worst of both worlds. José finds out what happened *and* I have an abortion."

"Sounds like you've decided."

Biting her lips, Sunny nodded.

"Do you want me to help you? Go with you?"

"Would you?"

"Of course. Whatever you need."

"Good. I want to do it soon, as soon as possible."

Maggie put her hand on top of Sunny's. "Let me know when the appointment is. If I can do anything before then, just ask. Will you do that?"

Sunny nodded. Maggie walked her to the door and gave her a hug as she left.

The elevator's antique brass doors opened slowly. The elevator operator said, "Good morning, miss," but, before she could step in, she heard Maggie's voice.

"Sunny, come back! I've got an idea."

CHAPTER 47

November 2, Sunday
Maggie

M aggie grabbed her hand and pulled her into the foyer.
"I figured out how you can nail Jack Slattery's ass."

"I like the sound of that."

"Have a DNA analysis done on the fetal tissue. That'll prove it's his baby."

"Right, right. *You're right*. That's great. But . . ."

"But what?"

"We can't prove anything without a specimen that's definitely his."

"Of course not. But I can get that."

"What? Are you going to have sex with him?" Sunny lifted her eyebrows.

"I love you, but not that much. No, I'll gather a specimen— two or three, to be sure—from Slattery's office."

"His office? How can you do that?"

"Remember he took over Bryce's office? I doubt he had the lock changed. It's not like he's expecting Bryce to return. I've got a key. Undoubtedly, Slattery has a toothbrush and comb in there. Probably a razor. Maybe a used handkerchief or nail clippings. He might have a gym bag in there with sweaty clothes from a squash match." Maggie wrinkled her nose. "There's lots of possibilities."

"You must really love me to go through his personal stuff." She giggled.

"That I do *and* I'm going to love seeing him kicked out of the firm. But there's no point unless you're willing to take the results to Andy."

"Take the results to Andy? I'll plaster them to his forehead."

"Good girl." Maggie paused. "I know this has been a terrible experience for you, but you've changed. It's made you stronger, tougher."

"Like they say, what doesn't kill us . . ."

"Well, it's going to *slay* Jack Slattery."

CHAPTER 48

November 4, Tuesday
Maggie

Maggie figured the firm would be thinly populated on election night. The race was close. Given Slattery's personal stake in the outcome, he would definitely be glued to the tube. This was her best chance to waltz into his office and grab some specimens.

Simple.

No problem.

But ropes of tension knotted across her shoulders.

Looking at the menu at Felidia, she almost abandoned her plan to have a light dinner before returning to the firm to wait out the janitors. Her stomach waffled as she considered each item. She managed to down most of the pear ravioli and all of the sorbet sampler. Skipped the espresso. She didn't need to amp her anxiety.

As she sat at her desk watching the election returns, she unconsciously worked the thumb of her right hand against each fingertip. She caught herself and snorted. It was as if she were a safecracker getting ready to twist the dials on a combination lock. *Silly.* All she needed was a key, and it lay nestled in her upper right desk drawer.

Initially, she'd pictured herself as a secret agent in black leotards creeping along the mahogany wainscoting that lined the firm's corridors. Rationality returned. She realized her best disguise was simply being one of the firm's lawyers. And if she chose to dress in black from head to toe, so what? Half the City's professionals did every day. Her Jil Sander pantsuit with its elongated silhouette and cigarette pants was perfect. She'd be as inconspicuous as a shadow.

But there *was* a mission to be accomplished, and she had prepared for it, stocking her briefcase with Ziploc baggies in a variety of sizes to protect the specimens she gathered from contamination. The briefcase had the added benefit of bolstering a claim she was in his office on business if she were challenged.

She watched the returns with growing excitement. O'Toole's opponent, John Finley, was gaining on him. She fervently hoped Finley would win and spare the country an attorney general like Andy.

The walk to Slattery's office from the elevator seemed interminable. She tried to appear purposeful but tired, the appropriate demeanor for a lawyer working past eleven. With a lowered gaze, she checked for light seeping under the crack of the door to his office. Nothing. She slipped the key into the lock and turned it.

She stepped into the office, flipped the light switch, and threw the dead bolt. The bathroom had the most potential. If she struck out there, she'd look for hair on his desk chair. But the probability was too low to start with such a time-consuming task. *No need to worry about time.* Slattery wouldn't visit his office at . . . She glanced at her watch. 11:12. No way.

But her desire to limit the window of exposure propelled her toward the bathroom in quick strides. The fluorescent light over the bathroom sink flickered on. The beige marble countertop was vacant.

Disappointed, she yanked open the first drawer below the counter. *Yes! An electric razor. The son of a bitch was going down.* She grabbed the shaver but froze just as she began shoving it into a plastic bag.

He'd notice it was gone. Not that he'd ever suspect her, but he'd blame the cleaning crew. That wasn't fair. They were hard-working immigrants at the bottom of the ladder. She put the razor back, laid the bag on the counter, and hoped her search would produce something disposable that wouldn't be missed.

She pulled the drawer all the way out. A cord for the shaver. A charger. No help. The ballast in one the fluorescent lights began to buzz. The noise gnawed at her frazzled nerves.

Before she gave up, she leaned over and reached until her fingertips hit the end of the drawer. She wiggled her hand from corner to corner.

"Damn!" She'd nicked her finger on something sharp.

Instinctively, she jerked her finger away and into her mouth. She sucked the blood, salty and metallic. After wrapping her finger in toilet paper, she reached carefully for the source of her cut.

An old-fashioned double-edged safety razor. Excellent.

But her makeshift bandage was leaking. She riffled the medicine cabinet for a bandage. She found Band-Aids *and* a toothbrush. Excellent.

She bandaged her finger, tossed the wrapping and the bloody toilet paper into her briefcase. Now for the prize: Slattery's toothbrush. She paused. He would surely notice it had disappeared. *Not good.* Then she noticed at the bottom of the cabinet an unopened box with a fresh toothbrush. She swapped it for the used one.

As she stowed the safety razor and toothbrush in her brief-case, she calculated the odds she had a specimen that would yield DNA. She'd done her homework on the Net; the success rate varied wildly for different objects. The yield on razors was only about 40 percent but toothbrushes were higher. Maybe as high as 70 percent.

The ballast's buzz grabbed her attention, interrupting her calculations. *Shit.*

She needed to focus. It would be terrific to have one more potential source of DNA but she wanted to get the hell out of there. She glanced at her watch. *11:28.* She should go.

But she'd come this far. She couldn't leave without a defini-tive sample.

Bingo! The next drawer yielded a pair of antique silver men's hairbrushes and a comb. She laid them out on the counter, quick-ly plucked auburn hairs from each, and transferred them to a plastic bag.

Enough. Not every specimen would yield DNA but surely some of them would. Returning the brushes and comb to the drawer, she heard a soft, muffled thump from the office. Her hand stopped in midair. It was probably just—

A faint grating noise followed.

A key.

The thunk of the sliding dead bolt.

Someone was coming in.

CHAPTER 49

November 4, Tuesday
Maggie

Slattery. It must be Slattery. And she was trapped in the bathroom. Maybe he'd stay in the outer office by his desk. But the bathroom door was open, the light was on. Reflexively, she clicked the switch and hoped she'd been quick enough he didn't notice.

She had to hide. Inside the shower or behind the door separating the bathroom from the office? She chose the shower. Its frosted glass door would at least blur her outline.

She grabbed her briefcase and took a step toward the shower but her arm jerked backward. What?

The briefcase strap was hung up on one of the faucets. She tugged it free.

Despite the urgency, she forced herself to walk lightly, avoiding the clatter of her stilettos. In two quick strides she was at the shower enclosure. She tried to ease the door open, but the latch clicked softly. A pulse pounded in her neck. She tiptoed to the corner away from the showerhead and laid her briefcase, buckle down, on the tile floor. No good. If he turned the light on, its chestnut leather would contrast with the tan tile.

She pressed it against the black fabric on her torso. Better but still too exposed. *She* was too exposed.

She turned to face the corner. With her black hair brushing the shoulders of her black outfit, she was a void. A human-shaped void, but still indistinct behind the cloudy glass. At least she hoped so.

She'd been so intent on hiding that she'd lost track of Slattery's movements. Where was he? He had opened the door, hit the light switch, and then what? She tried to soften her breathing so she could concentrate on noise from the office.

Nothing.

Then approaching footsteps. Not loud. Leather soles on thick wool carpeting. But each footfall was more distinct as he came closer. Then the flash of the overhead lights. The clatter of leather soles on tiles.

Her mind wailed, *No, no, no. Go away.*

She heard the crack of the toilet seat flipped against the lid. A zipper being lowered. The splash of urine against water.

He muttered, "What the hell?"

Her heartbeat revved to double time. He must have seen her. But he was facing away from her. How did he know? She stood motionless, waiting to be ordered out of the enclosure.

The next thing she heard was the clang of the metal handle and the rush of water filling the bowl. The zipper being raised. A footstep toward the door.

"What the fuck is this? Blood? Those bastards better not be shooting up in here."

But it was *her* blood from the razor. She'd hidden the bloody toilet paper in her briefcase, but she'd been so intent on his toothbrush that she'd forgotten to clean the droplets on the counter.

The lights flashed off.

The knot in Maggie's chest loosened. He hadn't seen her. She was safe. Or she would be if he'd just leave. But the next sound she heard was a low rumble; he was rolling his desk chair against the plastic floor protector.

"Shit. Where the hell did I put it?"

The sound of a drawer rattling open and sliding closed. Another drawer rattling open and then closing. "Goddamn it."

The sound of a drawer opening. "There you are, you pain in the ass." The sound of a drawer sliding closed.

He'd come into the office to pick up something. He'd found it. Now he'd leave. *Please, God, let him leave.* She waited to hear the chair rolling.

Nothing.

Then the static of an open line on the speakerphone. Two rings.

"Hey, Mary Pat. It's me."

"Oh, Jack, did you find my necklace?"

"Got it right here. No problem."

"Thank heavens. I was worried someone would steal it."

"What? In my office? Don't be silly."

"I've told the ladies so much about the necklace. Black South Sea pearls! Oh, my God!" she squeaked. "You know I really want to wear it at lunch tomorrow. I was such a silly goose to break the clasp the first time I put it on. You're a doll to take it back to the jeweler."

"A doll? Yeah, that's me all right. Got to go. Be home soon."

The line buzzed for an instant, then he tapped in another number.

"You have one new message and four saved messages. To hear your new message, press nine."

Beep.

"Jack, Andy here. I received a disturbing message from Bull. He tells me you've refused to meet with the gender sensitivity coach. I must insist. For the record, you understand. I'm too close to the finish line to let your—to let anything interfere. Just do the training and keep your pants zipped until I'm sworn in. Then we'll both get what we want."

"To replay—"

The line went dead.

"Son of a bitch! Who the hell do you think you are? *Keep my pants zipped! Keep my pants zipped?* Jesus H. Christ." Maggie heard a rumble followed by an angry thud. Probably his chair hitting the credenza. "Don't get righteous with me, you old fart. I'm the one who buried your dirty laundry, you fucking prima donna."

The sound of heavy footsteps gradually faded and the light went out. The door slammed.

Maggie exhaled. She was wrung out from the adrenaline surge.

After waiting five minutes, she climbed out of the shower and hurried to leave the office. She stepped into the corridor, pulled the door shut.

"Maggie, what are you doing here so late?"

She jumped, her pulse racing. She turned to see Sam, Jack's neighbor.

"I . . . I . . . It's confidential."

"Huh? You were in Jack's office. Working on Davidoff with him?"

She bit her lip. Lying could be risky. Sam might say something to Jack. "No. I can't explain now. I will soon, but not now. Please don't say anything to Jack. Please. It's very important."

He frowned. "But he's the managing partner. He didn't give you permission to be there? What were you doing in his office without his knowledge?"

She laid her hand on his arm. "Trust me, *please*. When I explain, you'll understand. All I can say now is that your silence is very important to me."

He paused, studied her face. "Okay, Maggie May, if it means that much to you, I'll be quiet. Just don't make me an accessory after the fact." He arched his left eyebrow, the one interrupted by a scar.

Maybe he wasn't such a tool after all.

"Thanks. You won't regret it."

"So when will I get the explanation?"

"A week. I promise."

CHAPTER 50

November 5, Wednesday
Maggie

Maggie shivered as she and Sam ran across Fifth Avenue. Winter might not have officially arrived, but cold dry air from Canada had enveloped the city. Her eyes stung and her nose dripped.

So far, the only good thing about their run was that Sam had discreetly avoided any mention of their meeting outside Jack's office.

"What do you think about the election?" Sam asked.

"It sucks. Finley would have been much better for the country than O'Toole. And, if Finley had won, Andy would be out of contention as AG."

"But he lost. So Andy will probably get the nod." Sam stared at her with open curiosity.

"Yeah." She pitched her voice low and flat to close off the topic. If she said more, raving demons would fly out of her mouth.

Last night they'd streaked through her mind relentlessly as she'd steamed about Andy's conspiracy with Slattery.

Sam seemed to get the message and shut up. They ran in silence for almost a mile, passing shrubs etched with frost, their feet crunching dead leaves. The air was so cold it burned her lungs.

Finally he said, "It's not a done deal. O'Toole still has to nominate him and then there are confirmation hearings. Don't look so down." He ruffled her hair, tugging strands free of the knit headband that covered her ears.

"*Ouch.*" She slapped his hand. "What? You going for pain as a distraction?"

"Sorry. How about this? Let's talk about the confirmation hearings. What kind of things might knock him out of the box?"

"Good. Let's start with what we know about him."

"Besides his years of public service and distinguished tenure as chairman of one of the country's most prestigious law firms?"

"Hey, are you going to help me or not? Look, he could be like Eliot Spitzer and frequent prostitutes. Or John Edwards and have his mistress on his payroll. Or—"

He laughed so hard, snot shot out of his runny nose. "Mrs. Lord? Jesus, who the hell would want to have sex with her?"

"Maybe she's a dominatrix. Can't you picture her with a whip and high leather boots?"

"Andy's so into control, I can't believe that's his thing."

"Well, what *is* his thing?" She'd been trying to answer that question most of the night. Because Andy's admonition to 'keep his pants zipped' had infuriated Slattery, she figured the secret had to be sexual. About two in the morning, she'd flashed on Andy having touted Slattery's ability to "resolve delicate matters discreetly" with the Manhattan District Attorney's office. That had to be what Slattery meant about burying Andy's "dirty laundry."

She said, "Maybe he's a pedophile or a flasher. A necrophili-ac?" She bobbled her eyebrows. "Does he have a turn-on that's so vile, it would knock him out of the box?"

"I shudder to think. Worse than picturing my parents do-ing it."

She smiled coyly. "I've never had so much trouble getting a man to think about sex."

"Okay. Just for you, Maggie May, but I've got to say I draw a blank when I try to picture him with a hooker, or any other woman for that matter."

"Then maybe he's gay. He's never been married. There was a rumor to that effect years ago, but Bryce said it was wrong."

"Could be, but I don't think that would disqualify him. He's so uptight, I can imagine he'd want to keep it secret, but, by itself, it wouldn't be enough. Not nowadays."

"No, probably not unless he did something illegal like . . . I don't know, hiring a gay prostitute." Her gut tensed with excite-ment. They were on the right track. She could feel it.

"Maybe cottaging."

"Cottaging? Guess I missed that in *The Joy of Sex*."

"It's what gays do in public restrooms when they want to make contact. You know, footsie under the stall."

"Yeah, like that senator from Iowa. No, Idaho. Anonymous sex in bathrooms is gross, but what was the criminal charge?"

"Public lewdness. A friend of mine didn't know her husband was gay until he got busted for going through the foot-tapping, hand-signals drill in a public bathroom."

"That's rotten. Must have been hard for her."

"Devastating."

She asked, "So cottaging is still an offense in New York?"

"At least as of a year ago when my friend's husband was arrested."

"Mmm. Public lewdness. I'd say that'd be disqualifying."

"Sure. But if Andy had it on his record, he'd never have put his hand up for the nomination," said Sam.

"Right. *If* it's on his record."

"So?"

"So, thank you for cheering me up." She gave him a quick hug. "Now I can head back."

"Giving up so soon?"

"I'm freezing my ass off. And, I've got a doctor's appointment." That wasn't precisely true, but close enough.

"You sick?"

"No. I'm kind of helping out with some medical research."

"Sounds mysterious."

She chuckled. "If only you knew."

CHAPTER 51

November 5, Wednesday
Maggie

After dropping Slattery's DNA specimens off at the lab, Maggie headed into the office. For the first time in weeks, she looked forward to legal work. Research was usually viewed as drudgery reserved for associates, but this morning she'd be eagerly drilling into New York criminal law.

As the elevator doors opened on Maggie's floor, Nancy Holstein stood waiting. Maggie grinned at her outlandish outfit. Nancy was decked out in platform stilettos, tangerine tights, and a dress in a psychedelic purple and orange print cinched with a wide violet belt. She'd topped it off with a shaggy jacket.

"Wow! Look at you."

"Hey, Maggie, I was just at your office. I thought I had missed you."

"Let's go back." She laid her hand on Nancy's arm. "I love this jacket. What's it made of?"

"Monkey fur."

Maggie jerked her hand away.

"Don't worry, it's vintage. It was dead long before even you were born."

"I'm going to forget you said that and offer you a seat." She closed her office door behind Nancy.

"I just wanted to say good-bye before I left the firm."

"Where are you going?"

"TechniVerse. I'll be the associate general counsel. Doing mostly licensing agreements, I think."

"I'm sorry things didn't work out here. You must be very disappointed."

"Yes and no. It burned my ass to hear Andy say I didn't have the 'gravitas' to become a partner because I slept around. Frankly, I think gravitas is code for 'white male.' But there it is." She sighed. "On the upside, he ponied up enough cash for me to buy a great loft."

"Andy ponied up cash?"

"You betcha. A million bucks." She beamed. "Georgia Albright said I did good."

"You mean Andy—I guess *the firm*—agreed to pay a million dollars to settle your sex discrimination claim?"

"Yeah." She opened her eyes wide. "And I wanted to make sure you knew about it."

"This is the first I've heard."

"I suspected as much. I had to arm-wrestle Andy to get the partners excluded from the restrictions of the confidentiality clause. When he balked, I figured he was going to try to brush it under the carpet. He's such a scumbag." She clicked her tongue. "You're fighting the good fight, and I wanted to be certain you knew. Use it as ammunition for other women."

"Thanks. Maybe it means they'll start treating women better." After all, a million dollar settlement was a hell of an expensive precedent to have out there tempting other disgruntled associates. "Do you have the money?"

"Abso-freaking-lutely. The check cleared this morning. Otherwise, I wouldn't be here telling you. My only regret is I'd signed the agreement before I got the call from the *Journal*. I would love to be a source off the record. But it's not worth the risk."

"The *Journal* knows about your situation?"

"Not mine, specifically, but it's doing a piece on life in a big law firm, namely Sweeny Owens."

"I wonder what we did to merit that."

"Probably anticipating Andy's nomination as AG. But I don't think merit is the word I'd use. Target might be more like it."

"Not a puff piece, huh?"

Nancy laughed. "Given the questions the reporter wanted to ask, I'd say it sounded more like an exposé."

CHAPTER 52

November 5, Wednesday
Maggie

As soon as Nancy left, Maggie focused on exposing Andy's criminal record. She was absolutely totally convinced it existed.

In less than an hour, she learned she could get his criminal history record from the New York State Office of Court Administration. The "history" would pick up what he had been charged with, the ultimate disposition of the charge, and the sentence. If Andy had been arrested and Slattery had intervened to get the charges dismissed, the arrest would still show up. Dismissal was, after all, one kind of disposition.

The only way the arrest could be buried was expungement. If Slattery had gone the extra mile after dismissal and gotten the record sealed, the charge would remain secret. But expungement wasn't available for all charges. Even if it were, Slattery might not have gone for it or might not have done it correctly. A long shot, but well worth filling in the form and forking up the sixty-five buck fee.

All she needed was Andy's exact name and birth date. The website warned that the search was based solely on an exact match of name and DOB. She checked the firm directory to see if Andy had a middle name, but he was listed simply as "Erling Anderson." She pulled his birth date from Wikipedia. Reading his bio there heightened her sense of urgency. A lawyer with glowing credentials like his—White House counsel, member of the 9/11 Commission, president of the American Bar Association—would sail through confirmation unless she found his "dirty laundry."

She printed out the form, completed it by hand in capital letters as required, and wrote a check on her personal account for the fee. The firm's messenger service would deliver the paperwork to the court administration offices on Beaver Street later that day.

CHAPTER 53

November 11, Tuesday
Maggie

Maggie squinted at the Criminal History Search Report. Nothing, nada, not a single charge, was found for Erling Anderson, born August 22, 1946. The form contained a boilerplate reminder that the results were valid only for an individual whose name was spelled exactly as shown on the search request and who was born on the date specified.

Damn, damn, damn.

That answer allowed for four interpretations: one, Slattery had succeeded in getting the charge sealed; two, the name Andy was charged under was a variation of Erling Anderson; three, she had his birthday wrong; or, four, he was never charged with a criminal offense.

She immediately rejected the fourth possibility. Slattery's response to the voice mail coupled with his sudden rise inside the firm hierarchy all but guaranteed Andy had been caught with his pants down. The third possibility was equally unlikely: his birth date was unambiguous. The second possibility had potential. She remembered thinking it seemed odd that he didn't have a middle name. Maybe he'd been charged as "Erling Middle-Initial-What-ever-It-Was Anderson." That was a lead she could pursue. But, if the first possibility, a sealed record, was indeed what had happened, she was screwed.

She pulled a yellow pad out of her drawer and started a list of approaches to find out what variation of his name Andy might have been charged under.

CHAPTER 54

November 13, Thursday
Maggie

Sunny burst into Maggie's office and shoved the door shut behind her. "You got the results?"

"Right here." Maggie waved the white envelope. "You should do the honors."

Sunny snatched it, jabbed a finger under the seal, and tore it open as if she were ripping Slattery's heart.

"Hey, keep it in one piece. You plan to plaster it to Andy's forehead as I recollect."

Sunny's eyes skipped over the pages. "*Hah*! 'Probability of paternity greater than 99.9 percent.' I got you, Jack Slattery, you son of a bitch!" Her smile flashed with triumph and malice.

"Couldn't ask for a better result. Can I see it? I negotiated some wording about not providing ID for his specimens. Hope they got it right."

Maggie read from the first page. "Our analysis was performed on DNA extracted from fetal tissue identified as the product of an electric vacuum aspiration performed on Sunny Star-Perez—"

Sunny sighed but said nothing.

"—and on DNA extracted from samples (a toothbrush, six strands of hair, and a safety razor) allegedly obtained from John Emmet Slattery. We can confirm that the DNA derived from said toothbrush and hair was identical. (No DNA was obtained from the razor.) However, we have no irrefutable evidence as to the source of these samples or their chain of custody before we received them. Therefore, our conclusion of probable paternity would not be admissible in a legal proceeding."

"Just the facts, ma'am." Sunny said in an acid tone, then exhaled. "It's correct, but, you know, I really hate admitting I had an abortion. It was totally the right thing to do, but, after wanting a baby for so long, it almost killed me. That prick Jack Slattery should have his balls cut off."

"You won't get any argument from me, but I doubt Andy will elect that remedy." Maggie returned the letter. "Sit down for a minute. We need to talk about next steps."

Ready to do battle, Sunny perched on the edge of a chair, her body taut. "It seems clear to me: I take the letter to Andy and demand that he kick Slattery out of the firm." She punctuated her statement by tucking a lock of hair behind her ear. *A lock of chin-length hair.*

"Sunny! You cut your hair! It looks great. I was so preoccupied by the letter, I didn't even notice. When did you do it?"

"Yesterday. I decided all that long hair made me look like a little girl or a hippie or . . ." She hiked a shoulder. "Just didn't feel like me anymore."

"You certainly look more professional. It's wonderful."

"Thanks. It feels good." She fluffed the back of her hair.

"Well, going to Andy is definitely the right course. One thing you should be prepared to address is where you got Slattery's samples. I have no prob—"

"I've thought about that. I'm going to say I got them from his office. There's no need to get you involved. It's perfectly plausible that I went in there while he and his secretary were at lunch."

"Okay. If that's what you want, but I don't mind—"

Sunny stood. "Look, it was terrific that you got them. I don't know if I would have had the guts to do it. I kinda wish I'd had." Her voice wobbled. "I *want* to say I did it, if you don't mind my taking credit."

"Fine by me." She paused. "Sunny, I'm so sorry about all this. Sorry you had to have the abortion. It *was* the right thing to do, but maybe you should talk to someone, like a therapist, about it. Just because it was . . . logical and appropriate doesn't mean there aren't feelings attached to it."

"Maybe. But first I want to talk to Andy and get Slattery the hell out of Sweeny Owens before he does to someone else what he did to me."

"Okay, but think about getting help. I can see you're hurting. I imagine José can see it, too. You don't want him asking questions."

"Don't worry. I can handle it."

CHAPTER 55

November 14, Friday
Sunny

Sunny rushed through the pleasantries with Andy. The smiles they offered each other as greetings were equally disingenuous. She knew he didn't give a shit about what Slattery had done to her except as a potential problem. She was delighted to be able to present him with a problem squared.

"Bull told me Jack Slattery denied raping me. I—"

Andy raised a finger as if he were a schoolmaster correcting a student. "More than that, Sunny, Jack denied having had a sexual relationship with you."

"I have proof that he lied." Her heart hiccupped. Time to go into her memorized lines. She'd practiced them again and again in her office so she wouldn't falter. "He not only raped me, he impregnated me. My husband is sterile and Jack is the only other man I've had sex with."

"You're pregnant?" His voice jumped an octave.

"I was pregnant. I terminated the pregnancy. A comparison of the fetal tissue to Slattery's DNA proved there was a greater than 99.9 percent probability he was the father."

"I . . . How unfortunate for you. I'm sorry."

"I didn't come for your condolences. I want you to expel Slattery from the partnership."

"I see." He raised a hand to his face, pinched the bridge of his nose, and sagged against the back of his chair. "I understand your desire for redress." He paused. "Now, as to the matter of proof. You say a DNA analysis was performed. Do you have a copy of the report?"

"Of course." She extracted the pages from the leather portfolio she held on her lap and extended her arm. If he wanted it, he had to get off his butt and reach over his desk. She was done with being the good girl.

He stood and grasped the document. Minutes ticked by as he read the report word for word.

"The laboratory had no evidence other than your word that the samples came from Jack Slattery. How did you come by the"—he flipped a page—"the razor, the strands of hair, and the toothbrush?"

"Simple. One day when neither he nor his assistant was around, I went into his bathroom. Do you require a description of the precise location of each item?"

"No. That does little to establish their authenticity."

"Do you honestly doubt these samples came from Slattery? Having been embarrassed by his denial, would I risk looking foolish again? If you don't believe me, have Slattery give the lab a specimen. They'll get the same answer." Her taut lips shaped each word into an angry projectile.

"I doubt that will be necessary. Obviously, I need to consult with Bull about this."

"And, while you're at it, consult with him about expelling Slattery. That's the only remedy I'll accept."

Surprised by her own forcefulness with the firm chairman, she rose and marched from the office.

CHAPTER 56

November 14, Friday
Andy

Relieved to hear Bull was on his way, Andy walked to a window and stared vacantly at the snarled traffic below. He didn't need Bull to tell him Slattery had to go as managing partner. That was a given. He doubted even Slattery would contest that. But surely Slattery would threaten to play his trump card to squeeze some advantage out of the situation. The only prize in play would be keeping his partnership.

When Andy finished his recital of the facts, Bull cocked his head in amazement. "Slattery is a total douche, but I got to hand it to him for chutzpah. What a piece of work."

"So you accept her account?"

"Yeah. Like she said, she'd have to be nuts to make up this claim if it wasn't true. I can tell you she was totally humiliated when she heard he denied having sex with her."

"But we should give him the opportunity to submit a DNA specimen to the lab if he wishes."

"Sure. Subject to it being done kosher, of course. I wouldn't put it past him to hire some homeless guy to go in and say he was Jack Slattery."

"For now, let's assume the specimens ascribed to him are genuine. If that's the case, we must consider him a liar and an adulterer, but, beyond that, I expect we will be left with a he said, she said as to what actually happened between them."

Bull rubbed his lantern jaw with the back of his fingers. "I suppose that's right."

"His lie impeded our investigation of the matter, but, even if he'd owned up to the sex, we'd still be at a credibility impasse." Andy paused and lifted a shoulder in a deliberate show of indifference.

"But what about Sunny?"

"Sunny? She aborted an unwanted child that may or may not have been the product of consensual sex. More than that, we'll never know."

"True."

"Given Slattery interfered with firm administration, his punishment should be stripping him of administrative responsibilities. At least temporarily."

"Temporarily?" Bull's voice sounded hollow with surprise.

"It's not as if his lie worked some irreparable harm."

"Guess not, but it really tore Sunny up." His heavy brow knotted. "I mean, she was on the edge of hysterics when I told her Jack denied having sex. She must have gone berserk when she found out she was pregnant."

"Yes, high drama indeed." He paused as if to consider Bull's point. "But I don't think the firm should deny itself the services of a highly capable administrator because her feelings were hurt. The greater good, after all."

Bull's bovine eyes blinked behind his thick glasses. His expression cleared. At last he'd realized where Andy was headed.

"Right. You're right. So, uh, how long do you think he should be suspended as managing partner?"

"Not long. The suspension itself will send a powerful message. Let me consider it further and discuss the entire matter with Slattery."

"Sure. I'm good with that . . . unless you want me there to witness the conversation. Create a record."

"No, that won't be necessary."

"Okay, but it would be good if you wrote up a memo about it. I think we'll need to put something in his personnel file."

"Certainly."

Bull pushed himself out of the chair cautiously, as if the seat held a spring-loaded IED. "Yeah, well, let me know how it comes out, all right?"

"Of course."

He turned as he reached the door. "So, will you follow up with Sunny?"

"I'll let you know the result of my meeting with Jack. It may be better if you talk to her."

CHAPTER 57

November 17, Monday
Andy

Andy slid into an armchair, unbuttoned his jacket, and smoothed his tie. The feel of the sleek Dupioni silk was soothing.

"To what do I owe this honor?" Slattery said. He swung his feet off his desktop and resettled himself.

"Jack, I'm afraid I have some difficult news. Sunny became pregnant as a result of your liaison and—"

"*Alleged* liaison. Nothing happened between us. If she's pregnant, it's not mine."

"Yes, I expected you would say that." Andy withdrew a copy of the report from his breast pocket. "She terminated the pregnancy and had a lab compare the fetal tissue to your DNA. Its—"

"What? *My* DNA?"

"Its analysis indicates a greater than 99.9 percent likelihood of paternity."

Slattery grabbed the document from his hand and scanned it quickly. "Ridiculous. I never provided any DNA specimen. The lab says as much. The comparison isn't worth the paper it's written on." He flipped it onto his desktop.

"I realize you didn't volunteer the specimens. Sunny says she removed the items noted in the report from this office. However, if—"

"From my office?" He snatched up the report. "A razor? A toothbrush? So she went into my bathroom. That's a place where I have an expectation of privacy."

"We're not talking about whether her search complies with the Fourth Amendment. If you insist you're not the father, you can submit a DNA specimen yourself."

"Damn right I'll submit a specimen. I won't be railroaded." He flushed, his complexion one shade short of apoplexy.

"Fine, but you do understand that the specimen will be taken by an independent third party in a way that assures its authenticity?"

"Of course I do."

"Then you also understand that, if you did indeed have sex with her, there is nothing to be gained by prolonging this process."

"Process? What process? Where are you going with this?"

"Sunny demands that you be expelled from the partnership."

"For screwing her? Who the hell does she think she is, the Virgin Mary?"

"She is a partner who, in the course of providing legal services to a client, agreed to travel with you to Azerbaijan, a Muslim country where she had no connections and no recourse to legal authorities to seek redress for being raped by you."

"*Raped?* I did not rape her. Absolutely did not rape her. If you could see what happened in that room—"

Andy held up a hand. "I'd prefer not to."

"Right. Wouldn't want to offend your delicate sensibilities. I mean, have you ever even seen a woman's pussy?"

Andy paused to strip any emotion from his response. "Jack, that is neither relevant nor helpful. If you remain civil, I believe we can work our way through this process to a resolution satisfactory to you."

"I'm telling you right up front, you fudge-packer, expulsion will not be a satisfactory resolution."

"Because it is no longer feasible to determine if Sunny's recitation of events is correct, I agree. The matter does not hinge on whether or not the sex was voluntary. It hinges on whether you lied to Bull about having relations with Sunny."

Slattery leaned across his desk. "The issue is whether or not I lied? Whether I broke the goddamn ninth commandment? That's what this is about?"

"Indeed. Lying to Bull in his capacity as firm employment counsel during the course of an investigation would be akin to obstruction of justice or impeding an official inquiry. It would be a serious offense for any partner but a grievous one for the managing partner, totally antithetical to his high office."

"You've got to be kidding me. Is this your way of weaseling out of our deal? Because if it is, I'll—"

"I appreciate the weight of your threat." He stared solemnly into Slattery's eyes. "I am on the cusp of fulfilling my lifelong ambition. I do not intend to jeopardize that. But, you must realize that if I fail to take any action on Sunny's complaint, it will cast a shadow on both my nomination and your future tenure as chairman. It is unfortunate that we are in this situation, but, remember, it is a situation you created."

"You better have a goddamn good solution if you want to achieve your 'lifelong ambition.'" His tone was cruel, mocking.

"Once my nomination is announced, I will inform the partnership that, in anticipation of the coming election for firm chairman, you have resigned as managing partner to level the playing field. While that will be the public message, Sunny will be told that your resignation is pursuant to my request, that, in the absence of proof of rape, such action is the most forceful I can possibly take, and I am most sorry for her distress."

"That's it?"

"That's it." Slattery didn't need to know about the memo in his personnel file. Andy could instruct Bull to overlook it, but he didn't want to appear negligent should the situation be somehow discovered.

Staring disconsolately into the corner, Slattery tapped his knuckles on his desk. He turned his gaze to Andy. "You'll endorse me as a candidate for chairman?"

"That I cannot do, but I will praise you lavishly in my memo announcing your resignation as managing partner."

"Yeah, well, you fruits know how to dress things up, so I'll expect a pretty package."

CHAPTER 58

November 20, Thursday
Sunny

Sunny was relieved when Mrs. Lord summoned her to Andy's office. It had been almost a week since they'd talked, and she'd spent a lot of time rehashing the conversation. Maybe she'd been too strident. That stunt, making him get up for the report, had been juvenile. She had intended to be forceful, but that had been over the top.

She sucked in a deep breath as she sat in front of Andy. He smiled solicitously, but the best she could do was lift the corners of her mouth.

"Sunny, I want to tell you how sorry I am about what you've had to endure recently. It is a testament to your character that you've come into the office every day with a smile on your face."

Her throat clotted up. She mumbled, "Thank you."

"There is nothing I can do to change what happened in Ordubad or its painful sequelae. I cannot imagine the distress you have suffered."

She couldn't believe it, but Andy seemed to understand. Tears pooled in her eyes.

"If I had the authority to impose physical punishment on Jack Slattery for what he has put you through, you can be assured that I would. *Intimate* physical punishment. That, however, is not my prerogative."

"Too bad. It's what he deserves."

"I am most frustrated that the events in Ordubad are beyond my purview. I do not for a moment doubt your account of what happened there, but we lack proof to craft an appropriate punishment."

Oh, my God. He believed her. She covered her eyes with her palm to hide her tears.

She heard him walk around his desk and sit next to her. He extended a white handkerchief. "My dear, I am so, so sorry."

She swiped her eyes and bit the inside of her cheek. She silently vowed, *No more tears.* Crying was such a feeble, girly thing to do. She coughed. "Thank you."

"You're most welcome. Take your time."

After a few breaths, she turned to him again. "I'm okay. Thanks."

"Good." He nodded. "I want to assure you that you are not without redress. By lying to Bull about what happened in Ordubad, Slattery undid himself. That is an affront he cannot deny. With that act, he interfered with an official firm investigation, in effect, obstructing justice. He has no defense to that charge and will be punished for it."

She nodded, not quite trusting her voice to remain steady.

"I have demanded his resignation as managing partner. He cannot impede firm administration on the one hand and be responsible for it on the other. That would be a totally unacceptable result."

"That's right. Exactly."

"Excellent." He put his hand on her shoulder. "If you have any more concerns about Slattery or any other matter, I hope you'll come directly to me. We haven't had the opportunity to work together, but I hope we will in the future. Perhaps you'll consider working with me in the Justice Department." He smiled. "There'll be an announcement in a few days. But keep that to yourself."

"Thank you. Thank you very much."

She walked slowly out of his office, exhausted by the emotions. Such a relief that he got it. He was a decent guy after all. He'd even tipped her off about becoming attorney general. She didn't want to go into government service, but it was kind of cool to have the inside track.

CHAPTER 59

November 24, Monday
Maggie

"Son of a bitch!" Maggie read the news alert glowing on her computer screen. President-elect O'Toole had concluded his press conference by naming his first two cabinet nominees: Wilbur Quimby for secretary of state and Erling Anderson for attorney general.

Now the only thing that would keep Andy out of office was the confirmation process. He sure as hell didn't belong there, but she didn't honestly believe she had enough to keep him out.

Andy's nomination scorched her but what could she do? She was totally pissed and thoroughly powerless. At this point, her only alternative was a mind-numbing diversion. *Think about something else.* She sorted through her mail. That worked for a whole thirty seconds until she found a memo to all attorneys from Andy.

I am most gratified to inform you that President-elect Michael O'Toole has nominated me for the office of the attorney general of the United States of America. I am humbled to have this opportunity to serve my country.

Although the confirmation process will demand much of my attention over the coming months, I will continue to act as chairman of Sweeny, Owens & Boyle until my successor is chosen. It is my hope that the selection will be completed by January 15.

I have asked Tom Beresford, Arnold Westing-house, Francis Carpenter, Skip Hayes, and Marty McSorley to serve as members of a Nominating Committee. As is our tradition, my successor will be chosen by consensus with these partners identifying the ultimate nominee based on a series of discussions with all members of the firm.

The partnership is fortunate to have many excellent candidates for the office of chairman among its ranks. One of those candidates is Jack Slattery, a man who has served with distinction as managing partner since Bryce Chandler's untimely death. Ever mindful of considerations of fairness and propriety, Jack has tendered his resignation as managing partner to create a level playing field for all who wish to be considered to succeed me.

Marty McSorley has excluded himself as a candidate because of his age. He has agreed, however, to serve as managing partner until such time as a new chairman has been selected and has designated his own managing partner. I have the utmost confidence in Marty and am deeply grateful for his willingness to serve in this capacity.

I have appreciated the opportunity the partnership has given me to lead the firm over the years. I can only hope that I have lived up to your trust and confidence.

Andy had given Slattery a pat on the goddamn back. "Served with distinction." The only thing he'd done to distinguish himself was rape Sunny. And the reference to Slattery's sense of "propriety" was ludicrous. Andy had transformed Slattery's demotion into a paean, into campaign propaganda. *Total bullshit!*

She had built up a head of steam by the time Sunny burst across her threshold, a sheet of paper clutched in her hand.

"Did you see this?"

"Andy's memo?"

"Yeah." She crumpled it into a ball. "The bastard. He said he was going to suspend Slattery, but this . . ." She glared at the memo. "This . . ." She choked on her anger.

Maggie put out her hand. "Here. Give it to me."

Sunny ignored her, paced back and forth in front of the desk, shaking the wad of paper at the ceiling. Her eyes were frantic. She deserved to be furious, but her brain had redlined on anger.

"Come on." Maggie put her hand on Sunny's shoulder and gently pushed her into a chair. "Take a deep breath."

Sunny collapsed onto the seat. "This is so unfair."

"Absolutely. I guess we shouldn't have expected Andy to live up to his word."

"But, if you could have heard him when he told me about

the suspension, he was pissed, really pissed." Her voice was thick with tears.

"I hate to say it, but it was probably an act. He was trying to placate you."

"This is wrong. All wrong. Slattery should have gotten kicked out of the firm. But now, now he could end up chairman." She paused, straightened her spine, squared her shoulders. "I'm not going to put up with this. I'm going to go complain to Andy. *Right now.*"

"No. Don't do that." Sunny was on the verge of a meltdown. She might well auger in if she had to deal with that tight-assed, insensitive bastard. "Let me confront him on this. As a member of the Gender Equity Committee, I have a little more influence with him."

Maggie glanced at her watch. "Hey, it's after five. Let's get out of here, go get a drink. How about Solera? Wine and tapas might be good." Sunny needed to chill.

"No, I'm tired. Besides, I thought you were going to talk to Andy."

"I am, but I'll catch him tomorrow. Today, he'll be preoccupied with basking in the glory of his nomination."

CHAPTER 60

November 24, Monday
Sunny

Slattery banged open Sunny's office door. She bobbed back in her chair. He slammed the door shut, planted himself a few inches from the front of her desk, his hands fisted on his hips.

"Well, *Ms*. Star-Perez, I hope you feel vindicated. You fucked me over good, didn't you?"

"What do you mean?"

"Don't give me that. You know exactly what I mean."

He'd startled her, but she wasn't going to come unglued. He'd pushed her around for the last time. "Your resignation as managing partner, is that it? Given the halo Andy painted over your head, you can hardly complain."

"*Halo*? You're nuts. He stuck it to me good. 'Served with distinction' was the best he could come up with. The only other thing he said was that I was 'ever mindful of fairness and propriety.' Christ, his tongue was so far in his cheek on that one, it almost came out his ear."

"Too damn bad. You raped me, you got me pregnant, and you're still a partner. You got off lucky. Too lucky if you ask me."

"So my getting canned as managing partner wasn't enough? You still want revenge?"

Angry static filled her mind. She was done being intimidated. "Yes, I do."

He placed his palms on her desk; his ruddy face loomed over her. He reeked of whiskey. "Two can play that game. My revenge will be telling José."

"*No!* Don't do that." A rush of fear flooded through her. "Let's call it even. No more revenge."

"Don't kid yourself. I'm just getting started," he scoffed, exhaling menace.

"Please, please don't do that. I'm begging you. It'll kill him. *Please.*"

Slattery jerked the door open without a backward glance.

Sunny's eyes filled with tears as she imagined Slattery confronting José, taunting him, rubbing his nose in her betrayal. She remembered Maggie's disdainful comment about Slattery cheating on his wife when she was getting chemo: *Cheating is vile anytime, but doing it when your spouse is hurting . . . That's a capital offense.*

What Sunny had done was even worse. She'd had sex with Slattery while José thought he wasn't a man because of his infertility. Sunny thumped a fist against her forehead. She was a selfish bitch who didn't deserve José. Didn't even deserve to live.

CHAPTER 61

November 26, Wednesday
Maggie

Despite her insistent phone messages, Maggie had been unable to speak with Andy on Tuesday. The ever-protective Mrs. Lord allowed only that he was "taking a well-deserved break over Thanksgiving" and was out of cell phone reach. In his absence, Maggie decided to tackle Bull about Slattery's status.

Maggie chose the ungodly hour of 7:00 a.m. in hopes of avoiding a cloud of smoke. The empty office smelled like furniture polish. She must have been the first one to step inside since the maintenance crew had left the night before.

She scowled at the massive guest chair that had all but swallowed her during her previous visit. Had he chosen them to intimidate normal-sized humans, or were they an unconscious statement that the world needed to adapt to him? Either way, she wasn't playing. She turned a straight-backed wooden chair away from his conference table to face his desk. The downside was, it put her in the corner of the room farthest from the door, but she didn't think she'd need a speedy exit.

She was seated there with a yellow legal pad open on her lap when he walked in ten minutes later. He'd made it to his desk before he noticed her.

His eyes blinked wide. "Jeez, Maggie. I didn't know you were here."

"I wanted to talk to Andy about the firm's so-called punishment of Slattery, but he's not available so I thought I'd start with you."

"Right. Right." He shrugged off his jacket, hung it over the top of his chair, and sat behind his desk. "He told me you have questions."

"*You* heard from Andy? When? When was that?" So she couldn't reach Andy but Bull could? Mrs. Lord had to get her story straight.

"Yesterday afternoon. Anyway, let me tell you what we did. Andy put Jack on notice that he had to change how he deals with women and removed him as managing partner. Also—"

"Removed him? No one would know that was the case from Andy's memo. Slattery came off sounding like a prince."

"You could hardly expect Andy to spell it out. Airing the situation inside the firm wouldn't be in anyone's interest."

"Slattery should be expelled from the partnership."

"Nope, you're wrong." His voice was flat, as if the conclusion was so obvious it didn't merit any inflection. "I put a notation in his personnel file about the situation. That and his resignation as managing partner are enough."

"So you're saying Slattery's punishment is appropriate? It's not a sweetheart deal?"

"It's appropriate. Not lax, not harsh. Right down the middle of the road."

"You're serious, aren't you?" She shook her head with inflated dismay. "Can't you see that the result of this *illusory* discipline is to allow Slattery to remain a partner and continue to prey on women?"

"Prey on women? That's a little melodramatic."

"Not at all. What he did to Sunny could be prosecuted as rape in most jurisdictions."

"You think Sunny didn't want it? Is that what she told you?"

"Yes, and I believe her."

"It's a classic he said, she said. Besides, she concedes the relationship continued after they got back. That doesn't square with it being rape."

"You know as well as I do, rape doesn't have to be at knife-point. It includes sex under duress or coercion. Threatening to ruin her career meets that standard."

"Oh, please." He flapped a hand at her. "More he said, she said." He swiveled his chair toward his credenza, lifted the lid of his humidor, and plucked out a cigar.

Maggie said, "If Sunny were willing to go public, Andy's response would be very different. After all, the firm paid Nancy Holstein a million bucks to settle her sex discrimination claim." His focus flicked up from the scissors at the end of his cigar. "And Lily Ching got two hundred fifty thousand to go away."

"So now you're saying compensating women for the harm they've suffered is wrong?"

"Of course not. I'm saying the firm's apparent solicitude for women is limited to situations where they can hurt the firm's reputation."

"Come on. You're a corporate lawyer. You know it's standard practice for companies to pay claimants to keep quiet."

"Yes, but I've never heard of a company *seeking out* claimants so it could pay them off. That's what this sham Gender Equity Committee is about."

"I have no idea what you're talking about." He lit his cigar.

"Oh, no? The firm—namely Andy—wanted to bury any bad news. You used the committee to identify potential claimants."

"So we found out about Nancy through the committee. Big fucking deal. She got a great payday and she's happy. End of story."

"Andy wanted to be sure that story and the rest of the firm's dirty linen stayed hidden. When the press began to pick it up, you put on a full-court press to find out who was talking. Andy must have leaned on you hard, so you stooped to wiretapping."

"Wiretapping? Absolutely not." His gray complexion turned crimson.

"You had my line bugged."

"*Bullshit!*"

She stood and offered him a close-lipped smile. "Now there's an articulate defense. I wonder if you'll be able to come up with something better when I sue you for invasion of privacy."

"Righteousness is funny coming from the woman who slept her way to a partnership. If it weren't for Bryce, you'd be in some fourth-rate firm litigating which car ran the stoplight." He blew a long stream of smoke at her.

"You asshole! How appropriate—a smokescreen, just like the Gender Equity Committee." She snatched the cigar out of his fingers and jammed it into the potted plant. "And, just for the record, your accusations are totally untrue. Bryce always recused himself whenever I was being evaluated."

"So, you're purer than the driven snow?"

"I had sex with the man I was going to marry." Maggie's voice quivered with rage. "You, on the other hand, are married to one woman and having sex with another. Your affair with your secretary is no secret. No wonder you can't see the damage Slattery's doing."

"My relationship with Kim isn't harassment. It's consensual. Besides, she came on to me."

"Oh, really? You're not exactly cover material for *Men's Fitness*. You're a married man with kids. You'll never leave your wife. Why would she come on to you?"

"Kim doesn't care about any of that. She knows I'll never leave Beverly. She likes me for my big dick." He smugly cupped his crotch. "And I like her 'cause she gives a great blow job. I don't need a mental giant under my desk."

"What you need under your desk is a land mine!"

She marched out and came face-to-face with Kim McSwain, pressed against the wall. She looked shell-shocked: her skin was pale, her eyes popped wide, one hand covered her mouth. Maggie gently squeezed her shoulder. "I'm sorry you had to hear that." Kim's gaze dropped to the floor.

ⓘⓘⓘⓘⓘ

Still fuming, Maggie shoved her office door shut. She paced as she replayed Bull's accusations. *If it weren't for Bryce, you'd be in some fourth-rate firm . . .*

Maggie stared at Bryce's photo. He had captivated her with his knowledge of the arts, law, and, most particularly, law firms—namely Sweeny Owens. She'd relished his insights into firm politics and personalities, his quick judgments about who had the "right stuff" and who didn't. When they'd handicapped her partnership prospects against those of her classmates, he'd said Bull didn't have it. But, somehow, Bull had made partner, and now he was saying *she* didn't have the goods.

Outrageous. Bryce had spent twenty years watching associates run the partnership gauntlet. If anyone knew who'd make the grade, he did.

Suddenly, she felt sick; her stomach dropped as if she'd been upended in a carnival ride.

She had married Bryce because he knew the secret handshake, the heavily camouflaged path to partnership. She hadn't consciously thought he could—or would—put his thumb on the scale. But, lurking below the surface, her ambition had embellished his qualities, burnishing them until he became the ideal mate.

Now she could see why their relationship had become barren. For some time, she'd known he had married her for her looks and talent, adding her to his portfolio of prized possessions. Love hadn't really been part of his emotional repertoire. But she'd maintained the illusion she had truly loved him for who he was as a person, not where his name sat on the firm's letterhead.

They had cheated each other. Neither one had had a loving spouse.

CHAPTER 62

November 26, Wednesday
Maggie

Maggie's secretary ran into her office. "There was a shooting in Jack Slattery's office. Sam was there—"

"What?"

"I'm not sure what happened, but my friend Sunita said the police are there and the paramedics." The words rushed out in a high-pitched torrent. "They took Mr. Slattery out on a stretcher. He was bleeding. There's another—"

Maggie was already out the door. She ran down the corridor to the elevator bay, jabbed at the button.

What could have happened? Had Sam been shot? She'd always thought of him as tough, almost invulnerable. But he wouldn't be a match for some nut with a gun. She banged the elevator button again.

Who could have done this? What lunatic would shoot up a corporate law firm?

She stabbed the button again. Gave up and jerked open the door to the staircase. She ran up four flights of stairs, stopped to gulp in some air, and jogged quickly up two more.

The hall outside Slattery's office was choked with people. She saw cops, medics, secretaries, lawyers, messengers—but no Sam. She shoved her way through the firm personnel but the cops were unyielding.

"Sorry, ma'am. It's a crime scene. You can't go in there."

"I just want to know if my colleague Sam Forte is okay."

"The Champ?" He smirked. "Yeah. The only thing that's wrong with him is some bruised knuckles."

"Oh, thank God." She sagged with relief, started to turn away.

"Maggie." Sam looked out over the heads of cops and EMTs. "Are you okay? I heard about the shooting."

"Yeah. I'm fine."

"You're sure?"

He nodded. "Can I come talk to you when I'm done here?"

"Of course."

Making her way back through the crowd, she remembered her screaming ascent up the stairs. Why had she been so worried about Sam? He was a friend, a good friend, but that was all.

▦▦▦▦▦

When Sam stepped into her office forty minutes later, gooseflesh blossomed on Maggie's arms. A large blood stain colored the front of his shirt. "Tell me that's not yours."

"No. It's Jack's. I gotta go to my office to change my shirt. My secretary went out to get me one. Be back in a few, okay?"

"Sure. Of course. Whatever you need."

True to his word, he returned quickly. He sagged into a chair.

Still shaken by the bloody shirt he'd discarded, she said, "So you're really okay?"

"Yup. Tired from the adrenaline roller coaster, but basically okay." He blew on his knuckles. "I left a little skin on José's jaw, but—"

"José? Sunny's husband, José? He was the shooter?"

Sam blew out a long breath. "Yeah. I guess Jack raped Sunny—at least that's what José said—when they were in Ordubad."

"How did he find out?"

"Sunny told him," Sam said.

"I can't believe that. She was desperate to keep it from him."

"So you knew about it?"

She nodded. "But the last thing in the world she would do is tell him. I don't get it."

"It almost *was* the last thing she did in this world. She tried to kill herself. He—"

Her eyes widened. "Is she okay?"

"She will be. She's hospitalized. She was out of it when he found her, and that's when she told him."

"Oh, my God. What a mess." She rubbed her forehead with her fingertips. "So José tried to kill Slattery to avenge her honor."

"I don't think that was why he went to Jack's office originally. When José first came in, he said he wanted Jack to know he could never come between them. But then Jack ran his mouth, trashed Sunny *and* José. Called him a Spic . . . Christ! You wouldn't believe the garbage he spewed. It was like he was asking for it."

"And José gave it to him." She sighed. "Did he kill him?"

"Almost. His first shot hit Jack in the shoulder. Second one, it's hard to say. It went into Jack's head, that's for sure. Looked like part of his jaw was hanging off but there was so much blood . . . I decked José before he could get off any more." He glanced at his hand. "The EMTs said Jack will pull through."

She came around her desk and crouched by his side. His knuckles were red and swollen. They had to hurt. "Can I get you some ice? Would that help?"

"Nah, it's okay."

"Isn't there anything I can do?"

"Yeah, sit down and talk to me. I don't feel like working."

"No wonder." She sank into a chair beside him. "How's José?"

"Better than Jack, that's for sure."

"I don't give a damn how he is. I wish José *had* killed him."

"But that wouldn't have been too good for José, now would it?"

"No, I suppose not. But at least now the truth will come out about what a pig Slattery is. Instead of that crap Andy had in his memo."

"Did Andy know? Is that what the resignation was about?"

Maggie poured out the whole story, then added, "Andy's pedaling so hard to hide the dirt before his confirmation hearings, he's lost all sense of right and wrong. This time it's going to come back to bite him in the butt."

ооооо

"Don't worry, Sunny. I'll take care of him." Maggie hung up the phone.

Things finally made sense. Sunny's suicide attempt had been prompted by Slattery's threat to tell José.

Slattery was truly evil. If Andy didn't kick him out of the partnership after this, she would go to the confirmation hearings and spill every bad thing she knew about Andy, or even suspected she knew.

Maggie walked the two blocks to the Seventeenth Precinct as daylight faded. She'd never represented anyone charged with attempted murder before, but she knew enough to get José through this stage.

As she waited to see him, she picked up a discarded copy of the Post. Buried in the business news was a short article announcing the EEOC was suing O'Malley & Mortimer for failure to rein in two senior partners notorious for sexually harassing female employees.

She chuckled. Andy's angst had been misplaced. Sweeny Owens wasn't the target after all—although it certainly could have been.

Maybe an anonymous call to the EEOC would be the best remedy for Andy and Slattery.

CHAPTER 63

November 26, Wednesday
Andy

Listening to Bull bleat in his ear about a confrontation he'd had with Maggie was like a bee sting on Andy's frayed nerves. He fought the temptation to toss the headset onto the passenger seat. The shooting had turned his planned holiday celebration to dross. He'd been on his way to Burlington when Mrs. Lord called about the incident. He'd had no choice but to turn back. The situation was too complex and too sensitive to leave in anyone else's hands. Clearly, not Bull's.

Andy's line beeped with a waiting call, but he ignored it even after it sounded twice more. When the line beeped again, he told Bull he'd call him back.

"Jesus Christ, where in the blue blazes have you been?" The gravelly voice of Howdy Pickens, O'Toole's campaign manager, blasted into his ear. "I been trying to reach you for the last goddamn hour."

"Actually, I've been speaking with one of my partners. I'm sorry if that's inconvenienced you."

"Inconvenience ain't hardly the word. Are you familiar with the principle of making sure your superiors don't get surprised?"

The only one Andy considered his superior was President-elect O'Toole, but he resisted the temptation to say so.

"Yes, I am."

"And you didn't think, you peckerwood, you should give us a shout-out about the shooting?"

"The motivation seems to have been personal. The firm's only involvement was as the venue."

"So you say. But when a female partner's husband shoots a male partner, it sure as all hell sounds like there's some hanky-panky going on. The very last thing you need is a sex scandal."

Andy's breath caught in his chest. He forced himself to exhale, inhaled slowly, and said, "I can assure you there's nothing to worry about."

"You better be right. President O'Toole doesn't want an attorney general who can't keep order in his own goddamn house."

Andy hung up and considered his options. If he were lucky, Slattery wouldn't recover. If Slattery did, as the doctors unfortunately predicted, Andy wanted to separate him from the firm. His wounds would make that easier. Reconstruction of his jaw was expected to take months, so the possibility of his succeeding Andy had been neatly foreclosed. And, while his recovery seemed certain, his ability to practice law was not. Perhaps he would never again darken the offices of Sweeny, Owens & Boyle. His absence should placate Maggie, who kept insisting she needed to talk to Andy about Slattery's relationship with Sunny.

Maggie felt much more strongly about women's issues than he'd ever suspected. His misjudgment was a bit of a disappointment, but he could use it to his advantage. Knowing what mattered to her was the first step in figuring out what it would take to buy her silence.

CHAPTER 64

November 28, Friday
Andy

Andy enjoyed receiving the congratulatory phone calls that continued to trickle in. He was feeling quite chipper until the intercom buzzed and Mrs. Lord said, "Micah Levin of the *Times* is on your line."

His stomach shriveled. He was too close to allow anything to derail his nomination. He picked up the handset, determined to shut down the press speculation.

"Mr. Anderson, thank you for taking my call. I was hoping to get more information on the shooting that took place at the firm."

"There's not much I can tell you. The firm had no more involvement in the shooting than the Texas Book Depository had in the Kennedy assassination." He'd come up with that analogy last night when he couldn't sleep.

"Then perhaps my understanding of the facts is wrong. John Slattery is a partner, correct?"

"Yes."

"And the shooter, José Perez, is married to another partner, Sunny Star-Perez. Is that correct?"

"Yes."

"So the obvious conclusion is that the animus between the men somehow relates to his wife's employment at the firm."

"Come now, Mr. Levin, you're a bright fellow. You must understand that what seems obvious, sometimes proves to be untrue."

"Occasionally that is the case, but this conclusion is warranted given Mr. Slattery was sexually harassing Sunny Star-Perez."

"You're most assuredly wrong about that. Any lawyer knowledgeable about such matters would tell you it's virtually impossible for one partner to sexually harass another."

"How is that, Mr. Anderson?"

"A typical element in sexual harassment cases is a power differential between the parties that is used coercively. No power differential exists between partners."

"Let me get this straight. You believe that even though Mr. Slattery was the managing partner and Ms. Star-Perez was a very junior partner, there was no power differential between them?"

"Correct. They both have the same rights under the partnership agreement."

"Hmm." Levin's skepticism was obvious. "Are you saying Mr. Slattery and Ms. Star-Perez had a sexual relationship, but that relationship was outside the scope of sexual harassment laws?"

"I most certainly am *not* saying that. If they had a sexual relationship—and let me be clear I'm not confirming that—it would be a personal matter, something entirely inappropriate for me to comment on as firm chairman."

"Do you have any other explanation for Mr. Perez's attack on Mr. Slattery?"

Andy's mind froze up; he was out of excuses. "I suggest you make that inquiry of the police. Good day, Mr. Levin."

CHAPTER 65

December 1, Monday
Maggie

As Maggie approached her office, she was surprised to see Bull's assistant camped out in one of the guest chairs. Maggie closed the door.

"I'm sorry you heard my conversation with Bull."

Kim twisted the corner of her mouth. "Better I know where I stand. That prick's been promising to leave his wife for years."

"Relationships are hard."

"Yeah, well, he made it a lot harder than it had to be by lying to me all this time." Her voice wavered.

"You must be very hurt."

She nodded. "I think it was President Kennedy who said, 'Don't get mad. Get even.' I may not be 'a mental giant,' but I know a thing or two about what's going on here at the firm."

"What do you mean?"

"For starters, you're right about the whole Gender Equity Committee thing. Bull dreamed it up as a way to find out who was unhappy."

"So the firm could make it better? That's what Bull claimed."

"Nah. It was to get rid of them before they sued. You know everybody thought the EEOC was investigating us, but it turned out to be O'Malley & Mortimer. Funny, huh?"

Maggie was getting excited. "What about Andy? Did he go along with it?"

"Go along with it?" she cackled. "Them two are thick as thieves. But I got worried that, when Andy goes to Washington, Bull would get blamed for the weird stuff that's gone down so I—"

"What weird stuff? What do you mean?"

"Started with the detective Bull hired to snoop around some of the women's homes."

"*What*? For what?"

"Well, he found a couple of letters in Nancy Holstein's apartment from attorneys she'd interviewed about suing the firm."

"So *that's* why Bull was in a hurry to get her to sign her settlement agreement."

"Yeah, he called me one night and wanted me in before dawn the next morning to type it. And the bastard shows up two hours later without so much as a cup of coffee for me. But that was only the beginnin'. He hired another detective to tap some of the women's phones."

"I knew my line was bugged when Andy accused me of being the leak. So Bull was behind it?"

"He sure as hell was, and Andy egged him on. Kept yelling at him to find out who the leak was."

"Andy knew about all this?"

"You betcha. That's what I was startin' to tell ya. I got worried if the shit hit the fan, Andy would try to put all the blame on Bull so I got him this miniature camera to wear when he talked to Andy. It was in his tie bar." She lifted the envelope from her lap. "And these here are transcripts of the recordings."

CHAPTER 66

December 1, Monday
Maggie

Shafts of light from the setting sun hit Maggie's face as she lodged herself in one of Andy's guest chairs. Mrs. Lord might have scheduled her for only five minutes, but she wasn't leaving until he'd agreed to her demands.

"It's a pleasure as always to see you, Maggie, but I'm a bit tight on time today. Mrs. Lord said you needed to discuss an urgent matter. Jack Slattery, I believe?"

"Originally, but now a broader discussion is in order. I have received evidence that you conspired with Bull to perpetuate a workplace in which women are discriminated against and harassed. The firm is unquestionably a hostile environment, actionable under Title VII."

"How interesting." He offered a patronizing smile. "As lawyers, we must be careful about the words we use. The term 'hostile environment' is a broad one. Isn't your true concern Jack Slattery?"

"It was until I received videotaped conversations between you and Bull." She raised a thick manila envelope and returned it to her lap.

His face hardened. The furrows and bags became frozen features on a winter landscape. "I have never agreed to be recorded, so, whatever evidence you think you have is inadmissible. No probative value whatsoever. Further, it would be protected by attorney-client privilege given I was consulting with Bull in his capacity as firm employment counsel."

"But a court's standard of admissibility isn't relevant." Her turn to flash a condescending smile. "If President-elect O'Toole saw these, he would immediately withdraw your nomination."

"A brazen assertion. I can recollect no conversation with Bull that would justify that reaction."

"Somehow that doesn't surprise me. Perhaps you'd like to read these transcripts?" She lifted the menacing package. "I'm happy to wait. We can continue our discussion when you're done."

He extended his hand. She had to admire the iron will it must have taken to keep it steady.

After picking up the *Journal* from the corner of his desk, she sauntered to his silk-upholstered settee. She didn't expect it to be any more comfortable than the antique chair she'd abandoned, but the move sent a message. So did the snap of the newsprint as she jerked open the pages. She was prepared to wait to get the results she wanted, and get them, she would.

Minutes passed. Much more time than he needed to review the pages.

"Shall we continue?" His voice was pinched as if it were coming from the top of his throat.

"Of course." She returned to the guest chair to face him across his desk.

"Taken out of context, these conversations could be misleading. Rather than debate their significance, why don't you tell me why you are here?"

"Fine. I will agree not to disclose these tapes if you expel Jack Slattery and Bull Holbrooke from the partnership." He didn't flinch. "Additionally, you must withdraw yourself from consideration as attorney general and retire from the firm."

"Withdraw? That's not possible. My nomination is already before Congress. It would be an embarrassment for President-elect O'Toole."

"It would be a much greater embarrassment to have these transcripts come out at your confirmation hearings."

"Maggie, I understand your frustration about the treatment of women at the firm, about the whole Sunny-Slattery debacle, but keeping me out of the attorney general's office won't solve that."

"No, but it will keep a criminal who is indifferent to human suffering from serving as the country's chief law enforcement officer."

"Your characterization is grossly unfair."

"Let's see, conspiring with Bull to tap women's phones, to break—"

He raised a hand. "Enough. If you care about the firm's women suffering, do something constructive about it. Ousting Jack and Bull won't really change anything. Change begins at the top. Become firm chair. You can clean house, establish Sweeny, Owens & Boyle as a model law firm, and carry that message to your counterparts in other firms across the country."

She felt disoriented and leaned forward to try to understand what she was hearing. "What are you suggesting?"

"Surely you know I control the process of naming my successor. While it is described as consensus, in reality it is my discussing with the Nominating Committee the possible candidates and informing them of my selection. That is how members of the Management Committee have always been chosen."

"Yes, I understood as much from Bryce."

"So, I will suggest to members of the Nominating Committee that your name be raised in the discussions held with individual partners to prevent your selection from being too much of a surprise. When it is announced, I will hail the committee's strategic choice of a groundbreaking leader to take us into a new era. I will take office as attorney general. Bull and Jack will leave the firm. What could be a better resolution?"

Her mind latched on to the proposal, refusing to entertain any another resolution. *Chair. Chairwoman. The chair of Sweeny, Owens & Boyle. Me, the girl from the wrong side of the tracks. The chair of Sweeny, Owens & Boyle.*

Eventually her reptilian brain sensed his avid scrutiny and jolted her mouth into action. She muttered, "I don't know what to say."

"Just tell me you'll think about it. I'm sure you'll come to the right decision after you weigh all the factors."

She nodded, slid to the front of the chair. "When do you need my answer?"

"I'd like to hear by Friday. I hope the overriding factor in your deliberation will be what you can accomplish for women here at the firm and around the world."

His oratorical flourish jerked her back to reality. *Around the world?*

He was blowing smoke up her skirt. But that didn't render the offer meaningless. Just a little more suspect.

CHAPTER 67

December 1, Monday
Maggie

Maggie resisted the temptation to pull a celebratory bottle of Cristal from the fridge and opted for Pellegrino instead. She needed to be stone-cold sober as she considered Andy's offer. Settling onto the chaise in her study, she tried to weigh the pros and cons.

The advantages were enormous, starting with ridding the firm of Jack and Bull. Then there were the reforms she could make: hiring an ombuds for the firm as a sounding board for complaints of any sort of harassment or discrimination; mandating equal work opportunities for male and female associates; permitting part-time partners; fairly compensating part-time associates; prohibiting strip club entertainment. And that was just the beginning.

She could do so much good. It would be a battle to force the partners to accept change; she wouldn't have Andy's imprimatur.

But the struggle would be well worth it. Sweeny Owens could become a model law firm with her at the helm.

The disadvantage would be allowing Andy to become attorney general. The man had no conscience, no sense of right and wrong. He was morally incapable of being the country's chief law enforcement officer. His ambition had led him to deceive his partners, misappropriate money from the firm, put Slattery in a position where he ruined people's lives. Sunny and José would ultimately recover from their twin tragedies, but Andy's ambition had taken a horrendous toll on them. All for the sake of Andy securing the nomination. His goddamned ambition.

If she took his deal, his ambition would be satisfied. But as chair of the firm, she could . . .

Maggie hissed in disgust. She was falling into the same trap. Andy would feed her ambition if she fed his. *Bullshit!*

CHAPTER 68

December 2, Tuesday
Maggie

Maggie told Ginger about Andy's proposal over drinks at Bemelmans Bar. Lifting her Scotch from the black glass tabletop, Maggie watched reactions race across Ginger's freckled cheeks: amazement, amusement, then concern.

Ginger said, "You aren't seriously thinking of taking the job, are you?"

"I have to admit I was tempted. My ego tap-danced for hours, but the truth is, I abhor Sweeny Owens. I hate everything it stands for. Sure, being the chair would be prestigious, but it'd be like being the CEO of . . . of the world's largest diamond mine."

"No. Much better freebies there." Ginger chuckled.

"I would be in charge of a firm that expects its lawyers to bill three thousand hours a year, always put the clients' work ahead of their personal lives—*provided*, of course, they're paying clients.

After that, attorneys can spend any crumbs of free time helping poor people who've been screwed over."

"Hey, if you want to help people who've been screwed over, come work with me. You can do all the pro bono cases you want."

"Don't joke. I may take you up on it. I can't stomach much more of Sweeny Owens. The place is morally bankrupt."

"You're just figuring that out?"

Maggie thumped her fist against her forehead. "What can I say? I was blinded by the prestige, the power, the money . . ." She drained her glass and signaled the waiter for another.

"If you came on board, we'd be Eminem. Marshall and Mahoney."

"Wait a minute. Mahoney and Marshall. We'll do it alphabetically."

"Nope. That's a deal breaker. I founded the firm so I get to go first. Guess it'll never happen."

"What if I brought in a big case, a class action that'd get the firm lots of good publicity? Would that earn me top billing?"

"Would whacking this defendant set an example for a whole industry? Maybe inspire across-the-board reforms?"

"Do you think law firms need to reform?"

The sound of their high five echoed through the room.

CHAPTER 69

December 3, Wednesday
Andy

Andy spooned Mountbatten's breakfast into the monogrammed bowl; the dog sat patiently at his side. Monty had a hearty appetite, especially for his custom lamb and rice concoction prepared fresh twice daily. Andy had just placed the bowl in the microwave to warm its contents when the phone rang.

"Erling Anderson."

"What in hellfire is going on at that goddamn law firm of yours?" He recognized the boom of Howdy Pickens's voice.

"What is it you're concerned about?"

"Have you seen the *Journal* this morning, or are you dumb and blind? There's a story that Sweeny Owens is being sued for race discrimination by some black son of a bitch named Travis something or other."

"Just a moment. I haven't seen it." Andy frantically flipped pages.

Sweeny Owens Charged
With Race Discrimination

After spending ten years at Sweeny, Owens & Boyle, Travis Benally was passed over for partnership. In a suit filed Monday, Mr. Benally alleges the decision was based on his racial heritage. His ancestors were Native American, African American, and European American.

"Did you know about this?"

"I—"

"The answer better not be yes, because we sure as shooting should have gotten a heads up before it appeared in the press."

"Would you like my response now?"

"Of course I want your response now. Why the hell do you think I called?"

"I was unaware of the article or the suit until you brought it to my attention. Travis Benally is an excellent lawyer, but we had to let him go because he exposed himself to a secretary in a fit of pique."

"Tell me in plain English."

"His secretary made a very serious error. He was exasperated and told her the only thing she was good for was to suck his dick. I believe that's an exact quote. To underscore his point, he unzipped his trousers and produced his penis."

"Christ."

"We had no choice but to dismiss him. Before this incident,

we'd eagerly anticipated he'd swell the ranks of our minority partners."

There was silence on the other end of the line. Pickens clicked his tongue. "You need to get your PR people on this, pronto. It does not look good for a potential attorney general."

CHAPTER 70

December 3, Wednesday
Maggie

"You're sure you're okay with this? It may get nasty." Guilt nibbled at Maggie. When she'd called Rosalinda last night about becoming a named plaintiff in a class action suit against the firm, Rosalinda had agreed without reservation.

Ginger said, "It *will* get nasty. You can count on it. You'll be branded a troublemaker. It will limit your future job prospects. If you want to leave Sweeny Owens, it's unlikely another Wall Street firm will hire you."

"I'm brokenhearted." Rosalinda laughed, pushed her chair away from the conference table, and walked to the sideboard for coffee.

With its Mission furniture, Ginger's conference room was simple but much warmer than anything at the firm. An old library table had been refinished so the quartersawn red oak on its surface gleamed. The plain side chairs were framed in cherry with squared-off spindles and padded leather seats. Not fancy, but a place where Maggie would be proud to meet with her clients.

Rosalinda returned to the table. "I've been thinking about going back to LA anyway. I don't like these New York winters. I miss my family."

"Just so you know, a big LA firm won't want you either."

"It's okay. I'm tired of this shit. Somebody has to stand up to the old white guys who think they're above the law. I get to be that somebody." She sipped her coffee. "Hey, Ginger, this is great. What is it?"

"It's a Dean & DeLuca blend. Low acid but dark."

"You take a lot better care of your clients than the firm does."

"That's because I care about them." Ginger paused. "And because I do, I want to warn you about another unpleasant result of this suit. The other women at the firm won't support you."

"But they should." Rosalinda squinted. "I mean, it'll help them, too."

"Yes, that's logical, but it's not how it works. I've been doing this for years, and I've learned it's about emotion, not logic. Deep down, the women want to believe you did something to bring this on yourself. The—"

"But I didn't."

"Of course you didn't, but they want to believe that because it makes them feel safe, insulated from the same thing happening to them."

"I don't get it."

"They want to believe their world is orderly, their fathers—in this case Andy—are fair. In that orderly world, you would be harassed and targeted *only* if you invited it. If they don't invite it, they'll be safe."

Rosalinda slumped against the back of her chair. "Damn."

Ginger added, "You may be shunned by the women. The men, too. People you thought of as friends may not talk to you. By being the plaintiff, you're going against the tribe, the family."

"Sweeny Owens isn't my family."

"Maybe not," Ginger said, "but it's become family for a lot of its lawyers."

Maggie ruefully realized she had felt that way.

Ginger said, "Remember, I was there for ten years before I opened my own shop. The firm goes out of its way to create that image. The historical photos of Francis X. Sweeny and Judge Owens. The three generations of Sweenys who ran the firm. The firm outings—like a family vacation. Even the dining rooms and the gym give the illusion it's taking care of you. All of that creates loyalty and the kind of commitment that make associates bill three thousand hours a year."

"Which, in turn, cuts them off from their real families," Maggie said.

"Okay." Rosalinda sighed. "What else should I expect?"

"On the bright side, when you leave the firm, you'll get nice letters from people who were too scared to support you while you were there."

"The urge for self-preservation prevails." Cynicism roughened Maggie's voice. She leaned across the table. "Rosalinda, I want you to consider that principle long and hard before you do anything."

"I have." She turned to Ginger. "Call me when the papers are ready to sign."

CHAPTER 71

December 5, Friday
Maggie

Mrs. Lord helpfully told Maggie that Andy was having lunch at the Parthenon Club. For the last century, the classical limestone building had hosted meetings among the City's power brokers over indifferent meals. Maggie walked under portraits of the City's most notable white male citizens as she led a short, compact, young man with a red ponytail down an antique Persian runner to the main dining room.

She smiled at the maître d'. "We're here for Mr. Anderson." She tipped her head in the direction of the table Andy occupied.

"I'm sorry, madam. Women are not allowed in the main dining room. I can ask Mr. Anderson if he'd like to be seated in the pink dining room."

"That won't be necessary. It will be sufficient if this gentleman joins them." Maggie touched the sleeve of Rick Skillin, a college student eager to earn his tuition as a process server.

"As madam wishes." The maître d' lowered his head respectfully.

Maggie watched Rick thread his way between the linen-draped tables. He handed Andy two complaints: a class action with Rosalinda as the plaintiff alleging Sweeny, Owens & Boyle constituted a hostile environment for women, and an individual action with Maggie as the plaintiff alleging Andy and Bull breached their fiduciary duties to her as partners and alleging misappropriation of assets in connection with Nancy Holstein's settlement.

Andy scanned the documents. His chin and chest jerked upward as if he'd just gulped a gallon of air. He lifted his eyes; they narrowed as he locked on to Maggie's gaze. Once, his primal fury would have withered her. Now she stood indifferent but for her scorn. His ambitious deceit had wounded so many. He deserved exposure and punishment.

CHAPTER 72

O'Toole Ousts Anderson;
Turns His Back on "Cronyism"

THE NEW YORK TIMES. In his third press conference since the election, President-elect Michael O'Toole announced he had withdrawn the nomination of Erling Anderson, chairman of Sweeny, Owens & Boyle, to be attorney general.

O'Toole said he had met with the plaintiffs who had recently filed complaints against Mr. Anderson and Sweeny, Owens & Boyle and was deeply troubled by their allegations which center on the mistreatment of women at the firm and Mr. Anderson's attempt to hide these problems.

O'Toole went on to say he opted for swift and decisive action "to send a signal my administration will not be doing business as usual" with "rampant cronyism." He recognized what he described as Anderson's "deep and long ties to the party," but said he would not include anyone in his administration "who has less than the utmost respect for each and every citizen, rich or poor, well connected or nameless."

President-elect O'Toole also announced he has asked the current administration to commence an investigation by the Equal Employment Opportunity Commission of the treatment of women at Sweeny, Owens & Boyle.

CHAPTER 73

December 11, Thursday
Maggie

A blast of frigid air hit Sam and Maggie as they ran across Fifth Avenue.

He said, "About time I got my running partner back. You've been so busy making headlines, I began to feel neglected."

"It's not like I've been in the headlines myself. It's—"

"Not true. You made *Page Six* with the story about you and Ginger starting your own firm. Great idea. A law firm owned, managed, and staffed primarily by women. What kind of response did you get?"

"The best was the avalanche of résumés from female lawyers at Wall Street firms who want a personal life *and* challenging work."

"Sweet."

Maggie tugged her hat down over her ears. "Damn. It's cold. Why did I let you lure me back out here? I could be running on my treadmill."

"Yeah, but the company sucks. What, a morning talk show? Besides, I want to hear how you crushed the forces of evil."

"I just got the ball rolling. The latest is that Andy and Bull have been indicted by the U.S. Attorney for wiretapping."

He chuckled. "I guess that's strike three for Andy. Sued by you, sued by Rosalinda, and now the feds are on his case."

"Bull will catch up with him in about a week."

"How's that?"

"Ginger is representing his secretary. She's suing him for sexual harassment. Added to my suit and the feds' indictment, he'll be neck and neck with Andy." She smirked.

"And wait until his wife files for divorce."

"Whoa! Is that in the works, too?"

"That's the hot gossip inside the firm."

"Excellent. Any other news?"

"Marty McSorley is the acting chairman. Technically, Andy and Bull took leaves of absence but the reality is, they're history."

"Slattery?"

"Officially history. Even sent out a departure memo. Not as colorful as yours, of course." He winked.

"Yeah, mine might have been a little over the top. I was still steaming when I drafted it."

"But it was great. The title was a perfect summation of your experience at the firm: 'Eating Caviar and Dirt.'"

"It was, but I didn't want to give the impression everyone there was a jerk. Some of them are decent people, good lawyers."

"Glad to hear it. I was worried your dislike extended to all the partners."

"No, of course not. Certainly not you. You're my running buddy." She lifted her hand to sock him in the shoulder.

He caught her fist and wrapped her in his arms. "That and a whole lot more, I hope."

MAHONEY & MARSHALL
MEMORANDUM

This memorandum provides an overview of women's right to be free of sexual harassment and discrimination in the workplace.

The principal source of this right is Title VII of the Civil Rights Act of 1964, which was originally intended to address discrimination based on race. In a "humorous" attempt to defeat the proposed legislation, an amendment was offered also prohibiting discrimination based on sex. The bill eventually passed, amendment and all. Private employers, state and local governments, and educational institutions now must comply with its provisions unless they employ fewer than fifteen individuals.

The linchpin of the protections offered female workers today is freedom from discrimination. Sexual harassment is a form of discrimination, and hostile work environment and *quid pro quo* (Latin meaning "this for that") are two forms of sexual harassment.

Sexual Discrimination
Considered apart from its manifestation as harassment, discrimination is often easy to recognize. Put simply, it is treating a female employee differently in any aspect of her work including:

- hiring and firing;

- compensation, assignment, or classification of employees;

- transfer, promotion, layoff, or recall;

- job advertisements or recruiting;

- use of company facilities;

- training and apprenticeship programs; and

- pay, retirement plans, fringe benefits, and dis-
  ability leave.

Sexual Harassment

Sexual harassment is seen as a form of discrimination because it results in the affected employee either leaving the workplace or remaining but being less productive and, as a consequence, jeopardizing her potential for raises or advancement.

Sexual harassment is "unwelcome verbal, visual, or physical conduct of a sexual nature that is severe or pervasive and affects working conditions or creates a hostile work environment."

Unwelcome: unwanted; it bothers the employee and she wants it to stop. If conduct is unwelcome, the employee should be very clear about it, for example saying, "Crude jokes about sex make me uncomfortable."

Verbal: sexual or sex-based jokes; observations about an employee's body, clothes, or behavior; sexual innuendoes; requests for sexual services or repeatedly asking an employee out.

Visual: e-mails, drawings, posters, photographs, or screen savers of a sexual nature.

Physical: groping, patting, stroking, kissing, hugging, or other inappropriate touching of an employee's body or clothes; blocking or impeding movement of an employee; following an employee; looking up and down an employee's body; insulting gestures or facial expressions of a sexual nature.

Although each type of conduct described above is defined as being of a sexual nature, an exception exists for a female employee working in an all-male environment who experiences nonsexual conduct that interferes with the performance of her work. An example of this form of sexual harassment would be a female carpenter on an all-male crew whose tools are routinely hidden by her male co-workers.

Remember the definition of sexual harassment had alternative descriptions of the actionable conduct: either <u>severe</u> or <u>pervasive</u>. Even a single instance of egregious conduct—for example, attempted rape—may constitute sexual harassment. The less extreme the conduct—for example, comments on a women's appearance, lewd looks, and off-color jokes—the more prevalent it must be to constitute actionable harassment,.

Quid pro quo **harassment**: In return for some sexual action, the employer or supervisor offers an employment benefit or relief from some employment detriment. For example, in exchange for sex, an employer might offer a raise or might offer to exclude the employee from those being fired as a result of downsizing.

Hostile work environment: A hostile work environment is one which is "permeated with discriminatory intimidation, ridicule, and insult" sufficiently severe or pervasive to alter the conditions of employment. The conduct must have been offensive to the employee, and must also be of a kind that would offend a reasonable person of the same sex. Other factors include the frequency of the offensive conduct and how many employees experienced it.

Other Issues

Retaliation against employees who assert sexual discrimination claims or who testify on their behalf is itself a violation of Title VII.

Although the individual who has committed actionable sexual harassment is often a business owner or supervisor, conduct of a co-worker or a customer may also result in employer liability if the employer is aware of it and fails to take corrective action.

A worker may have a claim for sexual harassment even if the offensive conduct is not directed at her. One example would be an employee in a sexually charged workplace. Another would be an employee who is disadvantaged because her co-worker is providing sexual services to a supervisor and receiving favorable treatment in return.

Workplace romances are permissible if they are truly consensual. However, when there is a power differential between the parties, questions about the voluntary nature of the relationship may be raised in retrospect after the relationship is over.

What You Can Do

1. Say "no" clearly. Much better to say you're not interested in dating than to say you're busy. Don't spare his feelings; protect yourself. If the harassment doesn't stop, write the harasser a letter or e-mail requesting that he stop, and keep a copy.

2. Write down specifics of what happened, including the date, place, offensive conduct, and possible witnesses. If there are witnesses, ask them to write up the incident, too. Do this for each instance. Because your claim may boil down to he said, she said, this step is vitally important to enhance your credibility. The written record should not be kept at work.

3. Report the harassment to your supervisor, the human relations department, or other appropriate authority at work. Make the report in writing if possible. This step is particularly important if the person harassing you is a co-worker, client, or customer because, otherwise, the employer may be unaware of what is happening. Make notes about your meeting.

4. Avoid the temptation of talking about the situation, or you may be subject to a defamation claim against you.

5. Continue to keep a written record including the notes described above (#2), copies of all correspondence, and notes about any meetings about your complaint.

6. Review your personnel file. In some states, you have a legal right to make a copy of its contents.

7. Follow whatever "official" procedure your company has for handling sexual harassment complaints. Find it in your employee manual or ask human relations.

8. As these steps escalate, you may suffer physical or psychological damage. See your doctor for help and for documentation.

9. Involve your union if you're unionized.

10. File a complaint with the Equal Employment Opportunity Commission (EEOC), a federal agency, or with your state's fair employment agency. The EEOC hotline is 800-669-4000. Be prompt! The deadline for filing your complaint may be as soon as 180 days from the act of harassment.

11. File a private lawsuit after you have filed with a governmental agency. You can ask a court for money damages, to reinstate you in your job, or to force your employer to adopt practices that would deter future harassment. We would be happy to help you with this.

12. Prepare yourself for the results of taking these steps. Your employer may retaliate. You may have trouble finding another job; you may be branded a troublemaker; you may be shunned by other workers (including women); you may open up your personal life to scrutiny by others; you may incur legal fees; and you may feel anxious, isolated, and depressed. Consider joining a support group.

Understand that employers expect these consequences, as well as women's training to be "good girls" and not make waves, to deter prosecution of complaints. Employers embrace the motto, "You have to go along to get along."

We hope you have found this memorandum helpful. It is offered as general advice based on the law at the time we prepared it. Your circumstances may be different or the law may have
changed. You should consult your own counsel about the appli-
cability of Title VII to your particular situation.

Margaret M. Mahoney
Agatha C. Marshall

BOOK CLUB GUIDE

1. How effective is the suspense aspect of the plotline? How effective is the author's use of plot twists? Was there foreshadowing? What events in the story stand out for you as memorable?

2. Is the author equally invested in both character and plot? Were the motivations of the characters believable, or did their actions feel like a means to further the plot?

3. Did you think the characters and their problems, decisions, and relationships were realistic? Which of the characters could you relate to best, and why? Talk about the secondary characters. Were they important to the story? Did any stand out for you?

4. What are Maggie's strengths and blind spots? What does she come to understand over time? Apply these questions to Sunny also.

5. How did the author's use of multiple voices in telling the story affect your reading of the novel? Do you think the author did a good job with it?

6. Talk about the author's use of language/writing style. Was the language appropriate to the story? Did the dialogue sound realistic?

7. Were the author's descriptions of the settings effective? Evocative? Did the author provide enough background information for you to understand the significance of events in the story?

8. Which scenes or passages were especially memorable or interesting? Have each member read a favorite passage aloud.

9. What were some of the major themes of the book? Are they relevant to your life?

10. Did this book change your perception of workplace interactions? Are you aware of situations in which gender affects assignments or promotions?

11. Both male and female characters offer explanations for why women don't come forward with complaints about their treatment in the workplace. Do you find these explanations believable?

12. The book's title, *Terminal Ambition*, can be read as the final ambition or that ambition is fatal. When does healthy ambition become toxic?

Turn the page for a preview of EROTIC CAPITAL,
a new Maggie Mahoney novel coming soon
from Kate McGuinness.

CHAPTER 1

Maggie Mahoney swiveled her desk chair to face the television screen. Her compact digs at Mahoney & Marshall were comfortable, but not as spacious or elegant as her office at Sweeny, Owens. Her new firm was more egalitarian in every respect. Ginger Marshall had set the tone, and Maggie embraced it.

Maggie grabbed the remote and punched in the numbers for the Global News Network. Her new client Jae Jun was about to do a live broadcast. Maggie hadn't met Jae yet, but she recognized her name when the woman called three days earlier to schedule an appointment about a "highly confidential matter." Jae asked for a time the following week after she returned from her trip to Afghanistan.

Maggie said, "Afghanistan? Are you reporting on the progress of the war?"

"No. Not at all. Western volunteers have organized a conference about the epidemic of violence against women there. I'm going to cover that."

"It's great that your network is bringing attention to the problem."

"It wasn't the network's decision." Jae scoffed. "It was mine. Do you know a woman was strangled by her husband and mother-in-law for the crime of giving birth to a third daughter?"

"Yes. Absolutely barbaric." She tsked.

"I made up my mind when I heard about it. My boss doesn't like it, but I'll be at the conference." Her voice had a steely determination.

Maggie imagined the network wouldn't buck the current media "It Girl." Viewers loved the novel combination of fragile beauty and a hard-hitting—almost fierce—interview style. At five foot seven, Jae was tall for an Asian woman, but she was slender and moved with grace. The camera loved her face: a perfectly symmetrical oval with enormous doe-shaped eyes, full lips and a jaw strong enough to convey authority without appearing manly.

Maggie sighed. "Yeah, that murder—strangling her—was awful. But will you be safe?"

"Reporting from the Middle East has always been a problem for women. But the network is providing security. I should be okay."

As the television screen popped to life, Maggie hoped Jae's courage wouldn't be tested.

Instead of seeing the expected image of Jae in front of the building where the conference was to be held, Maggie saw an Afghani woman holding a toddler's stiff body. The lead-in to the conference had morphed into a funeral tableau.

The child was one of scores of children dead in refugee camps from hypothermia. The winter's extreme cold had proved too much for the tents and lean-tos that offered meager shelter at Kabul's six thousand foot elevation. A frustrated aid worker had pushed the mother in front of Jae as she stepped out of a dusty van.

After Jae hugged the bereft mother, her guard began to push his way into a crowd filling the field between the street and the meeting hall at the American University of Afghanistan. Tall with broad shoulders and a thick neck, he resembled a pork-fed football player drilled into fitness by the Special Forces. His heavy tweed coat added bulk to his frame. Even bundled in a full-length down parka, Jae looked like a waif as she followed him.

The camera zoomed out to show the setting: the snow-covered Himalayas gave way to the jagged Chagai Hills and the urban sprawl of the Kabul Valley. Beautiful, fascinating and . . . suddenly frightening.

The camera's focus had switched to the mob in the field. The crowd roiled with anger as Jae's security guard elbowed people aside. Maggie thought the young men dressed in scruffy jeans and jackets in the front might be students. The microphone picked up their chant in heavily accented English: "Our country. Our ways."

Milling behind them were older men wearing traditional garb, vests over dresses with leggings. They shouted "Allahu Akbar." Maggie knew it meant "God is great," but their faces and their raised fists conveyed fury rather than devotion.

Jae had been surrounded by the mob. Her gleaming black hair showed over the mass of turbans and kufi worn by the short Afghan men.

"Jae, get out of there!" Maggie whispered an urgent, but futile, order. Maggie was thousands of miles away, but her body switched to fight or flight mode: sweaty palms, racing pulse and tight muscles in her thighs.

The head and shoulders of Jae's guard turned toward her. His beefy face was puckered with concern. He pointed toward the street, shook his head at Jae's response, pointed again.

The image bobbed sideways and up and down as the crowd jostled the cameraman. The sound of their protests became an indecipherable roar of Persian, Pashtu and English.

Maggie caught a glimpse of Jae's forehead. Thank God! She was turning around. The guard surged toward the street. The crowd parted but immediately filled the space he'd occupied. Behind him, Jae was trapped in the middle of a furious mob.

Fists rose around her head. Fingers grabbed a hank of her hair. A hand seized her collar. She disappeared from sight.

Jae had been dragged down by men angered by Western insistence that women be respected. They would show her how women were treated in their country.

Kate McGuinness joined a major international law firm following graduation from law school. In seven years, she became one of only a handful of female partners. After spending ten years as a partner, she was recruited by a Fortune 500 company to serve as its General Counsel. Today she is a full-time writer who advocates for women's rights. Her work has appeared in *Jezebel, Women's Media Center, Fem2pt0, Ms. JD, The Girls Guide to Law School,* and *Role/Reboot.* She tweets about these issues as @womnsrightswrtr. Her website, www.womensrightswriter, includes her blog as well as women's rights resources and volunteer opportunities. She lives in a utopian community in the Midwest with her husband, dogs, and innumerable squirrels.

Self publishing Process

- publish
- proof reader
- Re Reads it

proof
- Interior design of
  The book

    Back
    Apply to Library of Congress
        control #

  . ISBN

  . Create Space — Amazon
        sends an online
            proof
                proof read it again!

  . e books — convert to kindle — $4.99
        The proof read again

    Amazon
    Promotions
    . promotion: 90 days
                  5 day to give away
                        for free

            Announce
              when pro

Est. Social Media presence — a year before publish
                Nathan Bron......
      rec. -

    Twitter — 7500 people
    Facebook — write on Woman's issues

pinterest — 3rd Social media

Made in the USA
Charleston, SC
08 July 2012